Gold Dust *of* Begum Sultans

Gold Dust *of* Begum Sultans

Zubaida Sultan

Translated by
Zakia Zaheer &
Syeda Saiyidain Hameed

इन्दिरा गाँधी राष्ट्रीय कला केन्द्र
INDIRA GANDHI NATIONAL CENTRE FOR THE ARTS
RUPA

Published in 2016 by
Indira Gandhi National Centre for the Arts
Central Vista Janpath, New Delhi-110001

and

Rupa Publications India Pvt. Ltd.
7/16, Ansari Road, Daryaganj
New Delhi 110002

Sales centres:
Allahabad Bengaluru Chennai
Hyderabad Jaipur Kathmandu
Kolkata Mumbai

ISBN: 978-81-291-4024-1

Third impression 2017

10 9 8 7 6 5 4 3

Printed at Replika Press Pvt. Ltd, India

Hum wajd mein baithey rahe aur rait ki manind
muththi se sarakti rahi taqdeer hamari…

We sat in a trance and like trails of sand
From our fist, our destiny slipped away…

—Sultan Akhtar, Patna

Acknowledgements

The late Zubaida Sultan's Urdu novel, *Sunehri Rait,* was the core that enabled us to write this text. The book recalls events of a historical, entrenched and tantalizing past. Our work is not strictly a translation, mostly because we have taken artistic license, adding drama to a narrative which was linear and factually written. Generationally, too, we remain close to her and indeed, bore witness to the era about which she wrote. In her last days, she extracted a promise from Zakia Zaheer to bring out an English translation of her novel. So this is also the fulfilment of a long due commitment.

Many other people played a role in the creation of this book. We want to thank Hameeda Srivastava, elder sister of Zubaida Sultan, who not only nurtured her entire family and preserved tradition, but also gave us valuable information that enabled us to write. We are grateful to her eldest sister, the late Mahmooda Sultan, from whom we gleaned insight into the principal characters of the book.

To Vikram Srivastava, we express our gratitude for being a source of information and encouragement.

The link between us and Zubaida Sultan was forged by the deep bond between a sister and a brother, Aziz Jahan Begum and Sajid Ali Khan, respectively our mother and Zubaida's father. We offer our salaam and *fatiha* to their departed souls.

We are grateful for the consistent and cheerful help given by our young colleagues Ruth Zothanpuii and Imsutoshi in preparing the manuscript.

To Rupa Publications India, whose team worked around the clock with utmost patience, we offer our gratitude.

We are very grateful to the Indira Gandhi National Centre for the Arts for their unstinting and continuous help in our venture.

Zakia Zaheer
Syeda Saiyidain Hameed
March 2016

Foreword

The Indira Gandhi National Centre for the Arts (IGNCA) is visualized as a centre encompassing the study and experience of all the arts. It is a premier resource centre engaged in research, documentation, publication and dissemination of knowledge in the field of arts.

The present work is part of Janapada Sampada Division's programme on 'Confluence of Traditions and Composite Culture'. It is based on an autobiographical novel set in post 1857 in the region of Rohilkhand. The original novel, *Sunehri Rait,* was written in Urdu by Zubaida Sultan. It was published in 1989 one year after her death. The present book is its translation by Zakia Zaheer and Syeda Saiyidain Hameed

The action takes place in the riyasat of Mohammadpur located in the Rohilkhand region. The setting is feudal but its three main protagonists are women who steer the destiny of a household which is otherwise embedded in patriarchal values. It is a story of a dying tradition and its transformative successor. The old patriarchal order is dying and the new emerging world is struggling to replace it.

Veena Joshi
Officiating Member Secretary
IGNCA

Preface

During the 18th century, bands of Pathan adventurers called Rohillas established their control over the wedge of country located between the foothills of the Himalayas, the Ganges and Awadh, and gave their name to the region—Rohilkhand. Earlier, it had been a rich Rajput-dominated province of the Mughal empire, known as Katehr. The Rajputs were supplanted by the Rohillas or Pathans under the leadership of Ali Mahommad Khan and Hafiz Rahmat Khan. The name Rohilla is derived from the word *roh,* which like *koh,* means a mountain. The Rohillas claim Coptic origin and also claim to have been driven out of Egypt by one of the pharaohs. Wandering westward, they say they arrived in that part of the mountains of Afghanistan known as Sulaimani Koh.

With their capital in Bareilly, the Rohillas ruled Rohilkhand until the war of 1774–75—known as the Rohilla War. The small kingdom of Rohilkhand wished to become independent, but, alarmed by the way the Marathas were eyeing its borders, the Rohilla leader sought protection from the Nawab of Avadh—who was only too keen to step in and 'protect' the nascent state.

One interpretation of why the Avadhis wanted to control Rohilkhand state is that they felt threatened by it. In his book *Hastings and the Rohilla Way* Sir John Strachey writes that though the large majority of the population of Katehr was not Rohilla, but 'peaceable and industrious Hindoos', the dominant class was a military colony of Afghans, otherwise generically called Rohillas or highlanders who were '...too notorious to require description; and it may be enough to say that, though some of their leaders were men of a certain amount of cultivation, they were, as a body, fierce, turbulent, treacherous, and unstable as water.' And while the Himalayas protected Avadh proper in the north, the Ganges formed a barrier in the south, and east, the proximity of the English was a deterrent, no natural barrier fenced it off on the west from the threat of Katehr, or Rohilkhand.

Another account states that the Nawab of Avadh agreed—for a sum of 40 lakh rupees—to help the Rohillas if the Marathas attacked them. Now while the Marathas did indeed attack Rohilkhand in 1773, they had to return without entering the battlefield due to the sudden death of Madhav Rao Peshwa, their leader. Since Avadhi soldiers did not actually fight the Marathas, Hafiz Rahmat Khan refused to pay the agreed sum to the nawab! Affronted, the nawab requested the English for help to attack Rohilkhand. Warren Hastings accepted the request. In 1774, the Rohillas were defeated and driven from Bareilly to the distant borders of the Terai by the Nawab of Avadh with the assistance of the East India Company's troops under the command of Colonel Champion. Hafiz Rahmat Khan, along with 20,000 Rohillas, was banished. In the same year, the state of Rampur was established under the Nawab of Avadh and the Treaty of Laldhang was signed between the nawab and Faizullah Khan.

Rampur remained a pliant state under British protection. The first stone of what became known as the Rampur Qila was laid by Nawab Faizullah Khan in 1775. The same year 1775, modern Lucknow City was founded by Asaf-ud Daula. It was first proposed to be named Faizabad, but there being many Faizabads, it was renamed Akbarabad alias Rampur. In 1784, the Nawab of Avadh, with the assistance of the British, had crushed all the Rohilla sardars, with the exception of Faizullah Khan. He had put up such a fierce resistance that the nawab granted Faizullah Khan the *jagir* of Rampur, an arrangement encouraged by the British.

A patron of arts and literature, Nawab Faizullah Khan ruled Rampur for 20 years. Then began a series of successions and assassinations in Rampur.

Faizullah Khan's son, Mohammad Ali Khan, had barely ascended the throne when he was ambushed and killed by rival Rohilla tribes. The succession went to his brother Ghulam Mohammad Khan—but British opposition to the new ruler resulted in his being dethroned immediately and the succession going back to Mohammad Ali Khan's son, Ahmed Ali Khan in 1794.

Ahmed Ali Khan ruled for 46 years, from 1794-1840. Since he had no male heir, succession returned full circle and Mohammed Sayeed Khan, son of Ghulam Mohammed Khan, became the ruler from 1840-1855. His son and successor Mohammed Yusuf Khan 'Nazim', ruled from 1855-1865. His younger brother Kazim Ali Khan was wanted by the British authorities on suspicion of having murdered a white noblewoman. To save him from a certain death sentence, his brother, the nawab surrrendered a large area of the kingdom to the white man as a huge compensation.

The next successor, Nawab Yusuf Ali Khan's son Kalbe Ali Khan, ruled from 1865-1887. He was given the title 'Bahadur' courtesy the British, and became known as the most learned of all the nawabs of Rampur. A scholar of Arabic, he was a collector of the finest art from the world over. He also wrote poetry in Persian and Urdu and during a pilgrimage to Mecca, brought back manuscripts of the Quran from the 7th and 8th centuries. Rampur boasts of the best collection of art and calligraphy due to his quest for the best. His love for Khwaja Gharib Nawaz led to his order to construct the dome of Hazrat Muinuddin Chishti's Dargah in Ajmer in pure gold.

Kalbe Ali Khan's son, the invalid Mushtaq Ali Khan Bahadur, ruled from1887-1889. He had the walls and pillars of the Ajmer Sharif painted in red, gold and blue.

Hamid Ali Khan Bahadur succeeded his father in 1889 and ruled till 1930. A minor at the time of ascension, the government appointed a regent, General Azeemudin Khan from 1889-1894, to oversee matters of state.

His son, Raza Ali Khan Bahadur, ruled long, over three decades, from 1930 to 1966. The last Rampur nawab was Murtaza Ali Khan who ruled from 1966 till 1971, after which the title 'Nawabat' was abolished. He died in 1982.

The story you are about to read is about an adjacent riyasat, *Mohammadpur, which was linked in many ways with the state of Rampur, sharing a common culture, the culture of the Rohilla Pathans.*

Chapter 1

IN THE DEPTHS of the night, the city slept. But within the huge expanse of Akbar Lodge, soft sounds could be heard, something stirred. Servants and orderlies, like shadows in the night, moved up and down. In the courtyard, horse carriages were being discreetly loaded with luggage… In the emptying house, Sahibzada Akbar Ali Khan paced up and down in great consternation.

The walls of the reception room in which he stood, had been stripped bare of the rare paintings and the royal coat of arms. In one corner of the room, lay piles of rolled up Persian carpets. Expensive handcrafted sofas were shrouded in dust covers. His large, sad eyes, growing moist now, lingered over all this before he shut them and silently asked for forgiveness. Forgiveness from Allah or from the home in which he had spent the best years of his life? He could still 'see' the splendour of this, his ancestral home, especially after nightfall when each stone came to life with music and each floor tile reverberated with the stamp of dancing feet. Tonight it was bereft of happy echoes.

Akbar Ali Khan was a handsome 45-year-old, his princely bearing framed in an off-white angarkha trimmed with gold, and matching gold and white shoes. In dim silhouette, he could have been mistaken for one of the many life-size sculptures, imported from Europe, which stood along the walls of the gallery circling the main hall. Brushing his hand over his eyes, he found it wet with tears.

Inside the haveli were the begums, the women of the family, anxiously waiting to be summoned. Two of them stood apart from the rest, the trains of their Farshi ghararas trailing on the floor. Behind them stood their maids, bearing in their hands all the immediate necessities of travel.

Akbar Ali Khan walked over to the front courtyard. A white carriage stood with its doors open, two liveried footmen in attendance, faces averted. Akbar walked up to the horses, patting them gently. He then lifted his hand, ordering the first posse of guards to proceed. Twelve front guards respectfully bowed their heads and jerked their reins sharply. The horses began to move, their hoofs tapping a staccato rhythm on the driveway. This advance personal guard swiftly moved to the corner of the driveway and turned towards the main gate. They were required to send the signal for the carriages to proceed.

'Escort the begums.'

Akbar Ali Khan motioned to the eunuch guard standing at the door of the zenana. Menservants bowed out of the room, leaving the passage free. From the inner chambers, the personal maids appeared, followed by the two begums, both wrapped in white chadors. Two elderly women followed, each escorting a small boy and a girl. Another posse of personal maids followed, carrying jewel-encrusted silver vanity boxes. The begums sat on cushioned seats in the front section of the carriage with the two small children seated by their sides. Their maids climbed into the back. The chief syce then moved to the left of the carriage while the master swung lightly onto the driver's seat, taking into his right hand the soft black leather reins of the white Arabian steed. Thus. in the very early hours, even before the muezzin's call to prayer, the small caravan began its journey to an unknown destination.

Akbar Ali Khan was linked in many ways to the Royal House

of Mohammadpur, a state adjacent to Rampur. His only daughter, Jahanara Begum, was married to Ammar Ali Khan, the younger son of Nawab Sartaj Ali Khan of Mohammadpur. The nawab's anxiety to see his grandson Asad Ali Khan succeed him, made him reject his younger son and place his elder paraplegic son, Mustanzir, on the throne. Asad became the ruler after the expected death of his father Mustanzir, within a few months of the coronation.Thus the younger son, Ammar Ali Khan, who should have been nawab, remained a sahibzada all his life while his nephew ruled.

Sahibzada Akbar Ali Khan was himself the uncle of Nawab Asad Ali Khan. His wife, Qamar Zamani Begum, daughter of Kazim Ali Khan who was the brother of Mohammed Yusuf Khan 'Nazim', was the nawab's great aunt; although he always referred to her as '*hamari behan*' (our sister). Akbar Ali Khan was also his Home Minister, his closest confidante and friend.

In the gullies and mohallas of the town it was whispered that there was no one who could match Nawab Asad Ali Khan for his love of luxuries and desire for women. His first wife, the daughter of a neighbouring princely state, quietly tolerated her husband's profligacies for many years. She had been trained to shut her eyes and mouth so long as the throne was reserved for her progeny. But having borne the nawab several girl children, she was castigated for the limitations of her womb. It was then that she had made her decision. Collecting her serving women, her jewellery caskets and her royal wardrobe, she had called for her father's guards and returned to her father's home.

Her departure had removed the nawab's only restraint. No sooner did she leave the palace, than a stream of wives and concubines began to move into the palace bedrooms. The nawab kept a sharp eye out for girls and women. If any one struck his fancy, she was forced to enter the palace and overnight, a nikah or *mutah* would bring her to his bed.

Bride-for-a-night… that's what they became, most women who were brought into his chamber. But once the bridal night was over, they were buried alive within the four walls of the palace. It was said that 39 bridal dolis had crossed the threshold of the palace but no funeral khatiya was ever brought out. These unfortunate women had been blessed with lives which were far too long! There was plenty to eat and the royal physician ever in attendance; so lives were prolonged. The unfortunate ones who did not conceive on the first night, did not get another opportunity to do so, and hence were denied even the joy of motherhood.

The nawab had a few favourites, several of whom bore him children, all girls. A male child was desperately desired, and every wife tried her best to catch his eye and bed him—but still there was no heir! The nawab moved from bed to bed every night, dropping his seed in multiple wombs, not knowing which would produce the heir, the Wali Ehad. Women reached their full terms and delivered one girl child after another. Then one day, the cannons went full blast and the royal physician announced the birth of a boy. At long last the Wali Ehad had been delivered in the zenana! He came, full of slime and blood, crying his lungs out and was handed in that condition into the waiting arms of the ecstatic nawab.

The other wives now had a common enemy. The new mother and her infant son were ensnared by royal intrigue. A web of lies and hate spun out from one end of the palace to the other. Meanwhile, to celebrate the birth of the Wali Ehad, the royal treasury was thrown open to the public.

The birth of one son whetted the nawab's appetite for more until it became insatiable! The nawab threw himself headlong into new 'sightings', as he liked to call these hunts for women. Taking the birth of his son as testimony to his manhood, he now became obsessed with nurturing it. Virgins were sought and summoned. His desire for young girls grew insatiable. Having seen his wife nursing the tiny royal infant, he became partial to nursing mothers—the blush of new motherhood on their faces was irresistible to him.

Under cover of darkness, he prowled around the city in his carriage, peeping inside homes, flushed with yearning for a fresh catch. One night, he passed by a house with a single oil lamp in the window. He asked his syce to stop the carriage. A young woman was sitting on the floor beside the mud choolha, making rotis, her face glowing with the heat and her hands smeared in flour. Next to her sat her young husband, who had just returned from work, and two little children ready for the evening meal.

The nawab descended from the carriage and entered the hut.

'What is your name, child?'

'Noor,' she said, trembling at this august appearance at her door.

Her husband cowered with fear. The children began to whimper. Nawab Sahib sat down beside her.

'What are you cooking, child?'

'Sarkar, makka ki roti.'

'We will taste your cooking.'

Noor placed the roti on the tava with trembling hands and then set the half-cooked roti on a battered plate. She offered it with downcast eyes to the man who was taking in the squalor of the hut. The nawab put one morsel in his mouth and just as he came in, so he left, without saying another word.

From his abject position, Noor's husband glanced up to make sure the nawab's carriage had left. He then embraced his weeping wife. Both were dreading the outcome of this visit.

Nawab Sahib could not wait until morning! Noor was lifted from the cottage, her hands still smeared with atta, and forced into the royal carriage. The first rays of the sun found her face-down in the nawab's bed, her eyes red from crying all night for her husband and little children...

Many such Noors with atta-smeared hands were brought to the

palace, their bodies first hennaed and perfumed, then groped and pounded, then forever buried alive in the white marble mausoleum of the palace.

Hakim Saeed was a renowned practitioner of Unani medicine as well as a special confidante of the nawab. Whenever the ruler felt his sexual performance weakening, Hakim Saeed was summoned to prepare potions of the rarest of herbs which were mixed with gold, silver and Basra pearls and these he carried personally to the palace. The nawab had grown used to this kushta. But then came the day when the kushta stopped working! The hakim was urgently summoned. Someone had whispered to him about the failure of his potion and Hakim Saeed knew that unless he could find a way out, he would be thrown into the darkest prison until he died. Summoning his wits and forcing a smile on his anxious face, he whispered in the royal ear:

'Sarkar, my inner eye tells me that at this time you need ebony in your bed, ebony; only then will this trouble be averted.'

No sooner had these words been spoken than Nawab Sahib ordered his special attendant Gulrez—'Ebony, Gulrez, understand? Go to each nook and corner of the zenana, find the woman with the darkest skin and bring her in our presence within 30 minutes.'

Gulrez went to the gate of the zenana. His knock brought the gatekeeper, Champakali, a tall hefty eunuch, to the door. She was dressed in a gold-trimmed dupatta, her wrists laden with glass bangles which clinked with her swinging walk.

'Yes, my dulha darling, what brings you to my humble presence?' she teased, tapping Gulrez on the cheek and winking coyly.

'Stop this nonsense, Champa. Huzoor desires that the blackest woman be brought this minute to his royal chamber.'

Hearing this, Champakali let out a peal of laughter. '*Ari* Juhi, Dilruba, Haseena, where are you? Sarkar wants to mount a black mare!'

Gulrez was surrounded with the other eunuchs who were chortling at this eccentric order. Suddenly, the inner door flew open and a tall eunuch in a flowing gharara appeared. The laughter died down immediately.

Bibban Bua was the head of the Eunuch Brigade. She was greatly feared by her juniors. She glared at them with her sternest look '*Ari mardood* girls, stop showing your teeth! Get back to your duties, damn fools.'

The 'girls' paraded back inside, making obscene gestures behind Biban Bua's back. The eunuchs were the only 'men' who had a free run of the zenana. No man was allowed to enter the precincts, not even a four-year-old boy. Bibban knew the nawab's every whim so when Gulrez told her his mission, she knew exactly where to find the dark-skinned antidote to his majesty's impotence.

'Azizan,' she said under her breath.

Azizan was at the bottom of the servants' hierarchy. By caste, she was a Kaharin, but she was also a nursing mother whose little boy was always clutched to her breast. Bibban Bua strode across the large quadrangles of the zenana towards the shagird pesha (the servants' quarters). She stood before Azizan's small kothri, wrapped head to foot in a white chador. Mother and child were asleep.

'*Uthh*!' Bibban rasped in her ear. Before the woman could say a word, another white chador was thrown over her dirty tattered clothes and she was dragged out. Azizan scratched and fought but Bibban was strong. Cursing and ranting at her fate, clutching the child to her breast, the unfortunate woman was heaved into the nawab's bedroom.

The nawab took one look at the woman, her face smeared with tears and snot, and felt his gorge rise. He ordered the attendant to take the child away from the mother and leave him with one of the zenana maids. But Azizan gripped her child and wailed loudly: 'Sarkar, do with me as you wish but I will die before I let my boy out of my sight!'

The nawab felt stumped. Gingerly, he reached into his pocket and took out his silk handkerchief to wipe the two runny noses. He approached the Kaharin hesitantly, promising not to separate her from her baby. Then he ordered a bath and bridal clothes for her.

'Azizan,' he addressed her in chaste Farsi, '*Ba* Khuda! If this is the only cure for my weakness, I will take you as a bitter pill.' Thus, Azizan with her clutching child, became his companion for one night.

After having had his fill of Kaharins and Domnis, the nawab looked for new diversions. This time he fancied a proper nikah and that too, with a poor girl who was a Saidani. No one in Mohammadpur was prepared to offer their daughter, so word was sent to nearby towns and a Syed family of Lucknow was finally located. For the 39th time, the nawab wore his wedding clothes and with a grand baraat, the aged dulha arrived in Lucknow. It was a solemn ceremony. Afterwards, the bridegroom was felicitated by a line of small talukdars and representatives of the elites of the city. An old man bowed his head, touching it to the royal feet of the bridegroom. 'Sarkar, I am a very poor man but of pure Syed lineage. I have seven unmarried daughters at home. May Allah make you flourish until the day of qayamat; please save me, an old man from a sharif gharana. Take one of my daughters as your kaneez. Let the very maulana who has performed your nikah, perform the ceremony for my oldest child, my Masuma.'

Copious tears flowed onto the *zari* of the nawab's golden sandals. The nawab was in a generous mood—if he could marry one Saidani, why not marry two? He issued his orders, the maulana sat down again and in one sitting, two Saidanis became the nawab's 39th and 40th wives.

At the Mehtab Bagh Palace, the two brides alighted from their respective dolis. And the night's revelry began!

Nobility from the town and nearby *qasbas* had assembled for the lavish feast, singers and musicians sang and played late into the night—it was dawn when the party ended. The bridal chamber was ready... Maids brought one of the brides to the room and placed her under the canopy of flowers to wait for her royal husband; the other bride waited for her turn in the adjoining room. Alas, she was forgotten in the fun and frolic! And in the morning, the maids saw her lying in a heap among her bridal flowers and finery... She had entered the palace a sixteen-year-old virgin, as the wife of the nawab, and seven years later, when the nawab died, she was the only one of the forty wives who became a virgin-widow. During those seven years, Masuma Begum never once asked to be taken into his presence. Strangely, she felt a strange contentment at being forgotten. She would send parcels of clothes for her sisters and small gifts from the overflowing stores of the palace for her father and mother. She made friends with the other wives, who harbored no jealousy towards her. She was known as the Siyani Begum, wise lady, who lived her life with dignity and contentment.

The mehfils of the palace were an all-night affair. The best singers were brought to entertain the guests. The royal ladies sat behind the jharoka to watch the dance and catch occasional glimpses of their husbands. With the first light of day, the nawab would rise from his royal seat and with him, the entire mehfil stood and then bent over to bow to him. No one stood upright from the moment of salaam until the nawab reached his bedroom. Once the door was shut, the nawab's subjects dispersed to the comfort of their chambers to sleep off a hard night's toil

These heady days seemed like they would never end but suddenly something happened that shook the entire durbar out of this splendid reverie. The nawab, ever the gamester, took a fancy to a memsahib! Stories of the royal carriage being seen at dead of night near the British Cantonment, made the rounds. The sounds of shots were said to have been heard and some swore that they had heard a woman scream. The upshot was that the nawab was held responsible for the abortive attempt to abduct the daughter of the British Governor. Company Bahadur's wrath was aroused; British honour was at stake! All hell broke loose! Nawab sahib tried his best to save himself, but the stakes were too high and he paid a heavy and secret price for his philandering ways—several small towns in the riyasat, all the way to the foot of the Himalayas, were stripped from his estate; only a few small towns remained in his control—even the beautiful hill station Nainital, the summer resort of the British, was not only taken away, even entry into this 'Queen of the Hills' was forbidden to the nawab on pain of arrest. Overnight, it seemed, the grand Mohammadpur State had shrunk to one third.

Having lost so much of his kingdom, Nawab Asad Ali Khan became distraught. He felt betrayed and abused by those he had considered his own. Fury built up in his mind until he began suffering from white rages. The impotence of his anger found other emotional and physical outlets. Hakim Sahib's prescriptions started losing their zing. Middle age hit hard and the nawab's outbursts became daily occurrences, randomly targeting unwitting servants, companions, friends... Some turned away, while others tolerated his fits out of respect or expediency.

Meanwhile, the Wali Ehad, Saleem, had just turned 14 years of age.

Saleem was a handsome prince, with a kind temperament. One day, the young royal witnessed the nawab's anger against his wife, Saleem's mother. What was her fault, he asked himself? He had heard that his other 'mothers' were always intriguing, filling the nawab's credulous ears with their false stories—perhaps one of the stories had hit home? When his mother was summoned before the nawab, no one dared to breathe. The royal edict of punishment was pronounced—'Shave her head, put her outside the palace gates, hand her a stick and let her scare away the crows!'

Wali Ehad was mad with anger. He threw himself on his mother, and then turned to his father, blinded with tears—'When I have the power, you will see!' he shouted. 'I will take my mother away and keep her under my protection!'

'Wali Ehad! You scum of my loins!' raged the nawab as he lunged forward, falling in his effort to grab his son and heir. 'How dare you! Praying for our death, you *haramzaadi ki aulaad*! We will fix you!'

People helped the stumbling nawab to his feet as the child ran away and the woman was taken away from his presence to serve her sentence.

The first thing the nawab did when he reached his chambers, was to send for his dear confidante and friend, Akbar Ali Khan.

Akbar Ali Khan was at his meal when the summons came. Not a moment's delay, said the letter. One servant rushed forward with a silver bowl of water for his hands, the other held out a perfumed towel.

'This morning I had a feeling that something evil was going to happen.' Qamar Zamani said, leaving her side of the table to walk over to her husband. 'My *istikhara* this morning was negative.' She religiously consulted her tasbih (prayer beads) each morning before starting her day. Eyes closed, she would place her hands on the beads after saying 'Bismillah.' If the bead count was odd the answer was YES, if the count was even, it was NO. This was her way of warding off evil for herself and her family before taking any decision. Today, the beads had been even so the signal was negative.

'Don't go!' she implored him, but Akbar Ali Khan brushed his hand over her cheek, gently moved her restraining arm, and left.

The nawab was pacing up and down. 'Now listen to me. You, who are dearer to me than life itself, dear, dear brother, listen...

Wali Ehad, you know he is my flesh, my life, my being. Please listen Akbar Ali... brother... he cannot, I repeat *cannot* be allowed to insult us and breathe the same air. Never!'

Akbar Ali understood the import of these words. 'No, Sarkar, no!'

Much as he loved the nawab, he could never be party to such a heinous thought. He sank down on his knees and begged. He tried to think of a rational argument because he saw the nawab remained impervious to his tears.

'Your Highness,' Akbar Ali said, regaining his composure. 'We are under British rule. You are the ruler but your reins are in the hands of the White Man. You will never, never be able to hide this bloodiest of all crimes. Not only the white ruler, even his queen will never pardon you. And Sarkar, if I may make bold to say, what face will you show to the Almighty on the Day of Judgment? Whatever is left of your riyasat on earth will also be finished forever. Sir, in the name of Allah and his Rasool, please give up this madness. It is momentary, it won't last. Wali Ehad is the spitting image of your Abba Huzoor. I beg your mercy in the name of the progeny of the Prophet.' His eyes rained tears at the feet of his friend and master.

But even as he begged hard for the boy's life, Akbar Ali knew the futility of the exercise. The nawab was unrelenting—he was losing patience with Akbar Ali's pleas. 'Brother,' he proclaimed haughtily and with finality, 'if you can't help me in this small matter, there are others who will gladly do it.'

Akbar Ali Khan returned home and went quietly to his chamber. It was evening by the time anyone realised that he was there, sitting alone in his room. His eyes were red. The sound of small running feet made him look up. His grandson had entered the room—Mansoor Ali Khan, Jahanara's son. Mansoor sprang onto his grandfather's lap. Putting his arms around his neck, he buried his face in the old man's neck. For a few minutes, Akbar Ali sat holding Mansoor close to his heart. Then he sprang up and with the child in his arms, he walked with brisk, firm steps to the zenana.

The zenana was abuzz with activity. His wife was sitting with their small granddaughter, Mumtaz Jahan. All around her were dolls of different shapes and sizes dressed in fine hand-stitched ghararas. Sewing women, the Mughlanis, were sitting on the carpets stitching new clothes for the dolls. He took a look at his only daughter, Jahanara Begum. Being such a young mother herself, she, too, was totally involved with the dolls. Her job was to match the coloured pieces and hand them over to the Mughlanis for sewing. His eyes took them all in, the three precious women who made up his life. When Qamar Zamani saw her husband enter, she rose to greet him. The unshed tears in his eyes made her look at him with alarm—she had never seen him like this. Qamar Zamani was a petite woman with a royal bearing. Her eyes were large and ghilafi. As always she was dressed in a flowing gharara with a gilt-edged net dupatta draped over her thick black braids. Akbar Ali Khan gave Mansoor to Firozi Bua, his special nurse, the woman in whose arms he had been placed minutes after he was born. His wife was waiting for this sign that he wanted to be alone with her. She walked to her rooms, Akbar Ali Khan followed.

Neither Akbar Ali nor Qamar Zamani had ever been able to make themselves part of the nawab's profligate lifestyle. Ever since Qamar Zamani had heard about Noor, she had felt revulsion for the man. She had learnt that after the nawab was finished with her that night, she was thrown in a corner of the palace where, day and night, she wept for her husband and children. In the darkness of the night, Qamar Zamani had spoken to her husband:

'Sarkar, my heart aches thinking of that poor child, Noor. Can you find a way to restore her to her family? We, too, have a growing girl in our home. Today, she is just a child but how long does it take for girls to mature? Nawab Sahib freely walks into the house any time of night or day. I dread the moment he sets eyes on my little girl.' These words were resounding in his ears as he shut the door and came face to face with Qamar Zamani. She looked at him with questioning eyes, hoping he had some news about Noor.

While Qamar Zamani sat before him waiting for him to begin, Akbar Ali Khan's mind was elsewhere. Wali Ehad, heir to the throne of the Rohilla Pathans…that innocent 14-year-old face was imprinted on his mind. He recalled the child's birth and the revelry in the riyasat. He remembered having carried Mansoor and the Wali Ehad, one on each shoulder—those were some of the happiest moments of his life! What he had heard, he was about to repeat to his wife. No one knew better than he did, the obdurate nature of the nawab. He also knew, only too well, that by declining to participate in the nawab's plan he would be inviting his own certain death. He had no fear for himself; but thinking of Mansoor's innocent face made his heart stop. He saw his own lineage, the legacy of his forefathers, ending before his very eyes. It was this dread which had set his mind on the plan that he was about to confide to his wife, a plan that would involve leaving his beloved Mohammadpur forever.

'Now, listen to me carefully, my beloved wife, Qamar Zamani Begum….'

Chapter 2

WITH THE BREAK of dawn Akbar Ali Khan's small kafila had crossed the boundary of the riyasat. He knew that by the time the nawab found out, they would be well out of his royal reach. Nightly mehfils at the palace never ended before dawn—that was when the nawab retired to his chamber and once its doors were shut, no one dared to disturb him before midday.

Akbar Ali Khan's entourage had travelled 100 miles before the Terai area came into view. The snowcapped Himalayas appeared as the carriages circled the foothills. On the hillsides, the mustard crop was in green-gold bloom. Winding roads hugged the slopes, disappearing on the other side. The cool mountain breeze energized the kafila but did nothing to abate the discomfort of Akbar Ali's agonized soul. Wali Ehad's innocent eyes and boyish crop of golden hair were embedded in his eyes. Mansoor, who was sitting behind him on his saddle, felt his tension. He hugged his Nana's back with his small arms. Akbar Ali Khan felt in the little arms the cord which hooked him to life. He stopped his horse to bring the child forward and held him to his heart before moving ahead, towards a new home and a new life.

In a while his eyelids drooped with sleep, and the attendants helped him into the carriage. Here, reclining on the cushions, the last few years replayed in his mind. First, it was the birth of the heir and the palace in a frenzy of celebration like never before. All the elites of the riyasat were regaled with poetry and music as musicians played day and night in the halls and courtyards, even drowning the sound of Azaan, and master poets from all over the riyasat vied with each other to produce the best *qasidas* in praise of the nawab's newborn son. The royal treasury poured alms into the hands of the poor and made gifts to the rich. 'Begum,' he spoke softly in the darkness of the carriage, 'My eyes were witness to the magnificent celebration, and now, alas! My ears have heard the worst! If I close my eyes, the face of the Wali Ehad rises behind the closed lids. If I open them, I see my beloved Mansoor as a helpless victim of my refusal to obey the nawab. I am standing where the shadow of death has merged with mine.'

A new turn came within sight. They were both exhausted from the journey and elated with hope of new beginnings. But Qamar Zamani was filled with worries. She could not take her eyes off her husband's face, trying to fathom the storm behind those thoughtful eyes. He had not smiled even at the little Mumtaz Jahan who had settled herself in his lap. During her *maghrib namaz*, performed inside the carriage, she raised her hands. 'O my Creator, my Allah! What have you willed?' In her prayer, there was thought only of her husband; she asked nothing for herself. She did not much regret leaving the kothi which she had entered as a bride of nine years. Nine years! She had not tasted the pleasures of girlhood or played with dolls and other toys, when three years later, after her first menstrual period, she had found herself gripped in the arms of a loving husband. But once she was placed in this role, she had begun to enjoy it. Akbar Lodge had claimed her, body and soul. Within a year she had given birth to a daughter, a tiny, fair, doll—really the first toy she had possessed! She had played with her exactly as she would have with a toy. All the games of life-make-believe were played with this beautiful living doll.

The mountain roads snaked higher and higher, up to the top, and then began the descent. Suddenly, from the very top, could be seen a gigantic cup-shaped depression, with little houses nestling among the mountains. This mountain town was their destination. At the centre, was a large serene lake. Around the lake was the circular road, although sometimes hidden from view by the trees. At one end was a temple and even from this distance, its reflection could be seen in the lake's clear surface.

The caravan wound slowly upwards, halting at a gracious, sprawling house situated at an altitude of 6000 ft. After the 1857 uprising, an Englishman, Mr. Bowering who had lived in the mountains for 20 years, had decided to return home to York. He was known to Akbar Ali since he used to go down to Mohammadpur to play polo with the princes. Akbar had offered him a handsome amount for this house. The deal was done and instead of one, Akbar had bought two houses, side by side. The smaller one was for Mumtaz Jahan, the larger one, Mr Bowering's residence, for Mansoor. Bari Kothi, as it came to be known, had been prepared for their arrival. Flower beds had been carefully tended and weeded in the garden and creepers had been trained against the walls. The flowering trees and fragrant bushes had been trimmed. This garden would become Akbar Ali Khan's refuge during the remainder of the summer days. He would spend his time trimming, watering and fertilizing the flowers and shrubs. It was almost as if the garden had become a metaphor for his family and its state of health the blueprint for the well-being of his children.

The days and months passed and their lives had taken a new turn but Akbar Ali's sadness began to show on his soulmate, Qamar Zamani, as well. Lines of worry appeared on her forehead. He noticed how, day by day, she was becoming his own mirror image. In the feudal tradition, married life meant meeting in dark rooms at the dead of night and parting before the break of dawn. During the day, the husband and wife had separate lives, connected only through servants who carried messages back and forth. Akbar Ali and Qamar Zamani's marriage, however, was still touched with romance and firmly anchored in love.

It was a pleasant surprise when, on a bright sunny April morning, a servant brought a message that Sarkar was waiting for Begum Sahiba in the rose garden. She was to come at once. Screens had been placed around the garden to maintain purdah. Picking up the long and heavy train of her gharara, Qamar Zamani briskly walked to the garden. It was unusual that she had been summoned in the daytime. She climbed the stone steps leading to the elevated garden chabootra and tried to curb her curiosity while the servants served juices and fruits before withdrawing.

'Sarkar you sent for me?' she said with an anxious smile.

Akbar Ali placed a small champa plant before her on the table. 'Yes, I want to tell you something.'

Taking her by the hand, he led her to a corner of the garden where she saw a newly dug pit. He placed the champa gently in the pit and watered it with a silver watering can. 'I am entrusting this plant to you. Make sure you take good care of it. Nurture it like you have nurtured me.'

His eyes seemed to look into an unknown distance as he spoke these words. She even imagined the glint of a tear as she took her turn at watering the sapling. She noticed that the sky was a clear blue as she moved close to him. In the broad daylight, he did something unheard of—he drew her small frame close to his heart. She dared not ask him why. Battling her fears, she surrendered herself to the few moments they stood clinging to one another. Then Akbar Ali broke the silence. 'A messenger has arrived from the riyasat…' The rest of the words were spoken in a dull staccato. 'Wali Ehad is dead; the cause of death, unknown. The message is that my royal brother, the Nawab of Mohammadpur, needs my presence immediately. He wants me to leave for Mohammadpur this very moment.'

Qamar Zamani slumped in his arms. Lifting her up, he sat her down on a garden bench. 'Beloved wife, you know and I know what this means; there is no delay possible. I must go now and I must go alone. I am leaving a huge responsibility on your shoulders. I know you will bear it well. Give the best education to my beloved Mansoor. Cherish my little Mumtaz Jahan and when you get her married, give her the other kothi as a gift from us. Look after my unfortunate daughter Jahanara Begum. Until Mansoor becomes an adult, all this property is under your guardianship.'

Qamar Zamani's tears turned to sobs. Her dupatta had slipped She clung to him with all her strength. The only words she spoke were 'Never—never—never. Sarkar, never.' He could not loosen her hold. 'Qamar, please stop. As your husband and beloved I command, I implore you to stop. I want you to face this crisis, for the sake of the children. It is Allah's will. Surrender to it with grace, my beloved.'

For Qamar Zamani, it was the moment of qayamat. She realized the inexorable truth that she could no longer stand between her husband and the destiny which awaited him. Her uncontrolled grief at the news of Wali Ehad's death was also for herself; for the living death that awaited her. She went down on her knees and lifted her hands in silent prayer.

On the day of his departure there was the silence of death in the Bari Kothi. At last it was time. Akbar Ali Khan held both children to his heart. To Jahanara, he assigned the responsibility of looking after her children and her mother. He took one last look at his wife. Then he took leave of all the servants by turn. In the first light of the day, as he rode out, he turned his horse around at the gate for a last look. They were there, all of them arraigned in the entrance. A slight smile appeared on his lips and he lifted his hand to his forehead; this was the last time they saw their Sarkar.

Qamar Zamani lifted Mansoor in her arms. Her grip tightened,

Mansoor tried to wriggle out but she was impervious to his struggle. Only one thought remained in her mind; her promise to protect this precious household; if necessary, with her own life.

For the next few weeks, Qamar Zamani held unrelenting vigil. Most of her time was now spent on the namaaz chowki. When she was not praying, she was found tending her husband's champa plant. For hours, she would stand near it; it seemed she was actually conversing with the plant. As the days passed, the champa plant sunk its roots in the soil and began to grow; new leaves sprung and buds began to appear.

Qamar Zamani's smooth forehead acquired a black mark from touching it to the *Sijdagaah* during namaaz.

Chapter 3

SHE KNEW THE content of the sealed envelope before she touched it. The messenger from the palace stood at the door, his eyes glued to the floor. She did not wail or cry. The servants saw her glazed eyes. Then they witnessed her hands tearing the fine chiffon dupatta off her head. The jewels that she removed from her wrists and neck lay in a heap on the floor. Suddenly her voice shattered the silence—'Bring my shroud!' she shouted to Jahanara Begum.

Trembling from head to foot, her daughter came with a tray on which was placed a set of white garments. Only after she had worn them did she allow herself to vent her grief. Her cries struck terror in every heart, the servants falling to their knees, sobbing, uncontrollable.

Jahanara Begum picked up the letter. It was brief. 'Dear Sister Qamar Zamani,' the nawab had written. 'I am writing with the greatest sorrow that our dear brother is no longer alive. We tried every hakim and doctor but alas! No one could save him. Now you should return to the riyasat with Jahanara Begum and the children. To look after you is our duty. Help me to fulfill that duty forthwith.'

Qamar Zamani tore the letter to shreds. She turned on her heel and walked to her chambers. Something strange happened that day. Her eyes, which had been the most expressive feature of her face, kind and most loving to her family and servants, turned into orbs of fire. Her soft voice became harsh. The gentle Qamar Zamani of Riyasat Mohammadpur died that day.

In a trice, she had rejected the nawab's offer. What she had feared all along had now come to pass. She got word that within days of reaching the riyasat, Akbar Ali Khan had been offered, by the hand of Nawab himself, a glass of sherbet. Predictably, there was no trace of the lethal poison in the empty glass. The nawab had instituted an enquiry at the highest level; he had ordered that a petition be prepared for the Governor, and asked Qamar Zamani to become his co-petitioner. But even in the first stab of her grief, she clung to two convictions: One, that this was her safe place. And two, that the nawab would not dare to step in the Terai—his part in the old kidnapping case would ensure that.

When the emissary read out her message to the nawab, he was furious. But there was nothing to be done. He tried another manner of persuasion. At the dead of night, a cart was ordered into the courtyard of the royal treasury. Faithful servants loaded it with gold, silver and coin. Under the cover of darkness it was dispatched with a police escort. The next day, having safely traversed the Terai, the cart reached the stately home of Qamar Zamani. She asked the servants to lift the cover. Precious metal caught the glint of the sun. It was said that after a long time, a smile was seen on her face. She motioned to her servants. The cart was returned without a word of explanation.

The change in Qamar Zamani became evident with each passing day. It began with the metaphor of a stone. Often she said to her handmaidens and companions 'You know what beats in my chest? It is a rock, a stone. Expect no kindness from a dead organ.' Sometimes when dinner was laid on the table and the covers were lifted to reveal the most elaborately prepared dishes, she would rush out of the house. Then Jahanara Begum would search for her and often find her mother thrusting handfuls of gravel into her mouth; her way of punishing herself for being alive. Her anger spared none; no one dared to come in her way. Her only refuge was the champa plant growing quietly in the corner of the garden where her husband had spoken his last words to her.

Jahanara Begum was the only child of her parents. She was married at sixteen to Sahibzada Ammar Ali Khan, a handsome youth of 22, the younger son of His Royal Highness the Nawab of Mohammadpur. Everyone knew that Ammar was the rightful heir to the throne. But no one dared to dig out a past that was better forgotten. Only Firozi who had heard the story from her grandmother Putli Bua had whispered it to Jahanara Begum when she was applying the bridal mehndi on her palms. 'Bibi, your husband should have sat on the throne instead of Nawab Asad Ali Khan. I know that what I am going to tell you will endanger my existence. But I have tasted your salt, so I must tell you what I know.'

Jahanara Begum's curiosity had been aroused, no one had so far told her anything about the man whom she would call husband. She drew close to Firozi. 'Nawab sahib's Wali Ehad Prince Mustanzir, was the apple of his eye. He was the child of Mehtab Begum, daughter of the royal House of Jalalpur. All the other offspring of the nawab turned out to be girls; Nawab Sahib probably saw them only when they were born and never again. But one day, the impossible happened. My *naani* remembers the day when the news of your husband, Ammar's, birth came. It was *gulabi jara* (gentle winter). She recalled that she had covered me with a light *razai* when suddenly she heard the royal guns booming. The last time she had heard this boom was 19 years ago at the birth of Prince Mustanzir. The next day, the birth of Sahibzada Ammar Ali Khan was officially announced—a second son born to an ageing Nawab Sahib! His youngest wife, mother of Ammar, Begum Shahrukh, bestowed alms to the poor, lit lamps at dargahs and ordered a shehnai to play for forty days at the entrance of her mahal. The celebration of his birth extended into the marriage festivities of his older brother, Prince Mustanzir. The new Bahu Begum from the House of Banda was carried to the bridal chamber on an ebony *chhaparkhat,* borne on the shoulders of four black slaves. It is said that she conceived on her wedding night. When the news was brought to him, the nawab was thrilled. He started counting the days until the delivery; he prayed to live long enough to see another little Mustanzir playing in his lap. In this excitement, he forgot about his own son, Ammar, who had just started to walk.

Suddenly fate took a lurch and their world came crashing down. Mustanzir was struck with severe paralysis. He could neither sit nor stand. All the hakims from nearby riyasats were summoned but they could only wring their hands in despair. The nawab did not leave his son's side for forty days. In the meanwhile, the British sent their *firman* that the nawab would have to hold court and name his successor as per the rule of the British crown. The nawab looked at his helpless son and cried tears of blood. It was then that Sharukh Begum entered the royal chambers carrying little Ammar. 'Sarkar, you have forgotten. You have a son, your rightful heir, given that Mustanzir will never walk again.'

Her words stung the nawab!

'How dare she call my son, my jewel, my moon *apahej,* handicapped! I will show her.'

Mustanzir would be his heir! If not him, he would bequeath his throne to Mustanzir's unborn son! In his pre-dawn dream, he had heard that the unborn child would be male.

He summoned two of his tallest and strongest aides and placed them in Mustanzir's attendance. Planted on either side of the invalid, they were ordered to prop him up while the British Agent read the coronation order. No one would know that Mustanzir was crippled—the white man's law was immutable, a crippled heir was automatically disqualified from ascending the throne...

The rest, bibi, is history. Amidst great pomp, the crippled Mustanzir, held upright by the powerful guards, ascended the throne. Shahrukh Begum, with Ammar in her arms, cried tears of blood. Nawab Sahib lived his last days tending to his son at his bedside, literally dropping dead at the same bedside,' Firozi's voice trailed off, before she picked up the story again:

'Jahanara Bibi, this is how your husband was deprived from what was rightfully his. Mustanzir died within a few months of his father, but he was able to see the birth of his son Asad, who became Asad Ali Khan Nawab of Mohammadpur. Your future husband was relegated to the position of sahibzada, chacha, his senior in rishta but only two years senior in age. He always had a poetic temperament; he really did not care about ruling a riyasat. He also had deep affection for his nephew, Asad, who was a playmate and a friend. This, my child, is the story of the man you will call husband from tomorrow.'

Jahanara Begum placed her arms around the old woman whom she loved more than her own mother. 'Will he like me?' she asked, closing her large brown eyes to dream. Firozi spoke of how the moon paled before her radiant face and what Ammar would say and do when he caught his first glimpse of that face.

Akbar Ali and Qamar Zamani could not bear the thought of being separated from their only child. They also knew the subordinate position which was the fate of the younger brothers of rulers. Qamar Zamani spoke to her husband—'Our son-in-law will always remain a sahibzada, subordinate to the nawab. We cannot allow him to take away our only child to then live in subordination! Why don't you make him an offer? If he agrees to live with us, we will make him our heir. After us, he will be master of the entire estate. After all, Jahanara Begum is all we have.' Akbar Ali agreed and the agreement was prepared in the form of the nikahnama.

The wedding was a splendid affair, almost like a royal wedding. Akbar Ali wanted to show the entire city that his daughter commanded no less attention than a son. And that he was gaining a son rather than losing a daughter. The bridal chamber was decorated with strings of motia flowers, alternated with strings of pearls. The young bride emerged from her bridal chamber the next morning in a state of bliss. There was whispering among the servants that Sahibzada had captivated the young mistress and bets were laid that exactly nine months later, the kothi would see its first male heir. Firozi, being Jahanara's favorite maid, tried her best to get to the bottom of the wedding night but Jahanara just smiled and said '*Hato, hùm nahin batate...*' Those were happy days. Ammar became Akbar Ali's companion at shikaar in the day and chess at night. Jahanara would wait impatiently for hours for the game to be over. Ultimately, it was Ammar who would ask his father-in-law if he would let him go to his new bride.

Exactly nine months after the wedding night, Jahanara went into labour. Nawab Sahib sent Dr Franny, the British resident doctor, to stay on 24 hour duty. Qamar Zamani sat on her prayer mat and refused to rise until the delivery. Ammar stood at his wife's closed door, his hand resting on the handle, ready to rush in at the slightest sound. The sound came, but it was not the sound of a child's cry, it was the sound of wailing. Ammar rushed in. Jahanara had given birth to two stillborn boys. Qamar Zamani ordered that no lamps be lit for three days. The house was plunged into darkness. Ammar was kept away from his grieving wife—an unspoken punishment to the woman for failing in her duty to bear healthy heirs. Whenever he asked for her, Qamar Zamani said, 'Her bad fortune should not infect you, Dulha Miyan. You will plant healthy seeds; she is still discharging from her body the gore of her ill fate. Let the forty day cycle pass.'

Ammar grew restless. He wanted to console his wife. In those hard hours while she was in labour, he had prayed for her life at whatever cost. He felt tears choking his throat. He wanted to share her grief but Qamar Zamani's word was law. Akbar Ali patted him on his back but did not contradict his wife. Ammar felt suffocated.

Exactly one year later, Jahanara went into labour once again. This time the orders were to keep the delivery a dead secret. Qamar Zamani had summoned holy women from nearby dargahs who recited prayers to keep away the evil eye. Jahanara Begum's room was filled with incense and various charms were hidden in the nooks—Ammar found remnants of their ministrations much later when he was allowed to go inside her chamber at night. On the day of the delivery, he counted the hours at the door while his wife cried with pain inside.

At the birth of Mansoor Ali Khan, the celebrations were unprecedented in the history of Mohammadpur. The nawab came the very next day and stood by the cradle, marveling at the child's grey-green eyes. He left, bestowing diamond bracelets on Qamar Zamani and Jahanara and a property deed for a new *shikargah* in the name of Mansoor. In the days that followed, it seemed that new life was stirring in the grand old kothi.

Mansoor became the focus of the entire household's attention. All day, he was transferred from lap to lap; there were wet nurses, maid servants, nannies dedicated to his comfort. Jahanara found herself looking for opportunities when she could be alone with her child. Ammar saw him on very few occasions. He found himself at odds with his environment. Against all norms, he longed to hold and kiss Mansoor. One afternoon when he found him playing while the maid dozed, he swept him up in his arms and took him to the garden. Mansoor was thrilled to sit on his father's shoulder and stretched his little hand to pluck the orange orbs of Chinese oranges, grabbing fistfuls of new leaves from the low-hanging branches. But these moments were short-lived because someone always came running, looking for the child.

At night Ammar would whisper to his wife. 'Jaano. I am not

happy here. I love your father and mother, they do so much for us, they love us, but I feel suffocated. I wish we could live on our own. We could have Mansoor Miyan all to ourselves. I have a kothi near Kathgodam in the Terai. Let us go there. In the summer, we can go to the mountains…'

Jahanara would place her hand over his lips. 'It will break their hearts; Abba Huzoor will never survive the shock of separation from Mansoor.' She could not bear the thought of seeing her parents unhappy, she knew what separation from her would do to them. But not in her wildest dreams could she imagine what her refusal would set in motion in her marital life.

It began very slowly. Ammar started to withdraw from the daily activities of Akbar Lodge. At first there was his occasional absence from Jahanara's chamber. She did not take much notice; it was part of their feudal upbringing not to question the husband's absence during the night. But gradually, the servants' gossip reached her ears. Ammar had begun to spend his evenings at the palace. The nawab had been missing his uncle and childhood friend and sending messages, inviting him to the palace. So he was overjoyed at seeing him and welcomed him back with open arms. 'Let Sahibzada Ammar Ali Khan's return be marked as a day of celebration in the riyasat.' He ordered messengers to be dispatched to Moradabad and Bareilly to invite the most celebrated courtesans, including the famous Zenobia Banu Begum of Chhatri Mahal. This courtesan, much in demand in small princely states, sent word back to the nawab. She would come only if he sent her his personal carriage with 50 guards to escort her to Mohammadpur.

The entire gentry of the city was summoned.

Zenobia Banu Begum's mehfil began with the lighting of lamps. Nawab made Ammar sit next him on his own gaddi as a mark of respect. Zenobia arrived with her artistes and musicians and bowed low before the nawab. Taking a deep look at his uncle who sat with bowed head he waved the courtesan towards Ammar. The chords were struck, the tabla sounded, and the courtesan encircled her hennaed feet with ghungroos. From that moment onwards, the night seemed to whiz by with music, dance, and poetry in quick rhythm. Ammar's eyes strayed towards the musician's corner where a young man sat behind a pair of tablas, his fingers flying over the drums. Zenobia kept pace; the faster he played, the faster she danced. He played a piece, she danced it out, he played faster, she danced faster. It was a mad rhythm! Ammar could not take his eyes off the slim long fingers flying over the table—the boy was perspiring, his eyes closed in sublime concentration. Suddenly, the woman stopped; she conceded defeat. The mehfil burst into applause. Nawab sprung out of his chair. Zenobia motioned to the boy. He stepped up and bowed low. 'My nephew, Sarfaraz, at your service, your Highness.' Ammar was lost! He noticed that Sarfaraz was looking straight at him even as he stood in attendance before the ruler. 'Won't you reward this wonderful performance?' said the nawab, holding out a fistful of sovereigns towards Ammar. 'You do it, your Highness,' Ammar said absently. Then, removing his diamond ring from his index finger he placed it in Sarafaz's palm, closing the boy's fist over it with both his hands.

That night he appeared in Jahanara's chamber very late. Mumtaz Jahan Begum was born nine months later.

Aiwan e Akbar once again became a hub of festivity. Qamar Zamani had been granted her heart's desire—a doll to dress, to decorate and display. Jahanara held the newborn to her breast and would not let the nurse remove her for a moment. The wet nurse sat at the doorstep, waiting for the baby. Qamar Zamani realized that her daughter was equally strong-willed. Dr Franny had told her that Jahanara needed rest with her feet raised up so the bleeding would stop. 'Begum Sahiba, Miss Baba will bleed to death.' Madiha, the wet nurse, sat near the door not daring to nurse her own mite of a baby for fear of her milk being rejected by Qamar Zamani. Finally, the doctor asked if she could put Jahanara to sleep for a few hours so the baby could be removed and the placenta cleaned. Qamar Zamani motioned with her hand and the doctor pulled on her gloves.

When Jahanara woke up, she found Ammar at her side. She looked for the baby, then turned to her husband with anxious eyes. 'Mumtaz Jahan is well; she is with the new *dai*, Madiha. You lie quietly, *sab thik ho jayega*.' Jahanara sat up in bed, a strange expression on her face. Ammar recognised the same obduracy which he had seen in her mother. 'Nothing... nothing will be all right. They will never let me have my child. Take us away from here, me and my children, please. We will go and live in Haldwani, I promise.'

'Why are you crying my child?' Qamar Zamani had entered the room. 'Miyan,' she turned to Ammar, 'Who allowed you in the delivery room? This is not the time. See how you have upset her! Come back after she has completed *chilla* and is ready to receive you. Women need women to bring them out of the trauma of child bearing.'

Under the quilt, Jahanara was holding tight to his hand. He had to tear himself away. He walked out the door without once turning back to look at her face. He went straight to his chamber and closed the door. It was late evening when Akbar Ali Khan personally knocked and asked him to come for dinner.

After dinner, Ammar saw Firozi standing in the shadows outside the zenana. She fell at his feet, 'Sarkar, help her, my innocent girl. She is having fit after fit; tearing her clothes and hair, not allowing anyone to come near her. In the servants' quarters we all are crying and praying. Sarkar, for the sake of Allah, take her away, she won't survive!'

Ammar placed his consoling hand on Firozi's shoulder. 'Bua,' he said gently. 'Let me think. I know how she suffers.'

That was the last time anyone from the kothi spoke to Ammar. The next morning when the servant came with his morning tea, the bed had not been slept in. The news reached Qamar Zamani and Akbar Ali Khan while they were waiting at the breakfast table. 'He must have been summoned to the palace,' Akbar said to his wife. Qamar Zamani laid a hand on his. 'Sarkar, I am not at ease. This morning my *istikhara* was negative three times. I hope the news is good. Go to the palace and make certain. Too much is at stake.'

Qamar Zamani's premonition proved right. No one knew where Ammar had gone. Nawab Sahib dispatched his messengers in three directions; Jahanara began secret visits to the dargahs with Firozi. Qamar Zamani took to her prayer mat for prolonged *namaaz*. Ammar never appeared at the entrance of the kothi again.

Months passed. Mansoor and Mumtaz Jahan, were growing under the loving care of their grandmother and mother. But it was Qamar Zamani on whose orders their life revolved—their own mother featured nowhere in their upbringing, as if she was incidental to their lives. They were taught to call her Baji, meaning older sister. Slowly, Jahanara Begum became a shadow of her old self. At the age of 25, she began to attire herself as a widow. First, she removed her ornaments, gradually, so that her mother would get used to seeing her without them. One day, her bracelets came off. Another day, her slim neck became shorn of necklaces. The cast off ornaments were secretly stored by Firozi in an ivory box which lay in a concealed cabinet in her chamber. Every time Jahanara Begum handed her an ornament, Firozi would try to reason with her. 'He will come back, Bibi. As Allah is my witness, Ammar Miyan really loves you. It was Bari Begum's hukumat which drove him away.' Sometimes she used to reason with Jahanara Begum, sometimes she used her tears. 'Allah! Why did I live to see the day when my beautiful child would pluck all the plumes from her body and stand naked?' Wiping her tears, Jahanara Begum would smile and place her arms around Firozi. 'I promise to wear the plumes… when he returns.'

Days turned into months. There was no news from Ammar. Some rumors had begun to circulate. Ammar had been seen in the royal coupe of a train near Agra. He had been spotted at the Dargah of the Sufi Pir Hazrat Saleem Chishti at Fatehpur Sikri with a group of young qawwals.

Jahanara decided to send Firozi's son-in-law, Chhuttan, to the Haldwani house. He was given a purse and strict instructions to return with news. The man returned after a week. He was summoned to Jahanara's private chamber in the zenana. Firozi placed him behind the screen and narrated his story which she had been told. 'Chhuttan found the house in Haldwani closed. When he bribed the guards they told him "Sahib has gone to Bombay Presidency. His Munshi pays us salaries and keeps an eye on the property. We know nothing more".' Chhuttan added his '*Jee huzoor*', '*Baja huzoor*' from behind the screen.

Suddenly Jahanara got up and opened the screen; Chhuttan averted his eyes while Firozi tried to restrain her mistress. 'Bibi, please stop. Begum Sahiba will never forgive me for bringing him inside the zenana!'

Jahanara brushed her aside. 'Look at me!' She transfixed Chhuttan by the fire in her eyes, her voice harsh. 'Are you telling me the truth? On pain of death, tell me what you saw!' Then she turned to Firozi—'You have nursed me. I have called you Amma, a name I could never use for my mother. Swear by the milk which is running in my veins that this man is speaking the truth! Else may you live to see the day when you place my body in my shroud.'

Firozi was trembling. Chhuttan sank to his knees. 'Bitiya Begum, I beg you, forgive me. May all evil eyes cast on you be transferred on me. I saw nothing, I swear by my innocent children.'

'Everything, Chhuttan, each detail!' Jahanara Begum had removed from her waist the little ivory revolver that her father had gifted her the day Ammar left. With the muzzle in his gut, the man began to sob. 'Bitiya Begum, please spare me! I am your slave, but I am also Ammar Miyan's *namak halal*. But I will tell you, I will…'

Jahanara sat down, Firozi stood behind her trembling.

'It was a mehfil, the likes of which I have never seen. I had to bribe the guard with the pocket watch your father had given my father-in-law. It was very hard to part with it but I had nothing else. He took me to the attic and pointed at a small gap in the wooden floor planks. I could see two young boys playing tabla and sarangi. Music filled the air along with sounds of ghungroos. The dancing figure was veiled. The white *pheshwaz* swirled and the hennaed feet were flying. I was stunned at the grace and skill of the dancer. The music ended. I saw the dancer approach the *baithak*. And there was Ammar Miyan, reclining among the bolsters and pillows. In one had he held his cup of wine, in the other dangled a glittering necklace. The dancer approached him and bowed low, throwing back the veil. May Allah smite me, it was the young boy Sarfaraz who Miyan had first seen at the nawab's mehfil! His kohl-lined dark eyes were shining, there was henna on his palms and pearls in his ears. Miyan bent forward and kissed his forehead before placing the necklace around his slim neck. But the boy was too bold! Before the entire mehfil which consisted of a few boys, mostly local Talukdars from the Terai area, he slid into Ammar Miyan's lap! They laughed, another boy entered with a wine decanter and began pouring. Miyan now sat with his arm around the boy… I had seen enough. I prayed to Allah to restore Miyan's senses, cursed the entire lot of boys and came down from the attic.'

After she had seen Chhuttan go out of the *chor darwaza*, Firozi came back to see Jahanara sitting stone-like, still in the same posture. Jahanara's eyes were glazed, her body cold. The woman held her hand to her mistress' nose. 'My child, don't leave this servant, may my tongue burn, where have you gone?' she muttered and set about rubbing Jahanara's cold hands and feet. Suddenly, the young woman flung her aside and stood up, stretching to full height. Jahanara was tall and well-built, but she had always walked with rounded shoulders, to draw attention away from her height. Firozi had never seen her rise to her full height—she was an Amazon, a *Jadugarni* from a *tilism*!

'Amma, don't fret.' She spoke in a harsh voice 'Just stay by my side. Wait and see. We have a lot to do.'

All day Jahanara's room was shut. She had told the servants that she was on fast and was not to be disturbed on any account. Only Firozi was permitted to go inside to help her perform *wuzu* or lay out the prayer mat.

At *Iftar* time she emerged to break her fast, closing the door behind her. Qamar Zamani looked at her with an inquiring glance. The table was laden with Sherbat and *Iftar* food. After reciting the prayer, Jahanara Begum broke her fast with a date and glass of water.

'Why?' Qamar Zamani raised her brows. 'What was this *roza* for? Was it a *mannat* for Ammar Miyan's return?' Not once did the daughter look up or reply to her mother's anxious questions. She went back to her chamber and shut the door with a bang.

At some late hour of the night, two chador-clad women opened the front door of Akbar Lodge and stepped outside. One of them was staggering under the weight of a black trunk which was placed on her head. Walking briskly, the younger woman reached a clearing and ordered the other one to approach. They lifted the lid of the trunk and there was a rustle of silk as she took out armloads of clothes from the box. Ghararas, *angurkhus*, and dupattas all trimmed with gold and silver *lachka, gota, kali, karchob, bankri*... The splendid garments were heaped on the ground.

Firozi became very agitated. 'Bibi, *meri jaan*, what are you doing? These are your wedding *poshak*, each one has been hand-stitched by the kingdom's best tailors. The silks and satins have been imported from Damishq (Damascus). Why child.... You promised me that you will not harm yourself! Curse me for having listened to you! Now, for the sake of Allah and Rasul....Stop!'

Jahanara produced a box of matches from her cloak pocket. Firozi saw the stick light up the heap lying on the ground. The silver and gold gleamed in the semi-light. Jahanara's hand did not even tremble when she threw the burning stick on the heap. As the silk began to burn, Firozi threw herself on the pile trying to salvage the treasure from massive destruction. But Jahanara, tall and strong of limb, pulled the woman back and held her in a strong clasp. She watched the flames rise and felt Firozi collapsing to the ground, flailing her arms and legs, crying out her name. 'Amma!' she spoke, a haunted sound in the dark. 'This is what I wanted to do ever since the day I found Ammar missing from my bed. It had to be.'

In the early hours of the morning, Firozi slunk out of the house with two silver buckets. When she returned, the buckets were filled with silver and gold collected from the ashes of Jahanara's dowry. She got Chuttan to compress them into silver and gold bricks and stored them in a safe place for the girl's future.

As the days passed, Jahanara's persona took a different form. The truth about Ammar Miyan slowly leaked out from the servant quarters and reached her through different routes. She felt branded as a woman who could not satisfy her husband and who drove him into the arms of young men. She was ashamed of her failing and devised her own punishment... She began with dressing herself in the coarsest fabric, removing the little ornaments she still wore and secretly chopped off her thick braids, using her rough dupatta to cover her head so no one would know. Her temper tantrums deterred anyone who wanted to get close to her. 'Make them afraid and they will leave you alone' was her unthinking strategy. She was even able to stand up to her mother and challenged her authority, especially when it concerned her children. Now the two women of Akbar Lodge, stood face to face, eye to eye.

In this harsh matriarchy, Mansoor and Mumtaz were growing up.

Chapter 4

THE CHAMPA SAPLING had grown into a tree, laden with fragrant white flowers. Mansoor had also grown, passing from adolescence into a handsome, almost beautiful youth. Like most elite Muslim youth, he chose Aligarh Muslim University for his higher education, and presented his choice to his grandmother. Qamar Zamani could not bear any distance from her beloved grandson. The distance between Nainital and Aligarh was formidable.What was she to say? Day and night, she prayed to *Maula Mushkilkusha* to show her the way. After *chilla,* forty days of prayer, she consulted her tasbih for guidance. The answer was 'yes'—she had received a positive signal.

That day, she summoned her chief comptroller, Razzaq Ali. He had been her husband's loyal servant, now entrusted with managing the affairs of her estate. 'Go at once to Aligarh. The first available kothi close to the university should be purchased forthwith. Give the asking price and get nothing but the best for my family. Have I made myself clear?' Razzaq Ali boarded a train that very night.

Within one week, Qamar Zamani was in possession of a sprawling 13-bedroom mansion, within the outer boundary of the university campus. 'While Mansoor Miyan attends classes, we all will stay in Aligarh. During Mansoor Miyan's holidays, we will return to our home in the mountains. This is the will of Maula. May Mansoor live long and prosper for ever.' Qamar Zamani's firman brooked no argument. The move was imminent and Mansoor remained the pivot around which revolved the lives of everyone in the household.

ॐ

Mansoor graduated and then began preparing for the Civil Service exam. One day, seeing him immersed in studies, Qamar Zamani voiced her concern—'Why my love, you have finished your studies. What makes you so intent on these books now?'

'Ammajan, I have only finished my BA but I now have to think of my future. I want to sit for the ICS and become a civil servant. Please bless me and pray for my success.'

Civil Service! Qamar Zamani stopped telling the beads of her tasbih.

'Miyan, did I hear the word naukri? You want to *work*? Have you gone mad? You, who own this vast property, who employ hundreds of people? You, who are the only one who will carry our name? You want to serve others? Has there been anyone in our family who entered a service? Unheard of, my child! Don't ever ever mention this subject again." Having uttered her edict, she stormed out of his room, leaving Mansoor guilt-ridden and helpless.

Caught between desire and duty, Mansoor was in a fix. He could not think of hurting his beloved Naani. He had always been afraid of the woman whose writ ran all the way from Aligarh to Nainital and included 67 villages and innumerable lands in between. It saddened him to think that he could never perhaps follow his heart. His two custodians ran his life with an iron fist but were also his dearly beloved mothers. Left to himself, he had no interest in the affairs of his estate, he was not cut out for the financial management of landed property. The villages were looked after by old munshis and managers who collected the rents and taxes—he was not even interested enough to ask for accounts. The idea of forcing the poor to pay *lagaan* on their meager land holdings disgusted him. Only once a year, he agreed to go on a tour of his estate. When the farmers folded their hands before him in supplication, he thought nothing of foregoing the *lagaan*. The munshis silently fumed, but also saw their advantage in his generosity. 'He has no mind to take over the control from us,' they whispered to one another. 'His involvement is limited to annual visits. For the rest of the year, it is our show. This young fool will not miss a few mango groves or even a dozen fields of cane!'

Having given up his dream of joining the ICS, Mansoor had unlimited leisure. Other diversions took over his daily life. He played more tennis with friends, he also began to relish occasional sorties into the kitchen where he watched the preparation of delicacies for the *dastarkhwan*. His natural flair for cooking, a favorite past time of *nawabzadas*, deepened. On special days, he would call for the chief cook to bring his equipment and condiments into his personal veranda where he would supervise the preparation and even occasionally stir the pot. Qamar Zamani was content to watch the apple of her eye indulge in the sensual pleasure of taste and bring exotic dishes to the *dastarkhwan* of Akbar Ali Khan.

The silken cocoon was tightening. Every time he tried to break out, loving tentacles would jerk him back with immense tenderness but irresolutely. The comfort zone silently drew him in.

He was now at the prime of his life. His two mothers were dreaming of his marriage; the search was on.

In their reckoning, the noblest families and the most beautiful girls were not good enough. Qamar Zamani and Jahanara were on the lookout for a *koh qaf ki peri*—a celestial beauty from Mount Caucasus—for their precious child. In her solitary hill-top kothi, Qamar Zamani's was a lonely life. Her only entertainment was looking through the old and powerful telescope which her husband had bought for her from an Englishman. Nainital was a small cup-shaped hill station, a lake in its midst. Lush green foliage covered the inside of the cup, broken by the kothis and bungalows of the elite residents. Akbar Ali Khan would stand by her side at the highest point in the garden where his telescope had been mounted, explaining the landscape. She saw the winding road crawling with streams of cars and buses, bringing visitors to the valley. Like motorized toys, they disappeared around the bends in the road. Together, they watched boats in the lake, with their sails spread, swan-like. They would bet on the boat races, a bet he always lost! She could see right inside the gardens of the big kothis and marvel at the skill of other gardeners. Turning the instrument around, it seemed as if the circle of hills detached itself and passed through the glass of the telescope to lie scattered in their garden.

It was magic! A world miles away which one could stretch one's hand and touch. At night, the lights of the city would set the telescope on fire. The stars and moon descended from the sky and lay at their door. These were their own, very own, private moments. They spent hours taking turns to watch and marvel at their telescope world!

To dispel her loneliness now, Qamar Zamani had taken refuge in this colourful spectacle. She would stand for hours, hoping perhaps that one day she would see the image of her beloved husband. She had lost most other interests in life—eating, dressing, entertaining....Her recreated self was as hard and rough as the gravel she placed in her mouth at meal times, while her family waited for her at a table laden with the best of dishes.

Her only visitor was Dr Miss Gill from the General Hospital, who had lived in Naini most of her life. Living here so long, she knew all the elite families who came to spend the summer months every year. One day, arriving at the kothi, she found Begum Sahiba looking intently through the telescope. She stood behind her for a while, waiting for her to finish viewing. At last, growing impatient, she tapped the ground with her walking stick. Qamar Zamani did not move. Going closer, Miss Gill noticed that the Begum's gaze was fixed on a house on the opposite hill as if she was absorbing its every feature. 'Anything special?' she asked with her usual warm smile.

'Oh it is you, dear Miss Gill. Take this and follow my finger.' She yielded her place to the doctor and directed her gaze. While Miss Gill looked through the lens, Begum continued: 'For an hour, I had been looking at the garden and the riot of colour in the flower beds. Then suddenly I saw an apparition. Can you see her Miss Gill?'

The girl, with her back towards the telescope, was drying her hair in a corner of the garden. Long and shiny, it hung over her back in wet tresses. 'Yes, Begum Sahiba, I see the young lady. Now you look, maybe she will turn around.'

Qamar Zamani looked agitated as she moved back to the telescope.

The girl shook her head, sprinkling gold drenched drops of water all around, and turned to lift her face towards the shining sun, quite unaware that two eyes were riveted on her, taking her in from head to toe. She could not have imagined that her destiny was unraveling in those moments.

The girl was petite, with large blue eyes, and an almond-shaped face. Qamar Zamani was stunned at the beauty revealed before her eyes. Her first thought was Mansoor—she conjured up his face and form by the side of this girl. 'This is it. She is the one for my Mansoor,' she spoke out aloud. Then, turning to Miss Gill, 'Tell me dear friend, who is the child? Is she married, does she come from a good family, will they agree?' Taking her hand, Miss Gill sat her down, shaking her head in disapproval. She had known Qamar Zamani since the time she first came to this mountain resort as a young woman, so obviously in love with her handsome husband. She had seen her grow to become the reigning queen of both her houses in Mohammadpur and Nainital. She had been witness to her punishing herself for her failure to stop her husband from obeying the nawab's summons to go to his certain death. She had seen her devising ways to torture herself. But that day, the radiance she saw on her face was something she had seen after a long time. She asked affectionately. 'Begum Sahiba, your face is flushed. Come, let me check your blood pressure.'

'Oh Miss Gill, only you can bring joy into my life. Tell me, good woman, everything you know about that child you saw in the telescope. And promise me that you will help me get her for my beloved Mansoor.'

Miss Gill was astounded at her impetuousness. 'Begum, please stop right here. You know nothing about the girl! How can you be so impulsive?'

Qamar Zamani leaned back on the chair and closed her eyes. Her fingers were over her *tasbih*. 'But Miss Gill, if you value my life, if you have any regard for me, you must tell me all you know. There is not much use me dragging on my corpse of a body like this any longer.' She looked up at her friend with the saddest eyes. 'Speak now woman, or may you see my dead face!'

'You make it very hard for me, Begum Sahiba. I will tell you about her but promise me you won't unleash your imagination to plan a marriage. I won't let you hurt yourself any more than I have seen you doing for the last six years. Her name is Shehzadi. She has a distinguished lineage. Their household is known for the fact that during Moharrum, the Lucknow '*chup tazia*' is lifted from that *chokhat*.' Qamar Zamani's fingers tightened on her tasbih.

Miss Gill continued, 'Her family is from Lucknow. Her mother is my patient, she has been brought here to recover from a long illness. They have been here for several months. Both her parents are from *nawabi gharanas*. Her father, Mohammed Hasan Agha, is with the Provincial Government. Shehzadi, who just turned thirteen, is engaged to her cousin who has gone to London to study medicine.

I have advised them to stay here a little longer as the lady is still too weak to travel or to bear the heat of the plains.'

Listening to Miss Gill, Qamar Zamani was once again dreaming. She looked at Miss Gill with urgency and spoke almost pleadingly. 'Miss Gill. Ever since I have set eyes on this girl, I see her as Mansoor's bride. This *has* to be! And you are the one who will make it possible.'

'But Begum Sahiba, the girl is already engaged. You know how it is in such gharanas. Once they have given their word, they can never, never take it back.'

'We know this very well, Miss Gill,' Qamar Zamani said impatiently. 'And that is why we have entrusted you with this difficult task!' And so saying, she again closed her eyes. Miss Gill knew that she had been dismissed.

The begum would not give an inch, Miss Gill knew that much. There was no use trying to reason with one who was inured to any other reality but her own. She also knew that Qamar Zamani needed to be appeased, at least momentarily. So she left, saying softly to her inert form reclining on the chair by the telescope, 'Begum Sahiba, you dear, dear woman, I will see what I can do.'

Qamar Zamani spent the next few days gazing at Shehzadi. She showed glimpses of her to Jahanara Begum and to Firozi Bua—one the mother, the other the wet nurse and in a manner, more than a mother. Quickly, the news spread in the servants' quarters. One by one, the rest of the household servants took their turn at the telescope and left praying for the day to dawn when Mansoor would wear his wedding *sehra*.

Shehzadi was seen at her daily chores by occupants of the Badi Kothi. She would look after her mother, give her medicine, console her father or just sit between the two, trying to bring a smile by her innocent chatter. In the kothi everyone started calling her Miyan's bride, an epithet Qamar Zamani loved to hear. They all were watching a silent film, but hoping for a day when the silence would be broken by the sounds of the shehnai. '*Insha Allah* when she comes to this house in a doli, what a day it will be, Huzoor!' they would tell the Begum. 'Don't forget our gold bangles!' the serving girls would tease coquettishly. Qamar Zamani loved this prattle. But after a little banter, she would put up her hand to silence them and bow her head in prayer to almighty Allah.

Miss Gill was in a quandary. Qamar Zamani's obstinacy persisted. She had no idea how to bring up the matter with Agha Sahib. But something had to be done and done soon. Each day she found in her letter box a monogrammed envelop with a reminder. One day she reluctantly began the mission she had been saddled with. She had been called by Agha Sahib to examine his wife who had been feeling unusually weak. There, she found Agha Sahib pacing up and down in the garden.

'Don't be so agitated sir, let me examine her,' she said gently. After a while, she came out and found him in an armchair in his garden, blowing smoke rings from his hookah. She lowered her bulky body into a chair next to him.

'Agha Sahib, Begum is getting weaker by the day. I have prescribed some injections which the nurse from the hospital will come and administer. But what I am really worried about is her anxiety and depression. She needs to be happy, to laugh, to enjoy. Today she almost cried at the thought of Shehzadi Bitiya being left alone should any thing happen to her. She should not think such morbid thoughts. It adds to her illness.'

Agha Sahib sighed. 'But our Bitiya is already engaged! Its only a matter of time; her fiancé has gone to London, and as soon as he finishes his degree we will have the nikah ceremony conducted.'

Miss Gill bent close to Agha's ear.

'Begum is perhaps worried because she has heard that boys who go abroad marry white women and then come back to marry their parents' selection; the poor girl then becomes the second wife.'

'But Aijaz is not like that at all! He is from our family and has very high moral character. Begum is unnecessarily anxious and ruining her health!' Agha Sahib remonstrated.

This encouraged Miss Gill to speak about the subject which had been entrusted to her. 'I do not know if I should bring it up, but seeing Begum's condition I thought I should tell you something that may relieve her mind and help her recover soon...'

Agha Sahib sat up in his chair. 'Anything, dear Miss Gill, please tell us anything that will cure our Begum and we will be ever grateful to you.'

Miss Gill pointed to the sprawling red kothi on the hill right opposite. 'Do you see that double-storied house opposite?'

'Yes, we have been looking at it and admiring it. But who lives there?'

He was immersed in deep thought; all he wanted was his wife to get well... at whatever cost.

Miss Gill began the story of the inhabitants of the 'house on the opposite hill' not sparing any detail she could think of. Agha Sahib had heard about the Royal House of Mohammadpur, but knew nothing of the feudal intrigues which were woven around the majestic and lonely house he was looking at. Without realizing why the doctor was going to such lengths, he found himself drawn to these unknown people, in particular to Qamar Zamani.

One sentence spoken by Miss Gill made him sit up: 'Mansoor is a nice boy. He is the only son and will have a huge inheritance. I can't think of a better match for Shehzadi Bitiya. Please, Agha Sahib, you must meet them once, for the sake of our Begum Sahiba. She needs to calm down; such high BP is no good.

'What are you saying, Miss Gill? Do you expect that we will go back on our word? Bitiya is already engaged! In a year, Aijaz will return for the nikah and *rukhsat*. I forbid you, good woman!'

There was dead silence. Miss Gill looked embarrassed. She heaved herself up and made to leave. Agha Sahib was propelled with a nameless fear, as if her departure meant the end of hope. He held out his hand. Miss Gill saw in this gesture a faint hope. She took his hand in her firm grasp. 'Don't worry, sir. It will be okay. As Allah is my witness, I know this is His will for you, for our Begum and for Shehzadi.'

Long after she had left, Agha Sahib sat quietly smoking his hookah. As for Miss Gill, as soon as she had turned the corner, she made the sign of cross on her heart and prayed.

Chapter 5

THE NEXT MORNING, two *dandee*s stopped in the portico of Agha Sahib's house. Word was sent inside that two ladies had come to visit Begum Sahiba. The liveried palanquin bearers parted the velvet curtains. Firozi Bua and Saidani Bua descended gracefully, each carrying a silver tray draped with gold-edged silk covers.

Begum Agha Kaneez Zehra was reclining on her divan, supported by many pillows and bolsters. Her big silver *panadaan* sat next to her *khaasdaan,* which was filled with *paan gillories* wrapped in gold foil. A silver spittoon was placed by her side. She tried to get up for the visitors, but, feeling faint, sank back on the pillows. The women respectfully sat on the stools near her bed. She had been told that these two were close companions of Begum Qamar Zamani of Mohammadpur whose kothi across the hill she had often seen and admired. That is all she knew.

Firozi Bua furtively looked around in the hope of seeing Shehzadi. The girl was nowhere in sight. She then bowed her head and placed the two thalis on the takht and lifted the covers. The begum saw a gleaming red *Imam Zamin,* a plate of gold guineas, silver baskets of sweets and dry fruits. Looking at these elaborate gifts, the Begum was bewildered. She called out to her special attendant: 'Amina Bua, come here.'

A middle-aged woman in a Lucknow gharara and *chikan kurta,* her head draped in a light dupatta, appeared at her side. In the tradition of polite society, she was now the interlocutor between her begum and the women. She looked at Firozi and Saidani with questioning eyes. 'Amina Bua,' Firozi began, 'We have come from the house of Sahibzada Akbar Ali Khan. Our own dear Dr Gill may have mentioned about our visit.'

'Yes, Agha Sahib did mention to Begum Sahiba that your mistress wanted to meet her,' Amina answered, looking at her Begum all the time. 'But she did not come…?'

The begum gestured towards the *khaasdaan*. They picked up a *gilory* each and continued talking.

'*Insha Allah*, she will come here soon, not only once but many times. At this moment she has sent us to offer her salaams, her prayer for your quick recovery and… and…'

'Yes?' the Begum spoke for the first time.

'Her offer of a *paigham*, a proposal, for our Mansoor Miyan and your Shehzadi Bitia. We hope Begum Sahiba, you will honour us with favourable consideration."

Begum Agha was stunned! She looked at them and then at Amina Bua. 'You may not know,' she said gently, '*Masha Allah* our Bitiya is already engaged.'

'We know.'

Saidani spoke without raising her eyes. 'Still, our Begum Sahiba requests that you consider her proposal. She wants Agha Sahib to meet Mansoor Miyan once. Then it will be His will,' Firozi then turned to the Begum and for the first time in this visit addressed her directly. 'Begum Sahiba, if you refuse us today, our Sarkar… she will be very, very sad. She has seen many tragedies in her life and may not be able to bear this disappointment.'

Begum spoke her words haltingly, in a barely audible voice. 'Please give our salaams to your Begum Sahiba and tell her that I will talk to Agha Sahib. I promise. But there is one request. Take back these trays; we cannot accept them. She will understand. Let us just wait; whatever will be the will of God.' So saying, she placed her head on the pillow and closed her eyes. Amina Bua accompanied the women, escorting them respectfully to their *dandees*. She then handed back the trays while apologizing that her Begum, with her limited strength, could not have spent more time with them.

All the while they were gone it was not easy for Qamar Zamani. She stayed glued to the telescope, watching all the oncoming *dandees,* trying to spot the one with the liveried carriers. Tiring of her vigil, she started pacing up and down. She heard the gate clang open and the *dandee* entered. The two women descended bearing the silver trays. As soon as Qamar Zamani saw the trays, the dreaded frown appeared and she thundered. 'What do I see? Firozi, why do I see these *thalis* in your hand?'

Hesitantly, they narrated the story of their visit. They dreaded her temper but having served her faithfully for many years, they also knew how to calm her down. Slowly they described the fragile health of Begum Agha. 'Bibi, she could hardly lift her head from the pillow. She was in no condition to speak, leave alone take a decision about her only child. Allah *qasam,* she did not say 'No'. All she said was that she would talk to her husband. No, we did not see Shehzadi, nor did we ask to see her. We will now see her when we bring her here as Mansoor Miyan's bride. On that day, Begum Sahiba, on my bended knees, I will demand my reward, a pair of emerald earrings! As for Saidani bua, she has set her heart on a pair of gold *karas*!' By now, Qamar Zamani was smiling; she was promising whatever gifts they demanded, while her servants regaled her with grand plans for the wedding.

But the days passed without any word from Agha Sahib. Qamar Zamani waited with growing impatience, still unwilling to concede defeat. 'I will not take no for an answer,' she said after every namaaz. She kept up the pressure and every day, the two Buas trudged up to Agha Sahib's house with gifts and returned to the kothi carrying the untouched trays. Egos took over from niceties. Qamar Zamani was now adamant that no matter what, she would see Shehzadi as her Mansoor's bride.

The one in whose name these games were being played, was living his carefree life. Mansoor was beginning to look more like his father, Ammar Miyan. But no one dared say that for fear of annoying Qamar Zamani. Every morning when she went to wake him up, Firozi gazed at him. Fair complexion, grey-blue half-closed eyes, golden hair and slender body, if only Ammar could see him! Each day she prayed that his father may return to see his son, at least once. They were so alike, father and son. Like his father, he was gentle and kind, she had never heard him speak a harsh word to the humblest of his servants. Unlike his peer *nawabzades,* he was diligent in his studies. His best friends were serious and educated boys from modest families. But his social status demanded that he hobnob only with the children of the richest feudal families. Being an excellent tennis player, he was in great demand, men and women vying to be close to him. In Aligarh, within and outside the university, the parents of eligible girls saw him as a prize catch!

Some evenings, the central hall of the kothi would resound with western dance music. In their anxiety to please the British residents, the elite had adopted a few western norms which normally would be considered taboo, such as ballroom dancing. Young girls, daughters of government officials, arrived duly chaperoned by older or younger brothers and throwing off their capes and cloaks, took to the dance floor with ever attentive and nimble-footed young men, including Mansoor. Qamar Zamani and Jahanara watched this mehfil through latticed windows, proud to see their son weaving his way across the floor. Mumtaz Jahan, still an adolescent girl, stood behind her mother, cringing with awe and envy, never daring to ask why she had to be excluded from all the fun. It was only her unconditional love for her brother that kept her from expressing her pent up feelings by throwing tantrums to draw attention to herself. By Qamar Zamani's order, there was one restriction in these mehfil—liquor. Mansoor neither drank, nor served drinks. Sometimes his friends ribbed him for what they called his 'mulla habits'. But that did not keep them away from these dream parties. All the high officials, Indian and British, who came to Naini for the summer, were invited. The Governor, his wife and daughters asked for their favourite delicacies in advance. The table was laden with food prepared from secret recipes which the cooks were instructed never to reveal. Once Qurban Ali, Chief Khansaman, was called to the Central Hall at the request of Her Excellency, the Lady Governor, to explain the recipe for *Badshahi Raan*. Qurban, after elaborate salaams, presented his spiel and bowed out. At the door, he was accosted by Jahanara Begum. 'You rogue, how dare you reveal our royal recipe!' With cast-down eyes, Qurban softly said, 'Chhoti Begum, don't worry. I left out the most essential ingredient.'

Scintillating conversation, discreet flirtation and whispered declarations of love flowed through the evening. European and Indian girls vied with each other for Mansoor's attention and left for home as late as they could. They cast longing looks at the kothi, flushed with lights and music, Mansoor at the door waving goodbye.

A host of servants served the guests with quiet dignity but disliked any girl who tried to get too friendly with their Mansoor Miyan. Most of them had seen Mansoor through various stages of his life. Abid was the oldest serving bearer, Mansoor's personal servant. All he wanted was that Mansoor be 'safely' married and not be caught by one of these '*besharam*'girls. He equally disliked most of what he considered Mansoor's '*matlabi yaars*'—'taking advantage of *chhote sahib*,' he grumbled to Firozi. He was wary of all the 'party mems', especially of Rakhshanda, whom he called 'danger ladish'. Mansoor, like his father, was of a poetic temperament. Abid told

Firozi, 'Miyan is *husn parast*. Rakhshanda Bibi is not only beautiful but also very '*hansmukh*'. Just wait, Mansoor Miyan will be smitten by her. But Bua, she is only a glittering butterfly, no family, no pedigree. May Allah protect Miyan from her wiles.'

'Then do something Abid, my child,' Firozi urged. 'When you can't draw out the ghee with straight fingers, you must bend them. Catch him at the right moment and embed Shehzadi's portrait in his heart...'

One afternoon the two of them planted themselves outside Mansoor's chamber. They had seen Mansoor go inside for an afternoon nap. Hoping that he had not fallen asleep, they began:

'So Firozi Bua, have you seen Shehzadi Bitiya?' Abid asked in a voice that would carry into the room.

'Yes, *beta*. May my eyes turn blind, never have I beheld beauty such as I saw in her face and form. She is head to foot, Mughal princess. Her eyes are grey-green, her hair flows down to her hips, golden, silken. Her face is almond-shaped and her skin is liquid moonlight. She was made with His own hands by Almighty Allah, and guess what? She was made for our own Miyan. I wish he could see her, just one look to behold His miracle in human form!'

Abid heaved a loud sigh. 'Alas Firozi Bua, it is of no use. Miyan has eyes only for that angrezan, Rakhshanda Bibi. Maybe you can suggest one of Miyan's *nawabzada* friends for Shehzadi's hand. Wherever she goes, she will rule every heart...'

Mansoor, who had been listening to each word, smiled to himself. 'Rakhshanda...' he whispered into the pillow, thinking of her bare arms circled around his neck on the dance floor. But the description of Shehzadi had made him curious. He willingly played along with Abid's ploy and agreed with Abid's respectful suggestion to 'take a look at the hills' through his grandfather's telescope. Abid had focused the lens on the Agha Sahib's kothi. Luckily for Abid, Mansoor's first glance fell on Shehzadi as she stood beside her mother, feeding her something out of a cup. All he could make out was a girl in a lilac gharara; it was her hair that entangled his gaze. Loose and touched by the breeze, it shimmered as she tossed her head to throw back her hair back from her eyes and looked straight at the eye of the telescope. In a flash he saw her flushed face and large grey eyes before she turned away. Mansoor could not move. Abid had to almost shout, 'Miyan, for the sake of Allah, move! Begum Sahiba is coming this way!' Reluctantly, he let go of the lens. Who was this Shehzadi; and why was he feeling this overwhelming desire to gaze at her face and form?

Chapter 6

AFTER THAT INCIDENT, the kothi was not the same again. Gone were the late night parties, dancing and the 'babalog' women. Abid and Firozi rejoiced at their success! To further fan his desire, they took to calling him for viewing his 'dulha*n*' (as they like to call her) whenever Qamar Zamani and Jahanara were not around. They also kept feeding him with stories of negotiations between the two kothis. Mansoor grew impatient. He had never known a single wish in his life which had remained unfulfilled. Qamar Zamani was there to bring down the moon if Mansoor desired it. He looked at his ageing grandmother. How long could he bank on her, he mused. He had been told by servants that Agha Sahib was very firm about having given his word for Shehzadi. He also noticed that as Qamar Zamani's insistence increased in pitch, so were his refusals. He thought of cornering Agha Sahib—but where? The man did not visit the Naini Club nor the elite parties. Going to their house, uninvited, would never be acceptable. The only way was the one he had known from the day he was born; his grandmother's obstinacy and her strong will to get whatever she desired.

Poor Miss Gill! She was tired of running between the two hills. 'Alas,' she confided to Firozi, 'I feel so much for both begums. Our Begum Sahiba's intense desire to possess the girl who she believes is a perfect match for Mansoor, and Begum Agha's principled stand to keep her word. I hate to say this but the only slight hope is that Aijaz delays his return from London. Only that might break the resistance, at least of one party.' Dr Miss Gill, kind soul, *firangi* farishta as she was known in the servants' quarters, who believed not only in treating illness but shoring the spirit on both sides!

In July, the clouds had turned grey and mist lay thick over the hills. Sometimes it would drop right down to the lake and hide the entire cup, so nothing was visible beyond a few feet. It would envelop the houses and all the inside walls would become damp. Qamar Zamani stood for hours near her telescope waiting for the mist to lift.

Firozi Bua's daily trips to Agha Sahib's kothi brought nothing back which could offer the slightest relief. This time, however, she had an unexpected companion in her disappointment. She had observed Mansoor lurking around the terrace, hoping to have his go at the telescope! Sensing his discomfort, she loudly announced her prayers and disappeared inside even before the azaan was sounded, leaving the telescope free.

Miss Gill was again summoned by Agha Sahib. His wife was getting tired of the darkening skies and incessant drizzle, she was longing for Lucknow. Miss Gill could not find any excuse to delay her departure; she was worried that the cold and damp may affect the begum's fragile condition. So she agreed to let her go. But she had a promise to keep before the family left for the plains.

'Take me to Bari Kothi,' she instructed her *dandee* bearers. The four emaciated coolies hauled up the *dandee* carrying her bulky body and began the uphill trail. She turned her eyes to their bare feet treading the sharp gravel. She heard their heavy breath and saw the sweat trickling down their necks. Whenever the breeze blew in her direction she caught the smell of their sweat. 'Stop!' she ordered. Heaving herself out of the *dandee,* she handed a bunch of notes to the head coolie, 'I want to walk; it will be good for me.' Their burden thus lessened, they entered the Bari Kothi with a lighter step, set it down by the stairs of the Summer House and retired to steaming cups of tea and a quiet smoke.

Miss Gill climbed the steps and turned towards the wooden bridge that connected the kothi with the summer house, its dome-shaped roof set with coloured glass. The bridge was an enclosed walkway and on its walls, on either side, hung gold-framed paintings of ancestors. Its floor was covered with a red floral carpet. The walkway led to the living room where the fireplace was dispelling the grey feel of the mist outside. Miss Gill found Qamar Zamani sitting by the large bay window of the glazed veranda. She was talking to Saidani Bua while gazing outside, trying to peer through the thick sheet of the mist which had covered everything, lake, sky and hills.

Miss Gill lowered her bulk into an armchair next to Qamar Zamani and sighed deeply. 'Begum Sahiba I am just coming from Agha Sahib's house. They have decided to go back to Lucknow. I thought I should inform you.' The lines on Qamar Zamani's forehead deepened. She did not speak for a few moments; her gaze was fixed on the mist outside. Suddenly she stood up. 'We will go ourselves. Right now. Saidani, get the *dandee*s prepared and inform Jahanara Begum.' With a half smile at Miss Gill, she walked out.

The kothi coolies, the lucky few who not only had liveried uniforms but servant quarters for their families in the compound and less work since the begums hardly went out, prepared the *dandees*. As soon as the begums sat down, the curtains were lowered and the small caravan of three began its descent towards the lake. From there, they would climb the opposite hill towards the other Kothi. Their heads bowed, the coolies entered the main gate and gently placed the *dandees* in the portico.

Agha Sahib was reclining with the silver pipe of his hookah, enjoying the fragrant Lucknawi tobacco with which his servant had stoked the chillum. Suddenly, his personal bearer appeared before him without the usual knock and breathlessly informed him that the begums from Bari Kothi had arrived.

Glancing towards the portico, he saw Amina Bua escorting the begums and their retinue to the inner chambers, offering Lakhnavi salaams all the way.

Begum Agha was lying on the *takht,* lovingly instructing Shehzadi in the art of fine embroidery. Seeing such elegant ladies walking into her mother's personal chamber, followed by an obsequious Amina Bua, the girl quietly left the room. Trying to hide her surprise, Begum Agha greeted Qamar Zamani with great respect. She was stunned at the womens' regal bearing—Jahanara was no less imposing a personality than her mother.

Qamar Zamani inquired after Agha Begum's health, and said: 'We heard you were going back to the plains. All this while, we have been longing to meet you. You don't know us. But as Allah is our witness, you know what we want. And we both, mother and daughter, have come all the way, in the hope that you won't disappoint us.'

As if on cue, Amina Bua appeared with a silver tray, bearing delicate bone china cups and small plates of savouries and sweets. Qamar Zamani looked approvingly at the refinement and grace of the service. Begum Agha, with impeccable Lucknowi *tehzeeb* began an apology for not having taken the first step in visiting the kothi. 'I thought I would feel strong enough to come, but now that the weather is changing, I am afraid I may get worse.' Then, very quietly, she added, 'We are humbled and grateful for your proposal Begum Sahiba, but such matters are in God's hands.' She hoped this would signal the end of this conversation.

Qamar Zamani understood and dropped the topic. After a few formal exchanges, she motioned to her daughter. Jahanara spoke—'Where is our dear Shehzadi Bitiya? We would love to meet her.'

Jahanara Begum's tone was firm and Begum Agha could find

no excuse to refuse her guest's request. She gestured to Amina Bua. With her eyes glued to the floor, Shehzadi entered and sat near her mother. 'Come here child, come and sit next to us,' invited Qamar Zamani.

Shehzadi looked to her mother for permission. Seeing the slight nod, she politely came and sat next to Jahanara. Qamar Zamani bent over and kissed her forehead and before anyone could protest, she whipped out a golden *Imam Zamin* and tied it on Shehzadi's arm. 'It is our tradition, the *Imam* becomes our *zamin*. Whenever children go on a journey, the elders tie *Imam Zamin* for their protection.' Her words hung in the air; no one could object.

Then she stood up and all others in the room came to their feet. Casting a last longing look at Shehzadi, she climbed with Jahanara into her *dandee* and ordered the coolies to move.

The next day, the Agha family left the mountain resort.

Mansoor and Qamar Zamani both lost interest in the telescope. No more did the golden image of Shehzadi capture the lens. Then, one day, Jahanara discovered the instrument; she started to watch the Boat House Club races and gradually began to enjoy the spectacle. On one boat, she saw the captain pull the ropes to keep the sail open; he was always with his skipper, a woman. They would laugh as they caught the direction of the wind. How different was what existed on the other end of the lens from her own life; rudderless, directionless, dull. She would watch that 'unreal' world for hours, sometimes peering intently at the laughing men and women; occasionally, she could glimpse the moving forms on the dance floor in the Clubhouse ballroom. She had never known this form of abandon, neither as a child nor as a girl, and not even as a young bride and mother. After Ammar had walked out of her life, the only companions she had had, were servant girls, submissive puppets brought up to do her bidding. Observing life's effervescence around the lake increased her loneliness and bitterness gripped her like a vice.

Chapter 7

MANSOOR HAD GREAT affection for his sister Mumtaz Jahan. He wished he could give her everything her heart desired, but what she desired the most, his time, he could not spare . She treasured the few moments he came to spend in the zenana, knowing how lonely she was, that she had no one to play with but her dolls, her imaginary playmates.

The word of his marriage was the buzz in the servant quarters. Mumtaz Jehan, though, was not taken into confidence by her mother and grandmother, a fact which she always held against them. One day, she suddenly sprang up and much to the surprise of the attendants, ran all the way from the zenana to her brother's chamber. 'Bhaijan, am I not to be trusted? Why doesn't anyone tell me anything? You will be married, won't you? Then what will I do? What will become of me? You are the only one who cares, Bhaijan!' Tears welled up in her large green-grey eyes. Mansoor felt great affection for this little girl who was always cooped up in the kothi, her ivory complexion sallow and her golden hair lank under her covered head. He put his arms around her, desperately thinking of what he could say to make her smile.

'Mumtaz Jahan, I have an idea! Since the household is full of marriage buzz, why not arrange a marriage for Farah-Naaz?'

'Farah- Naaz, what are you talking about?'

'I just named your favourite blue eyed doll Farah-Naaz,' he said laughing, relieved to see Mumtaz Jahan smiling.

'Who will marry poor Farah Naaz?' Mumtaz Jahan asked wistfully.

'Why I will... I mean, my boy doll will marry your girl doll. Will that make you happy?'

'Oh Bhaijan, my best Bhaijan!' Mumtaz Jahan was ecstatic. 'Let us do it now, today!'

'Not today, my dearest. First I will have to find a *gudda* and then he will marry Farah Naaz with great fanfare. I will come with his baraat and take the bride away.'

Mumtaz Jahan's face contorted with pain. 'No! Never! I will never let her go away from me! Your *gudda*, Sartaj Miyan, will have to come to the kothi and stay with me forever! Only on that condition will I agree to your proposal!'

'Done!' said Mansoor kissing Mumtaz Jahan's forehead.

Firozi, who had followed Mumtaz Jahan to Mansoor's chamber, was listening to this exchange between brother and sister. 'History repeats itself, even in make-believe,' she sighed to herself.

With Mansoor joining in, the whole household became involved in the wedding preparation. Elaborate Farshi ghararas, *cholis* and heavily embellished dupattas were made for Farah Naaz. Silversmiths were called in to make small utensils from *paandans* to *pateelis* of silver. Jewellers were called to make jewellery sets including the *jhoomar* and *teeka*. Carpenters were engaged to make furniture for the doll house. All the Mughlanis of the household were kept busy stitching quilts, pillows and bed linen for the trousseau. Whatever royal brides needed, was produced for the wedding on a doll scale.

Qamar Zamani got new clothes made for all the staff. Everyone was furiously busy, in the arrangements. The baraat arrived with a 10-piece band playing happy music. From the main gate, through the Summer House, across the bridge to the main kothi, many of Mansoor's friends walked along the small pony which carried the bridegroom. Maulvi Naqi Saheb performed the nikah. Then the *arsi mushaf* was held, at which Sartaj Miyan beheld Farah Naaz for the first time in the mirror. Mumtaz Jahan was so completely immersed in the role of the bride's mother, she cried real tears at the *Rukhsati,* even though Sartaj Miyan was to stay with her! Then, Qamar Zamani came forward and placed the first *chhuwara* in Mansoor's mouth. The omen was that the one who ate the first *chhuwara* was to be married next! A lavish feast followed the *nikaah.*

For days after, everybody talked about Mumtaz Jahan and Mansoor's doll wedding.

After three days of festivity, Qamar Zamani found herself, once again, gazing at the thick shroud of mist. Jahanara applied herself with renewed vigour to stitching and knitting for the household to fill her empty days. Mansoor spent his day playing tennis, sailing on the lake, and playing bridge. Mumtaz Jahan kept the servants busy teaching the newly-weds the *taur tarike* of Bari Kothi.

It had been fifteen days since Agha Sahib and family had left but there was no news. Qamar Zamani sent one of her servants to Lucknow with a personal letter. After a few days, the man returned, but the news was not good. Agha Sahib had written that his wife had fallen very ill. He would only write back when she was better. Qamar Zamani could not make herself wait any longer. She decided that it was time to go to Lucknow herself. She took Jahanara Begum and Saidani Bua along, leaving Firozi to look after Mansoor and Mumtaz Jahan. Mansoor drove them up to Ramgarh from where there was an overnight journey on the small metre gauge train.

On reaching Lucknow, Qamar Zamani sent word to Agha Sahib that she wanted to visit Begum Sahiba. Promptly came an invitation saying that it would be an honour to receive her in their home. On reaching there, she found that the doctors had almost given up on the begum. Agha Sahib was very tense and Shehzadi's eyes were red from weeping. Amina Bua had not left her Begum's bedside for a moment.

On hearing that Qamar Zamani had come to visit, Begum Agha opened her eyes after many days and tried to speak. Amina Bua moved closer to listen. On hearing her words, she gestured to Qamar Zamani to excuse them for a moment and go to the next room. Then she ran to call Agha Sahib. Agha Sahib was afraid that the worst was about to happen—with a heavy heart, he approached her room. It had been three days since she had last spoken. He sat by her pillow and gently said 'Begum... please say what is it that will make you better...?'

The begum's lips moved weakly. 'I called you to say that I want to see my little girl married in my lifetime. I do not know how much time I have left...but I will die in peace, Sahib...' Her voice broke. She continued slowly. 'Aijaz has written that he will take three years to complete his degree. I may not last long; please Sahib, for my sake, listen to Begum Sahiba and accept her proposal. This is my last wish.' Then she closed her eyes and motioned for him to leave.

Agha Sahib had nothing to say. Within his wife's hearing, he told Amina Bua to go to the next room and tell Begum Sahiba, that it would be their honour to accept her proposal but the marriage had to be performed as soon as possible. Having compromised his principle for his wife's last wish, Agha Sahib went straight to his prayer mat. Everyone thought it was *namaz e shukrana,* but it was forgiveness that he was pleading for.

Wedding preparations began at once on both sides! Whether it was the excitement or a miracle, Begum Agha started recovering with good speed. She instructed the opening of the trunks in which she had collected Shehzadi's trousseau since the child was 40 days old! In 15 years, she had collected everything she wanted to give her only daughter.

Agha Sahib was quite concerned at the thought of sending his 15-year-old daughter to her matrimonial home. He was hoping that she would have been 17 or 18 by the time Aijaz returned. But once Agha Sahib had met Mansoor, he was a happy man. He was now convinced that besides the family wealth, his daughter was marrying a cultured and educated young man.

Shehzadi herself was too young to understand this great change in her life. She was happy with all the new clothes and jewelry and the fuss that was made about her. The fact of having to leave her home had not even registered in her mind.

Qamar Zamani and her entourage arrived in Lucknow two days before the wedding. Agha Sahib had arranged their stay in a big *haveli* and had spared no effort to make them comfortable. Qamar Zamani sent eleven trunks filled with clothes and jewellery for the bride, plus another 20 trunks filled with new sets of clothes for relatives and servants of the Agha household.

One day before the nikah, Qamar Zamani and Jahanara Begum arranged all the clothes and jewellery in large trays. Fifty-one were laid with Shehzadi's bridal outfits, seven silver trays had sets of jewellery—diamonds, pearls, Kundanwork and precious stones. Then there was *phool gehna*—flower jewelry—made with fragrant champa, chameli and motia flowers. Also five gold and silver *matkis* were filled with dry fruits and 101 boxes of *mithai.* Every tray was covered with a *zari khwanposh* (gold-edged tray cover).

All the begums and *buas* accompanied the *bari* to the bride's home where they were welcomed with garlands and taken inside with great pomp and ceremony. Shehzadi was bodily lifted into the mehfil by Amina Bua with two special kanee*zain.* Seven *suhagins*—married women—placed all the floral ornaments around her neck, arms and hair. Fruit and *meva* was poured in her lap. Mirasins, the singing women, sang, in typical Lucknow fashion, the choicest abuses for the baraat women and were silenced only by a large sum of money from the embarrassed *samdhins*.

It was late night when they returned to their *haveli*, a bright moonlit night. Gradually, all noise died down, the lights were switched off, the exhausted staff retired to their quarters. After much tossing and turning, everyone finally fell asleep and the haveli became quiet. Only two green-grey eyes were wide awake… gazing in turn, at the ceiling, the sky, and the moon which was visible above the casement. Qamar Zamani. With empty eyes, she sat mumbling quietly, as if talking to someone. Maybe she could see the shadow of her beloved Akbar Ali Khan, and she was telling him that at last, she had fulfilled the responsibility he had entrusted to her.

Suddenly, a loud explosion was heard outside. Qamar Zamani jumped to her feet from the chair on which she had been reclining. Everyone ran towards her room, the guards shouting—'*Daku*, Sarkar! *Daku*! *Ya Maula Madad*!' A small hand bomb had been exploded at the gate.

'Lie down and don't stir!' Qamar Zamani ordered. Everyone froze. 'Lie down, offer no resistance, let them take whatever they want.'

The doors opened and five men, their faces covered, entered brandishing their guns. No one breathed. Mothers cautiously placed their hands over the mouths of sleeping babies. The bandits moved from room to room where corpse-like people lay on the beds. Anything of value was taken; no one resisted!

When the last man was out, Qamar Zamani rose from the chair, stretched herself as if she had just woken up, and reached for her prayer mat. She placed her head on the *sijdagah* and thanked Allah. By His Grace, the most valuable things had already been sent to the bride's home! The box of all their personal jewellery Qamar Zamani had placed under her pillow, next to her prayer mat. There, even Sultana Daku would have never dared to look!

Mansoor's wedding was the fulfilment of Qamar Zamani's long-cherished dream. Not known for displaying her emotion, this time even she could not maintain her stoic front. She wanted to shout from the rooftops! She wanted all Lucknow-wallahs to say 'We have never ever seen such grandeur!' Perhaps even the dacoits came to try their luck, after hearing stories of the lavish wedding! 'But thank Allah, thank His Prophet and thank Muala Mushkilkusha,' she murmured, telling herself that *sadqa* was due in the name of *ahl-e-bait* for protecting her family

For seven days, the festivities went on. Each day, a new ceremony was performed. *Manjha* for Mansoor *Miyan,* for Shehzadi *Sehnak* and *Godh Bharai*; Nikah, *Rukhsati* and *Chauthhi* for both. Each day was a mini wedding. Alms and food were generously distributed; there was unbounded generosity with celebration and joy.

Mansoor willingly performed all the rituals but he had one reservation. He hated the smell of Mehndi. If a maid offered him a glass of water with hennaed hands, he could not drink it. He confided in Firozi 'Please Bua! No mehndi on Shehzadi's hands or feet. Do it whichever way, but don't bring her into my chamber with this foul smell!'

Firozi was in a fix. How was she to tell the begums to not allow henna?

'Was there any mehndi in Madinah?' she respectfully asked Qamar Zamani. 'Our Huzoor would never have permitted mehndi on the palms of his daughter during her marriage to Hazrat Ali! Begum, we must follow Rasool's *Sunnat* as a mark of thankfulness. You have not spared any expense or reduced any *rasam*; give up the mehndi, Begum. It will be well regarded in the annals of the Prophet (PBUH).' Finally Qamar Zamani gave up and conceded that the bride would go to her bridal chamber with 'naked' palms.

Festivities lasted two weeks. Both sides were competing, trying to outdo each other on the chessboard of this feudal contract. The best outcome of all this was the miraculous recovery of Begum Agha.

People whispered that she had been 'possessed' by the spirit of her mother-in-law who had extracted a promise to marry off Shehzadi before she attained puberty. It was the fulfilment of this wish that made her leave her daughter-in-law in peace.

At last it was the day of *Rukhsat.* Shehzadi was being beautified to leave the home and family she had known till now. Agha Sahib shut himself in his room so no one would see him cry. From a window overlooking the zenana, he watched his little girl seated on a chowki, hidden in heavy, ornate clothes and jewellery. He saw her being lifted from the *chowki,* flanked by both her brothers while they waited for the father to escort her to the *doli.* Begum Agha had a fainting fit and had to be administered smelling salts. Agha Sahib splashed water on his face and descended the stairs. The shehnai which had been playing joyful tunes all evening was now playing the bittersweet songs of *bidai* and farewell. There were sad faces all around.

Shehzadi's *doli* was decorated with roses and jasmine. Gold embroidered red curtains were lifted for her to enter the palanquin. Astride a decorated white Arab steed which stood beside the doli, was Mansoor On either side, his friends carried the strands of the six-foot long flower sehra. Thus with the band, the crowd of baraat*is* and splendid fireworks, the baraat finally departed from the bride's home.

And what about the 15-year-old bride, Shehzadi? A bundle of red clothes, covered from head to toe in a *sehra* made of flowers of gold, silver and pearls, she was red eyed and silent. Amina Bua, sitting in a corner of the doli, was now her only link to her past.

While the lights went off in Shehzadi's home in Lucknow, every window in Mansoor's home in Nainital was lit up. The valley and mountains, which had been witness to Miss Gill's journeys back and forth on her *dandee,* were in full bloom to welcome the new bride. The champa tree had spread out its branches and opened its arms covered with fragrant white blossoms to embrace her. Perhaps Akbar Ali Khan had planted it for this very day!

The bride stepped into her new home. She entered the main door where two senior women, family retainers, held the Holy Quran aloft for her to pass under. A group of Domnis sang to the rhythm of dholaks. Qamar Zamani and Jahanara threw handfuls of coins at them to ward off the evil eye. The most important ritual was the *Arsi Mushaf* literally meaning, 'countenance in the mirror'. Mansoor was shown, for the first time, the face of his bride in a golden-framed mirror which was placed between them as they sat under the canopy of an embellished red dupatta. No one except Firozi and Abid knew how many times he had seen this small innocent face through the lens of the telescope!

At last! The bride was bodily lifted by two maids and taken to her chamber. There she was gently lowered onto her canopied bed amidst the flowers strewn all over its damask cover. Mumtaz Jahan refused to leave her *bhabi*'s side. For the first time, she had a girl of her own status and age who, she had been told, would be her friend 'forever'.

'Bibi, now you will have your very own *humjoli* (friend),' Firozi had told her many times.

The lonely girl did not want to let go of her Bhabi's small hand, a hand strangely without henna. Her spontaneous love for Shehzadi instantly endeared Mumtaz Jehan to Amina Bua, who had been sent with the instructions never to leave Shehzadi's side. Her eyes misted at the thought of how she had nursed and nurtured this girl since the day she was born, when her mother was too fragile to breastfeed the infant.

Outside the bridal chamber, there were more *rasams,* more festivities, more visitors. The evening passed with visits from royalty from all the neighbouring states, each bearing expensive presents. The royal ladies came into the bridal chamber, lifted Shehzadi's veil and spoke words of praise. They were themselves beautiful and regal but no one could match the bride's unblemished innocence. They commented on Qamar Zamani's fine choice and left feeling a twinge of envy.

The whole day, Shehzadi had been carrying the heavy burden of her bridal clothes and jewellery. She whispered her discomfort to Amina Bua, which Mumtaz Jahan overheard. 'Bhabi, you rest,' she whispered back. 'I will bring Bhaijan.' So saying, she walked straight to where Mansoor was sitting with his close friends. 'Bhaijan ... !' she called out. When he came to the door where Mumtaz Jahan was standing, she whispered, dragging him with her—'Come at once before my *bhabi* falls sick with all the finery they have loaded on her!'

Much as he was tempted to follow his sister, Mansoor knew that he had to go to his bride via Qamar Zamani's room. The shadows of the evening had darkened. Mansoor and Mumtaz Jahan walked in. They found Qamar Zamani standing erect. 'Amma.' Mansoor said softly. She turned around, her eyes bright with tears. Holding Mansoor close while Mumtaz Jahan watched impatiently, she spoke some words of blessing over his bent head. Mumtaz Jahan felt that her grandmother's prayers were merely a ruse to hold Mansoor for a while longer, as if she did not want to let go of her beloved child. She also knew that Mansoor was too timid to break out of her embrace. So she swung herself into their circle saying 'Amma, how about me? I am also your child.' The spell was broken; Mansoor bowed his head and left the room.

Shy and hesitant, with expectation, anticipation and a fast heartbeat, Mansoor entered the bridal chamber to finally meet the girl he had been dreaming about.

The child transformed into a woman in the arms of a tender and caring husband.

Many days and nights passed.

Custom dictated that during the first forty days, Shehzadi remained confined to her rooms. She longed for the outside world but dared not express her desire. She considered herself lucky that Mansoor visited her every night and expressed his love for her body; but unlike what she had heard of the ways of the nawabs, he made her talk to him about herself, her life in her parents' home. She began to confide in this man who never tired of her confidences. In him she found a friend and companion—but only when he came to her at night. It was considered unseemly for a bride to receive her husband in the light of day. She also considered herself fortunate to have Mumtaz Jahan, her sister-in-law and confidante, who was always by her side. Both needed each other so their friendship deepened. Amina Bua hovered over them constantly, showering her blessings. Sometimes even during the day, Shehzadi managed to snatch moments with Mansoor, away from the eagle glare of Qamar Zamani and the stern oversight of Jahanara Begum.

One morning after Mansoor had left her side, Shehzadi drifted off to sleep again. Suddenly, she woke up with her stomach churning. She screamed for Amina Bua. After she had retched and vomitted, she fell back, exhausted, on her pillows. Amina bent down and kissed her forehead triumphantly. '*Mubarak*, my Shehzadi Bitiya! I will immediately go to Bari Begum and ask her nothing less than gold bracelets!'

Shehzadi blushed; at the age of fifteen, she had been told what the nights with Mansoor would yield. She and Mumtaz Jahan had whispered about the possibility and made a pact that if the first born was a girl she would inherit Mumtaz Jahan's entire *Gudiya Ghar*. 'Send Mumtaz Jahan!' she ordered Amina with a new-found voice of authority. But Amina first went straight to Qamar Zamani. 'Begum Sahiba, this humble servant brings good tidings! May Mansoor Miyan live long! A child has been conceived in this kothi! May your household prosper forever!'

Qamar Zamani looked at Amina, took off her gold *Kada* and threw it towards the woman. Then she raised her hands and pulled the strap which would sound a gong in the entire kothi. In a few minutes, the room was filled with servants headed by the Chief Comptroller of the estate. 'Open our *Tosha Khana* and let no one go empty-handed from our door today. Mansoor Miyan will be a father, by Allah's grace! Maula Ali be praised! Nawab Akbar Ali Khan's heir has been conceived.'

The word echoed in every corner of the kothi.

Qamar Zamani ordered that Bahu Begum was to be confined to her room. All precautions were taken to ward off the evil eye. No shadow of a widow or childless woman was to fall on the mother-to-be. From that moment on, Shehzadi's room was to become her prison; its veranda would be her *Lakshman rekha*. Shehzadi heard the words which sealed her fate, thinking earnestly of a way out of this forced confinement. She had Mumtaz Jahan in the day and Mansoor at night—that was her redemption; she was not unhappy. The two girls would spend the day planning for the child; she would ask Mumtaz Jahan to bring her dolls and they would play games of 'mother and child'. At night with Mansoor, she would recount her day and play games of love with her changing body.

One morning at the start of the fourth month, the axe fell.

While the young couple still lay together in the musehri, warm from their love-making, there was a rustle outside. The curtains flew open and Qamar Zamani appeared with her tasbih threaded through her fingers.

'Miyan,' she ignored Shehzadi. 'I came to tell you something which could not wait.'

There was an urgency in her voice; making it masculine, almost. Mansoor sprang out of bed, Shehzadi drew the quilt over her naked breast.

'It is the will of Allah. My *istikhara* says that from this day until the end of Bahu's *zachchgi,* she should not be touched by her husband. It will harm the child. So Miyan, say Khuda *Hafiz* to *bahu* and return to your chambers. You will see each other, *inshallah,* five months hence when the baby is born.' She then bent down to kiss his forehead, blew words of prayer at them both and left the room.

Mansoor could not console his weeping wife. He summoned Mumtaz Jahan, who came running barefoot. She found her brother bent over her Bhabi.

'Why do you allow this cruelty, Bhaijan?' Mumtaz Jahan demanded. 'Just say no! Say it to her face. Come… I will go with you!' Mumtaz Jahan was white with anger.

Mansoor looked at his sister in admiration. This was the courage he had never been able to summon. Shehzadi, too, was clinging to each word of Mumtaz Jahan. She looked at her husband with hope, but there was no spark in Mansoor's eye.

'No I can never do this—never disobey Amma. And I won't let you either. There are limits which we must not transgress. Are you mad? Promise that you will never leave Shehzadi's side. I want you to come to my chamber every evening to recount the well-being of your *bhabi* and our child.'

Mumtaz Jahan's eyes sparkled with anger. Tears welled up but she jerked them back. 'Bhaijan… let us go now and confront her… I wish—' Mansoor silenced her with a kiss on her forehead. He cast a farewell look at his wife and left the room.

Thus, the days passed. Shehzadi remained in her rooms. Amina Bua went in and out bearing trays of nourishing potions and other delicacies. Qamar Zamani, clad in white gharara, dangling a tasbih in her fingers took to pacing up and down in front of Shehzadi's room, guarding her next generation with her prayers. Her haughty demeanor had become intense, her voice raspier and her command more inviolable.

In another part of the house, Jahanara was busy all day stitching and knitting for the new arrival. Cloth merchants came bearing their best selection of materials. They came into the zenana and sat down respectfully, never lifting their eyes. Jahanara selected the materials for outfits for Mansoor, Shahazadi, Mumtaz Jahan, the Agha family and even the servants. An iron *guz* was taken out to measure the length. The merchants happily gave an extra half yard as a special gesture and having bowed themselves out, collected their dues from the *munshi*. No one asked the price or calculated the grand total.

While she sat with her head bowed over the needlework or the sewing machine, nobody could guess what she was thinking. Jahanara had taken her private decision for which she was gathering courage. There were too many vague, nameless emotions sealed in her heart. All she knew was that no one should get the slightest whiff of her mind's workings. Looking at her with a dupatta draped over her head, no one could have imagined that she was thinking of her love nights with Ammar Miyan every single night. When she uncovered her severely draped head to comb her long, now greying, hair, it was Ammar's fingers she felt combing the last strand. Once, it had framed her face in gentle curls. Now, the strands had been beaten into drab flatness by the dupatta. Those nights of love-making had given her Mansoor and Mumtaz Jahan. She still felt Ammar entering her room and lying by her side, tracing his long fingers along her yielding body. She often wanted to hug Mansoor to her breast, seeing in him the image of Ammar. Only once did she hesitantly express this desire. But Qamar Zamani brushed all her longings aside with one flourish of her tasbih 'Bibi, sit on the prayer chowki and ask the Almighty for forgiveness. We have all sinned and you are no exception.'

She wanted to lunge at her mother and clap her mouth shut! She wanted to place her head on her lap and cry out her barren life. But she thrust all these thoughts down, somewhere in her stomach, and looked longingly at her own children whom she dared not kiss or cuddle. Wet nurses, *ayahs,* nannies—they had everything. Everything but her caress which was dismissed as 'unnecessary demonstration, unbecoming of the high born.'

The moment she learnt about Shehzadi's pregnancy, Jehanara's mind went into overdrive. All her life she had seen children being traded around in the family like commodities. No one asked her when Mansoor and Mumtaz Jahan were whisked away to the chambers of Akbar Ali Khan and Qamar Zamani. Every morning, they appeared with their nanny to wish her. She would never see them again until the end of the day when they appeared at the dining table, seated between the grandparents while she sat at the foot of the table counting her morsels. When they fell sick, she heard from the nannies and ayahs. At night, they were attended by nurses while Qamar Zamani sat at the door on her prayer mat. Where was the space for her?

But now, a new space was opening for the first time in her life. Her son was going to have his first child. Girl or boy, Jahanara did not care. Mansoor's child would fill her empty life. She would uphold the family tradition of grabbing others' children. This child would be Jahanara's. Nothing, human or divine—nothing—would come in her way.

Meanwhile, oblivious of the undercurrents, Shehzadi was beginning to show the first glow of motherhood. Her face looked more radiant every day. She lived for stolen moments when Mumtaz Jahan would bring her brother and leave them alone for an hour in the afternoon while the household slept. Mansoor felt the baby's movements under his fingers. He kissed Shehzadi's stomach and promised happy times to come. She confided to him that Amina Bua had told her that Agha Sahib was writing to Qamar Zamani asking for her to be sent to Lucknow, to her *maika,* for the first child's delivery.

One morning, Amina came to her room, her eyes swollen with

crying. 'Bua,' she said 'What happened?'

Tears flowed down Amina's face as whispered about how Qamar Zamani had flown into a towering rage. First she had torn Agha Sahib's letter into shreds and thrown it at the messenger's face.

'Tell Munshi Saheb to write to our revered *samdhi*! Let him write that the first inheritor of our name will be born right here, in Akbar Ali Khan's estate!' she thundered. The messenger was dispatched by the next train to Lucknow.

When he got word, Agha Sahib became very thoughtful. For months, he had observed the changing attitude of Qamar Zamani. To his wife, he said that Shehzadi has been stopped from all travel by the doctor. Begum Agha, credulous and trusting, praised Qamar Zamani and thanked Allah for giving Shehzadi such a loving mother-in-law! As per the custom, she assembled an elaborate *chhochak* (baby's wardrobe) and filled the trunk with baby clothes, bedding and woolens. She also prepared new sets of clothes for Shehzadi, her husband, Mumtaz Jahan, her two matriarchs and the entire staff. Baskets of fruit, sweets, dry fruits and special pindis, the best that Lucknow had to offer, were sent with a servant. A maid was sent to massage the new mother post-delivery for 40 days or the *Chilla*.

When the *chhochak* arrived in the kothi, Qamar Zamani gave the contents of the trunks a perfunctory glance. Summoning Firozi she ordered—'Take this away and put it in the store-room. No need to show it to anyone. It is an inauspicious omen. Give this woman some *inaam* and send her away. There are enough maids to look after Shehzadi. Now go!'

The maid saw the hurt on Amina Bua's face and followed her to Shehzadi's rooms. She wanted to tell her Begum that she had seen Bitiya with her own eyes. But when she saw the sad shadows in Shehzadi's eyes, she decided she would not say anything to the anxious parents in Lucknow.

Amina sat in a corner of Shehzadi's room and quietly told

the maid the stories of Shehzadi's days and nights. The hukumat of Qaisar Zamani, the secrecy of Jahanara, and the struggle of Mumtaz Jahan to steal moments for her brother and her *bhabi;* so many stories. 'Bitya has been condemned to *qaid-e-tanhai* (solitary confinement). And what is worse, is Mansoor Miyan being stopped from visiting his wife. To make sure, Bari Sarkar makes him sleep next to her own bed. You saw Bitya—she has become a shadow of herself. In her condition, she needs love not discipline.' She offered her a *paan gillori* and continued, 'To tell you the truth, if it was not for Bitiya, I would not live here one moment. Even *my* visits to her are curtailed! I cannot go to her without Bari Begum's permission. She says I tire her out by talking rubbish.' Amina wiped her eyes and said, 'I do not want to stay here a moment longer, but how can I leave? I will never desert my Bitia, no matter what I have to put up with.' By now the tears were flowing. She missed the *haveli,* her *malkin*'s gentle ways, and the freedom to run the house as she wished. But her love for Shehzadi was an iron chain which she could never break, no matter how much she pined for Lucknow.

She sat with the woman for a long time, speaking quietly, till she heard screams from Shehzadi's room. Dr Gill, who happened to be visiting Qamar Zamani, was already at her bedside. Qamar Zamani was counting her rosary beads, pacing outside the room. She frowned at Amina, but this time, the woman ignored her disapproving look. Jahanara Begum kept her door ajar to keep up with the goings-on. Total silence reigned in the kothi, broken only by Shehzadi's piercing screams.

Mansoor, too, was pacing—downstairs in the garden. Every scream pierced his heart, but he could not go past his grandmother. He felt so helpless! If only he could go to her and hold her hand—but fear of Qamar Zamani chained him to the grounds below.

Suddenly there was an even louder scream, followed by silence. Then, the sound of a baby crying! Qamar Zamani stopped counting her beads and lifted her hands in prayer before moving towards Shehzadi's room. Jahanara rushed out from her room with a white cloth in her hand and she, who had never taken a step without her mother's permission, now pushed her aside to enter the door to her daughter-in-law's room. Even before Dr Gill could announce if it was a girl or boy, or could clean the child, she had wrapped the newborn in the cloth and disappeared back into her room, banging the door shut behind her.

Dr Gill, with bloody gloved hands, rushed after her while Qamar Zamani stood stunned.

In this commotion, Mansoor also ran upstairs. He was not bothered about the child, he only wanted to see his wife. He found her semi-conscious on her bed with Amina trying to revive her with smelling salts. Mansoor went to her and lovingly whispered—'Shehzadi my dearest, open your eyes, look at me, here by your side.'

Shehzadi opened her eyes to cast a glance at her husband, and in broad daylight, held on to his hand. She seemed at peace.

Outside the room, a drama was being enacted. Qamar Zamani was banging on Jahanara's door full force, ready to break it down. 'Jahanara Begum open the door this minute! How dare you!' she screamed.

At last, Jahanara opened the door, warily like a protective lioness. For the first time in her life, she stared straight into her mother's eyes. Her face was hard and voice harsh, 'Ammajan, this is my child and I will bring her up, all by myself, I need no one else, not even you.' She spat each word.

For a moment Qamar Zamani saw in her daughter the determined face of her husband, Akbar Ali Khan.

Dr Gill was caught between the mother and daughter, mediating, pleading, cajoling. Suddenly she remembered Shehzadi and returned to her room. She asked Mansoor and Amina to leave. Shehzadi was trying to grope the space by her side, but finding it empty, lifted her questioning eyes towards her doctor. Miss Gill had no heart to tell her the truth.

'You have a beautiful daughter, she looks just like you. You are still very weak. We have taken her to another room so you can rest.' Saying so, she gave the exhausted young mother an injection to sleep.

Miss Gill had no children of her own. But she had the satisfaction of having brought new beings into the world and placed them in the arms of their mothers. She felt a great grief for this young mother who was being deprived of the fruit of her hard labour. There was nothing she could do. These people had their own code of conduct; she was after all a foreigner.

Firozi had quietly entered the room. Miss Gill looked at her with questioning eyes. The woman could not bring herself to speak, her eyes were glued on the inert figure of Shehzadi who had fallen asleep.

'Chhoti Begum…' she whispered in the doctor's ear, 'She will never give the child back to the mother. She had planned every scene of this drama. Even Bari Sakar had no inkling. She is now the baby's mother in every sense. Except…' she hesitated.

'Go on,' Miss Gill ordered.

'She has called a wet nurse from Mohammadpur who is waiting in the servant's quarters to feed the child. It is so hard, Memsahib. But we are servants…what can we say? Nawabs, Memsahib, they are a law unto themselves.'

Miss Gill tried to quieten Firozi Bua, she was afraid just in case her voice reached the layers of Shehzadi's subconscious. She was now concerned about the infant who had been snatched from the nurse's hands before the doctor could examine her; and who was now taking her first breaths behind Jahanara's locked door. She went to the door and knocked softly. The door opened a crack through which she saw Jahanara Begum's grey-green eye. The maid opened the door and Miss Gill went straight to the baby cot. She saw a small face peeping from beneath a white lace-trimmed quilt.

'Rahat,' Jahanara said softly, 'Say salaam to Dr Sahiba.'

Hiding her emotions, Miss Gill first examined the baby with her best professional face and said that she was satisfied. She heard a sigh of relief behind her back. Then she examined the wet nurse and declared her clean and healthy. She then turned around to address Jahanara, but found her on the prayer mat, tears running her down her face. The maid gestured to her to be silent. Miss Gill realized that it would be useless to reason with her.

Qamar Zamani was pacing in front of Jahanara's room with glazed eyes.

'Begum Sahiba, don't worry. The baby is fine. This is Allah's will. Jahanara was never allowed to bring up her own children. That was your way; this is hers. Maybe after sometime when she has had her fill, she will return the baby to her mother.'

The next morning when Shehzadi woke up from her medicine-induced sleep, she opened her eyes and felt at her side again for her child. Finding the empty space, she sat up in shock and called out. Amina came running.

'Where…where is she? Is she alive?' she asked hysterically, dreading the answer.

'Don't worry my child, my bitiya. Your beautiful child is well. She has the grey-green eyes of her father and the pink of your skin. You are too frail at this time so Jahanara Begum is looking after her.' The woman cursed herself under her breath for lying to this innocent girl. But Shehzadi seemed relieved.

Mansoor and Mumtaz Jahan had been taught to call Jahanara, Baji Begam, which meant 'elder sister'. Since Qamar Zamani was their 'mother', they never knew Jahanara in any other relationship but that of 'sister'. Gradually, everyone in the kothi followed suit and started calling her Baji Begam.

Shehzadi's breasts were full of milk, and there was no baby to suck. She was in great pain. Miss Gill, Amina, Firozi, even Mumtaz Jahan who had stayed at her bedside all these days reporting every event to her brother, all avoided her pleading eyes. No one had the heart to speak the truth that Baji Begum would never allow her the pleasure of suckling her child. They appealed to Miss Gill to relieve her of her misery. The kind doctor took out the pump to draw out the milk and ease Shehzadi's pain.

Chapter 8

AFTER 40 DAYS, there was a grand feast for Shehzadi's *chilla* and Mansoor was permitted to visit her again. Shehzadi had not seen her child for 40 days—her eyes were swollen from crying! Deprived of her husband and child, all she wanted was to be free of this suffocation. When Agha Sahib arrived, laden with gifts for the *chilla,* she just clung to him and refused to let him go. But she could neither hurt her father by telling him of her misery, nor could she ever think of leaving her marital home, to say nothing of her love for Mansoor. She just cried her heart out, with her head in his lap. He looked helplessly at the women, Qamar Zamani, Miss Gill, Firozi, even Mumtaz Jahan. But his daughter's condition was described by the matriarch as 'normal post-partum depression'.

Baji Begum brought the baby, Rahat, outside her chamber for the first time to get her grandfather's blessing. This was the first time the mother saw her child. Instinctively, she stretched out her arms towards the child but Baji Begum stepped back and handed the child to Agha Sahib. Aching for his own child, Agha Sahib kissed the baby and handed all the trays of gifts to Baji Begum. He left the same evening after spending some time with Mansoor. When he came to say good bye, Shehzadi clung to him with desperation. With great restraint and promise to send for her, he kissed her, handed her to Mansoor and left without once looking back.

Life returned to normal. In the kothi, things began to settle down. Mumtaz Jahan spent many hours every day with Shehzadi. The mother asked her to report each detail about Rahat. Does she lift her head, does she smile, who picks her up, who cleans her who who who....? Mumtaz Jahan recounted every detail. This exchange was a constant source of pain and pleasure, one emotion flowing into the other. Mansoor was visiting her again in the silence of the night to share the pain of absence and pleasure of love. She was still very shy and had no means of expressing her real feelings for him or her resentment at the two matriarchs. All she felt was a great comfort when she lay in his arms; thus, the days passed in a melange of pleasure and pain.

Rahat was six months to the day when one early morning, Shehzadi vomited. Amina Bua instead of rejoicing, was most upset. She dreaded to think what may befall the girl this time. Will she, once again, have to go through the same ordeal? What new *zulm* would they wreak now? She just wanted to gather the 17-year-old child in her dupatta and run away to Lucknow. She forbade Shehzadi to speak to a single soul in the kothi about her condition. For hours she sat thinking about the next move she would make—how long could she keep the news away from Qamar Zamani? Should she abort the fetus this time and ensure that for the next delivery Shehzadi would be in Lucknow? She knew that in either case, she would have to pay with her life. She was an old woman without any support—she would have to beard the tigress in her den. One morning, after reciting *Fajr* she went to Qamar Zamani.

'What is the matter?' Qamar Zamani asked in a harsh voice. 'Why is your face like death? Is there news from Lucknow?'

'God forbid Sarkar,' she said, trying to smile. 'May she live long, once again your Bahu is going to give you good news.'

Qamar Zamani's fingers stopped telling her beads. A deep, enigmatic smile lit up the worry lines on her face. 'This is very good news. We are overjoyed. Why do you look death-washed? Now go and ask that the announcement be made soon after Maghreb prayers.'

Amina Bua did as she was told. That evening, to the sounds of shehnai, the announcement was made. Baskets of sweets arrived for public distribution. The only door that did not open to the festivity was Baji Begum's. She could not be bothered. Her world had one anchor, Rahat. That was all she could see, feel and love. At last, she had someone to call her very own.

Once again, excitement swirled through the kothi as Qamar Zamani began preparations for the new child. Mughlanis were summoned for sewing baby clothes and *poshaks* for the family. She personally supervised Shehzadi's diet. Her every comfort was the foremost consideration of the entire household staff. Instructions were issued. She was not allowed to climb stairs; thus no walks in the garden. Mansoor was asked to sleep downstairs and Mumtaz Jahan's visits were curtailed. Neither the brother nor the sister adhered to these orders and once Qamar Zamani retired to her chambers, they stole into Shehzadi's room and had their mehfils of songs, poetry, story-telling while Firozi kept a watch at the door.

Still, Shehzadi was intensely lonely. At the age of 15, she had been denied her childhood and thrust into a new life which she had to negotiate without any tutoring, any skills. But for Mansoor and Mumtaz Jahan, it was a hard sentence. All the gentleness and kindness she had seen in her parents' home was a fading memory; she, too, was slowly hardening. Unknown to her, even to Mansoor, the girl's gentle nature was being poured into a different mould.

And then one morning, something happened which tipped the balance of this carefully calibrated nawabi order forever.

Shehzadi came out of her room and stood in the veranda, breathing mountain air and looking out at the view of the valley. A dot in the distance was the house where she had come with her parents few summers ago, where her fate had been sealed in the lens of the telescope. Suddenly, she heard a movement—her little daughter had crawled across the veranda from Jahanara's room.

Shehzadi looked around furtively, and finding no one around, she rushed to pick up the baby in her arms. The mother hugged the little form tightly to her heart and showered many kisses on her small face. Impervious to the world around, she held the baby aloft to take in her fill of the small face, so much like her own. Strangely, the child must have sensed the mother's instinct because she cooed, smiled and babbled, giving no sign that this was a 'stranger' holding her. Hearing the happy sounds, Qamar Zamani emerged from her room and stood watching this little play.

Suddenly, the door opened on the other side and Baji Begum dashed out like a streak of lightning. Eyes blazing with anger, she roughly pushed the mother aside and snatched away the child. Shehzadi stood in a daze, guilty, caught red-handed, between the two mothers-in-law. The white rage that was simmering in each of the three suddenly burst forth.

Qamar Zamani had never accepted sharing her beloved Mansoor with anyone. Much as she had desired to see him as a bridegroom, she had not been prepared to see him actually belong to another woman. She liked Shehzadi, the doll with long curling hair—but at the other end of the telescope. She disliked her for actually entering their life and claiming her part of Mansoor. As far as she was concerned, Mansoor was exclusively hers, neither his mother nor his wife could lay any claim. Love wanted exclusive rights. It closed every other option.

Jahanara's was the slower burn. Her barren life, her empty womb, her drying body; she saw her mother's handprint on every one of her life's deprivations. But ingrained fear prevented her from ever opening her mouth to remonstrate. When she saw Shehzadi's face glow in the mornings after Mansoor left her, she found herself shriveling inside. She would vent her mounting anger in small bursts. On this day, however, between the two women, a scene was enacted in which all the veneer of cordiality was stripped.

Qamar Zamani was roaring—'Shameless slut, hugging your child in view of the whole world, and that too in broad daylight! You are almost ready to deliver—you could have killed the unborn! Have we lived so long only to see the day when the Bahu Begum of this family brings disgrace to this house?'

Jahanara had gone back to her side of the veranda and stood at her door, shrieking. 'How dare you lift Rahat! I have never seen such brazen behavior! Why are you crying girl? God forbid, nothing has happened to Mansoor. If you want to cry, better go to your mother's house.'

Shehzadi stood, bent head, tears welling. In a daze, she slowly backed into her room. As she heard both the mothers' doors bang, she made one resolve. With her swollen face staring back from the mirror, vowed—'One day... one day I will get my back on these two.'

That was the day when at the age of 17, Shehzadi became a full-grown woman.

Now, the mothers wanted to further tighten the noose. Qamar Zamani ordered that no one be allowed inside Shehzadi's room, nor would she be permitted to come out. She declared loudly within Amina and all the servants' hearing—'Bouncing the child in her arms at this stage of pregnancy! What if the baby had dropped in her womb? It is for her own good that she should stay in her room. Amina, woman, why are you standing here? Go at once and order her favourite food from the kitchen. Let our bahu have nothing but the best. Today we promise to look the other way; we won't instruct her on what to eat. May Mansoor live long; let him see her happy face.'

From that day on, Shehzadi imbibed one trait of her two mothers-in-law. She stopped smiling, no one ever again saw her happy face. Miss Gill, who came to examine her every week, saw her stony expression and cursed the day she had introduced her into this family.

Mansoor was involved in his own life and friends. A lot of his time was spent in reading and writing, poetry and prose, and music. These were inherited talents; both his father and grandfather were renowned authors of *Diwans* (poetry compendiums). He played tennis, bridge, and threw parties to liven the long, dull evenings. Never interested in domestic matters, he made no effort to find out what went on in the zenana. He did, however, feel increasingly constricted in his grandmother and mother's presence. So he tried to reduce the time of his visits. Every morning he appeared on the dot, paid his respects and hurried away after glancing briefly at his wife's closed door. He knew that the day he decided to take her side, all hell would break loose. Rebellion against their diktat was unthinkable. He said to Abid, his trusted aide, 'Why should I interfere? Shehzadi never complains. And the mothers… they may have a sharp manner, but they are all love. I only want everyone to be happy. Tell me Abid, is there anyone who can fault me?'

Abid bent down to remove his shoes and spoke the words Mansoor loved to hear. 'No one can blame you, sir, no one. A son or husband like you is one in thousands, rare, very rare.'

Chapter 9

IT WAS A letter which bore many stamps and seals. The envelope was addressed to Jahanara Begum, w/o Ammar Ali Khan. It was a sunny day in the mountains when a messenger from the GPO handed it to the chowkidar with instructions to give it to the Begum Sahiba.

'Who has sent her a letter?' Qamar Zamani inquired from the servants.

'Begum Sahiba shut the door as soon as the letter was handed to her. We don't dare to knock,' they replied.

Jahanara broke open the seal. She recognised Ammar's perfect calligraphy which she had read on pieces of paper on which he would write stanzas of poetry when she was fast asleep, after their passionate love-making. She would find a slip of paper near her pillow when she woke up. Ammar had been an early riser who loved to go to exercise the horses with the trainer on the grounds of Akbar Lodge in the small hours of the day.

My Dear Wife,

This is the last time I will address you as 'my wife'.
There is a talaqnama enclosed with this letter.
You will remember our nikahnama dated 1901. I, son of Nawab Asad Ali Khan, Firdaus Makani in my complete mental and physical health, promised to take you as my wife for a

mehr of rupees 21 lakh, sikka raijul waqt (which currency was current) and promised to stay with your revered parents as a 'Khana Daamaad' (resident son-in-law).

The events that followed this agreement have been eye witnessed by you and I. When I decided to leave you and my children Mansoor and Mumtaz Jahan, I was broken in spirit; I was leaving my family and also affectionate parents who loved me dearly, more like a son than a son-in-law.

My news must have reached you from time to time. I have nothing to say to justify or defend myself. I carry many regrets, many baggages of the past. That is all I can offer you, Jahanara Begum.

Tomorrow morning I will reach Kathgodam in the hope of seeing my family, perhaps for the last time. There is one train that comes directly from Delhi which reaches at 6a.m.. If all goes according to plan, I will reach the kothi by midday.

How you will receive me, is your decision. I will respect you and Ammajan until my last breath. The one soul who understood me better than even my own self, has now become Khuld Makani (home in heaven), your respectable father, Akbar Ali Khan. I wish he was there to receive me.

Ammar Ali Khan.

Mansoor left for Kathgodam at 4a.m. in Qamar Zamani's carriage, accompanied by his own personal guards.

Ammar Ali Khan stepped out of the first class coupé with the help of a liveried servant. There was nothing left of the broad-chested, black-haired poet-prince whose charm had taken Akbar Lodge captive and literally swept off her feet, the daughter of the house. On the dim platform, Mansoor saw a man leaning on the shoulders of two servants, looking for a bench on which he could sit down. Ammar saw an 18 year-old-youth in breeches and jacket, full boots and soft beret. His golden-brown hair was visible beneath the cap. Two pairs of grey-green eyes met each other.

'Mansoor Ali Khan, are you the son of Ammar Ali Khan, younger son of the Nawab of Mohammadpur?' The eyes were laughing when he posed this question. Mansoor's legs trembled, he felt a thrill in his spine ... ... 'Abba Huzoor, Abba Abba Abba!'

The servants who stood damp-eyed on both sides, watched the father and son clasp in a long embrace.

The kothi had been prepared carefully for Ammar's visit. A table had been laid with all the delicacies that were his known favorites. Qamar Zamani personally supervised Mumtaz Jahan's grooming. Firozi dressed her in a *Farshi* gharara, with a peach *kurti* and dupatta. Her thick hair was intricately braided and coiled on both sides of her head. Qamar Zamani hung a small *teeka* on her forehead and covered her head with the golden edge of the peach georgette.

When Mansoor brought his father into the house, he saw Mumtaz Jahan standing against the light, her face radiant and innocent. When she bent down to salaam him, he swept her into his embrace and sixteen years of separation flowed freely through his eyes.

Two pairs of eyes, grey-green and gold-flecked, watched this scene from behind the blinds.

Jahanara kept the shutters down; she never allowed Ammar to glimpse her face. Qamar Zamani did not receive him either, although she made sure that every courtesy was extended to her son-in-law. Mumtaz Jahan stayed close to him throughout the day. She refused to let go of his hand and cried when her brother helped him ascend the carriage later that day. He climbed on the seat next to him; several hours later, Mansoor saw Ammar off at the Kathgodam Station.

Chapter 10

MUMTAZ JAHAN HAD just turned eighteen; she was beautiful and accomplished, but locked within herself. She was witness to injustice and oppression but could not bring herself to speak out against it. The only way she knew, was to keep it tightly packed inside, giving no one an inkling of the real Mumtaz Jahan. She had in the past tried to take her brother into confidence, but.... 'Never mind all that,' she said to her dolls, 'Bhaijan is so good.'

From nearby riyasats proposals of marriage had been received from a few nawabs and *jagirdars*. But if Mansoor was firm about one thing, it was that he did not want his sister to get married into a nawab family. His instructions to his grandmother were firm—no proposal should be accepted without consulting him. Qamar Zamani was surprised at the authority she heard in his voice. She had never yet known him to be asssertive.

Among his circle of close friends at his university in Aligarh, Shahab was the brightest. He came from a good *qasba* family, with an impressive lineage of modest but educated men and women, several of them renowned scholars. He did not have much by way of landed property, but his family was amply endowed with intellectual property of which he was proud. Mansoor began to think of Shahab as the most suitable match for Mumtaz Jahan. He had no doubt that he would face vehement opposition from his mothers, but for once, steeling his gentle nature, he decided to assert himself.

His mind was in overdrive; plans were being churned.

Quietly, he bought some land near the university campus. He wanted to build two houses here. One would be his, and the other his beloved sister's. He already thought of names—*Ashiana* for himself, and *Mumtaz Jahan Manzil* for her. He planned the design, the layout of garden and even the furniture for both houses. He wanted to make sure that Mumtaz Jahan would not be deprived of any comfort.

Meanwhile, Nainital was deep in winter. Icy winds were blowing across the valley and all greenery had disappeared under a sheet of snow. From the chimneys, clouds of grey smoke merged with the mist and covered the valley in one grey blanket. The *dandee-wallahs,* out of work for the season, lit small fires and cursed the fog, praying that it would leave the valley so that they could begin earning again.

Aligarh had become Qamar Zamani's winter home so she could be near her Mansoor. Mansoor was on the lookout for the right moment to talk to her about Mumtaz Jahan. One day, he lingered longer than usual with Qamar Zamani while she was enjoying the winter sun and savouring the pleasure of Mansoor's presence.

'Amma, will you be angry if I tell you my heart's desire?'

'My love, my life, my child. Just say the word. Nothing that your heart desires can make me angry. My complaint is that you never ask for anything! A new car? A new hunting lodge? A new pair of hunting hounds? Just say the word.'

Mansoor went behind her and placed his arms around her neck. 'It is about my friend Shahab. Amma, I have found the best match for my sister.'

'Firozi, see my child's *zimmedari*!' she said to the woman who had been listening to every word. 'He thinks of his sister, first and foremost! Meri jaan, who is this young man? Which family? What is his worth—land, property, and of course his income? I have so many proposals from *nawabzadas*! He would have to be someone special!'

'Amma, he is a lecturer at Aligarh University. I don't think he has much property but he has a modest monthly income of 300 rupees.' Mansoor spoke, looking her straight inthe eyes.

The shock was evident in her abrupt reflex; pulling herself from his grasp, her small frame rose to its full stature as both looked at each other for a minute without blinking

'Miyan, are you her brother or her enemy that you want her to marry a man who is the servant of an institution? Has anyone in our family ever been in any *service*? You want your one and only sister, who has been brought up in the best of comforts, to live with someone who earns a mere 300 Rupalis! It takes more money than that to cover the expenses of her *paandan*! Never… !So long as I am alive, it will not happen. I will not allow you to push your sister into a living hell! Understand? This is the last I will ever hear of your foolish plan!'

Jahanara, who had walked in and had heard the last part of this exchange, spoke with bitter regret, 'Madness, Amma, Mansoor has gone mad. But for this, we have to thank you and your decision to send him to Aligarh. This is the bad influence of hostel life. I told you that this foolish decision of yours would haunt us. And it will.'

With both of them attacking him from different angles, Mansoor, who had never been very resolute, found himself on the back foot once again. But he saw very clearly that unless he struck now, this matter would be buried forever. Confrontation had become inevitable.

He had failed in using love to negotiate with his grandmother, so he tried another way.

'His salary may be meagre at this time, but with his education and intelligence, he is sure to progress very rapidly. I would not be surprised if he rises to the top of his profession. Amma, feudalism is dying; it is the professionals who will rule in the future. I promise you, Mumtaz Jahan will be happy. Then there are you both to make up for her lack of comfort. You can give her anything you want to ensure that she does not miss the comfort to which she is accustomed.'

Qamar Zamani retorted. 'So that is why he is keen to marry her! Three hundred rupali! Miyan, go and tell him we will not give her a *thing*... if that is what he is expecting.' Qamar Zamani looked triumphant. She had outwitted her child.

But this time, she had hit the wrong nerve. Mansoor, her gentle obedient child, suddenly lashed out. He shouted at the woman before whom he had never even spoken in a loud voice. 'Amma! Never, *never* say this again! When I asked him about my sister, he had only one hesitation... that she came from a wealthy family. He made me promise that there would be no dowry, not an ounce of gold, a thread of garment or a stick of furniture. He said, let her come only with the three clothes she wears over her body.' And let me make one vow before both of you. If Mumtaz Jahan is not given in marriage to Shahab, I promise I will not be there for her wedding.' He stormed out of the room.

The dice were thrown. Qamar Zamani was checkmated, stripped of hukumat.

Preparations for the marriage began slowly, reluctantly. Only Shehzadi was happy. She saw this as her moment of glory. With her husband at her side, she felt confident that she would arrange a beautiful wedding for the girl who had valiantly taken her side all these years, against the might of the matriarchs. She would show them, she would show them all! She would prove herself as the begum of the house; the tyrannical rule of the two mothers would ring out with Mumtaz Jahan's wedding chimes.

The day of the wedding dawned bright in the mountains.

Everyone in Bari Kothi was excited. Mansoor had organized a grand feast and invited all his friends—what he did not know was that Qamar Zamani had not invited a soul.

A simple baraat arrived at the grand gates of Bari Kothi, consisting of a few male relatives, some friends and a dozen girls and women in three closed carriages that had been sent by Mansoor to Kathgodam railway station—no shehnai, no fireworks, no decorated horses. The men were escorted by Mansoor into the Summer House. The ladies' carriage was ushered into the quadrangle where Shehzadi and her staff were standing with garlands. As the ladies stepped out, she placed strings of flowers around their necks. On two high chairs which were placed on a raised platform, sat Qamar Zamani and Jahanara. Firozi stood behind Jahanara Begum's chair holding Rahat who was wearing a little crown around her dark curls. Sounds of the shehnai could be heard from the men's side. Sherbet and sweets began to do the rounds.

Mumtaz Jahan was surrounded by brightly dressed girls, daughters of attendants and servants. By her side was Shehzadi, her only friend, sister, relative, confidante. It was she who sat holding Mumtaz Jahan's hand when the maulana appeared on the other side of the curtain to pronounce the words of the nikah.

'Bibi Mumtaz Jahan, daughter of Ammar Ali Khan, do you accept Khwaja Shahab Hasan, son of Khwaja Wasiq Hasan, as your husband?'

Each time, Shehzadi had to prod her sister-in-law; once, twice, thrice. At the third sound of acceptance, there was a big chorus of *Mubarak*. Men and women servants entered the mardana and zenana respectively, bearing large trays of *chhuwaras* (dates) and *misri* (crystalized sugar). Money was showered on Mumtaz Jahan and Shahab and steaming gold and silver dishes of the rarest delicacies were laid out on the tables. The feast had begun.

At last it was time for *Rukhsati*, the bride's departure. Mansoor

Ali Khan brought his sister out from the zenana. Her eyes were red with tears and he could barely control his own. Shehzadi was crying softly, the old nannies were tearful, even Miss Gill held her kerchief to her eyes. But the mother and grandmother had distanced themselves. Jahanara was tending to Rahat to the exclusion of all that was going on. While Qamar Zamani stood at a distance, haughtily observing this little crowd. As Mansoor was handing his sister into Shahab's care, her voice stopped them mid-gesture:

'Miyan Shahab! May you live long and be forever happy with our child. But let it be clear that we have nothing to give you. By the grace of Allah we have always adhered to the *Sunnat e Rasul* to give our daughters only *Fatmi Jahez* (Dowry that the Prophet gave to his daughter Fatima). Here it is—' she gestured towards the door. Four servants entered; each holding a corner of a huge tray. Placed on the tray were five claypots, five sets of clothes for daily wear, one prayer mat and one Quran in its *rehal*.

Even the servants could not conceal their shock—this stricture was unheard of even in their humble households! Mumtaz Jahan Begum was being sent out from the entire state, *Riyast e Mohammadpur* 'in tatters'. In the stunned silence, suddenly a girl spoke up. It was Saliha, Shahab's younger sister:

'Begum Sahiba we are grateful for your invaluable gift. Who can be luckier than a family which receives *Fatmi Jahez*? We are indeed fortunate to have as our sister Mumṭaz Jahan, about whose virtues we have heard from our brother. She will light up our home and fill it with the greatest gift of happiness for our dear brother.'

Mumtaz Jahan heard these words; she did not know it at the time but these words would come to her at times of great trial during her married life. She bowed her head before her mother and grandmother who tried to conceal their emotions. Mansoor took Shahab aside and pleaded with him to accept the newly-built Mumtaz Jahan Manzil as a gift from a brother. 'I want you and her to always be near me.'

Shahab saw the unspoken plea in his friend's eyes. He hugged Mansoor. 'Yes, of course I too, never want to live far from you.' The baraat left for Shahab's ancestral home in Panipat.

When the train pulled out of Kathgodam, Shahab and Mumtaz Jahan, surrounded by his family, began their journey together, a journey which would last as long as she lived. This had been a blind move—Shahab had listened to his instinct even though his family was very anxious about this uneven alliance. How would a girl brought up in nawabi luxury survive in his modest household? He looked at Mumtaz Jahan who sat across him, her face hidden behind her red dupatta. During the *arsi mushaf,* he had just caught a glimpse of her beautiful and innocent face. He knew that she had been taught at home by English governesses and by Urdu teachers. She had never seen the face of a school. How could he share his mind with one who had no formal education? How could he make her understand his dreams, his yearnings? He had heard that she was keen to learn, but kept a strict leash on her personal desires. He had seen Mansoor's lifestyle in the hostel—he had been a *nawabzada* with no nawabi arrogance. Would the sister be like the brother?

Within a week, he had his first vindication. On the seventh day, Mumtaz Jahan was preparing to go with her husband to Aligarh. Shahab saw that all the women of his family were crying at the parting. 'Saying farewell to her as if she were their daughter who was going to her *sasural*', he said to himself with a smile.

Chapter 11

SHEHZADI'S PARENTS HAD come to Nainital with both their sons, Aamir and Aalam, to participate in the wedding. Shehzadi was completely happy as she was released from her solitary confinement and allowed to be with her family. Begum Agha, the simple soul, was happy that her daughter was looked after so well—she found Qamar Zamani reciting prayers and blowing holy breath over her all the time. Jahanara, with Rahat in her arms, joined her mother in saying prayers for the expectant mother. They both said: 'Dulhan is expecting again, by the grace of Allah. She needs to be relieved of all cares.'

Amina Bua was afraid of upsetting her Begum by revealing the real story, so she clamped up. Agha Sahib, Aamir and Aalam were impressed with Mansoor's hospitality and found nothing remiss. As for Shehzadi, she had decided not to complain to her parents. It was all churning inside her; causing hot flushes and irrational bursts of temper.

After Mumtaz Jahan's *rukhsat,* the entire kafila returned to Aligarh for the winter season.

Summer's hot and relentless *loo* (hot summer breeze) was turning the green into shades of brown. Even slabs of ice and khus curtains could not cool the rooms. The *Pankhabardars* could not pull the cloth *pankhas* on the ceilings fast enough. The pregnant

Shehzadi was getting very uncomfortable. So Mansoor decided it was time to return to the hills, and saying good bye to Mumtaz Jahan, who was living next door in Mumtaz Jahan Manzil, the whole household traveled to Nainital.

Shehzadi was sad at being separated from Mumtaz Jahan. From the time she had entered her *sasural,* Mumtaz Jahan had been her constant companion and her confidante in her loneliness. In her solitary confinement, Mumtaz Jahan always found a way to sneak into her room and bring her word of how much her husband missed and loved her. Now she was bereft of her only support. And her pregnancy was at an advanced stage. One morning, she woke up in discomfort. By the evening, her pain was intense but she bit back the cries that sprang to her lips. At last it became unbearable; she called for Amina Bua.

Seeing her collapsed in pain, Amina rushed to Qamar Zamani who had just finished her evening prayers, 'Bitiya.. Bitiya... Begum, for the sake of Allah Rasul! Please call the doctor, I beg!' She bent down to plead, hands folded.

Qamar Zamani looked at her in great disdain. The black mark of *Sijda* was embedded on her forehead but she disliked such open expression of emotion as Amina was showing. *'Istikhara wajib hai.'* (*istikhara* is needed) she said matter of factly and closing her eyes, kissed the Tasbih and counted the beads. They were an even number; two by two they were pushed on either side of the string. 'This even number means 'No.' Not yet time. Don't make a fuss, woman. When the *istikhara* shows an odd number, we will call the doctor.'

Amina was hysterical with fear. Without thinking of the consequences, she dashed downstairs to Mansoor's room. She found him reading, oblivious to what was happening upstairs.

'Miyan, for the sake of Allah Rasul, please save my child! She is in agony. Bari Begum says she won't call the doctor as her *istikhara* says 'no'. Miyan, she will die! Have pity on yourself for once. Please do something.'

Mansoor took one look at the old woman and dashed out of his room. At the top of the stairs, he saw his grandmother dangling her tasbih.

'Miyan, miyan, not so fast! Miss a step and break a bone. What is the rush?'

'Don't worry,' he shot back and ran outside to his car.

'Curse that woman! I will deal with her later,' Qamar Zamani said to herself.

She heard Mansoor back out of the garage, the tyres screeching as he swung out.

'How dare you send my son out in this cold, you wretch! Where was the need to make such a fuss? Every woman bears a child, your Bitya is not someone special! If she did not want her husband to risk his life on these hilly roads, she should have waited until morning...'

By now, everyone from the kothi had gathered around Amina. Jahanara fueled the tirade:'There was no need! She has still two weeks to go! Getting Mansoor Miyan to drive out for the doctor. Mark my words, she will go back with her fees. May Allah protect him from evil eye... these winding roads of Nainital...'

Shehzadi was in her room, writhing in pain. Hearing Qamar Zamani screaming, she buried her face in the bed to muffle her own cries. She was exhausted with labour and almost passing out when Mansoor entered with Miss Gill. The woman rushed to Shehzadi and removed the quilt—the child's head was already out, the semi-conscious mother bleeding profusely! Miss Gill was furious. Her red face was perspiring despite the cold.

'Miyan, you go out, but remember, if you had not brought me in time, neither Shehzadi nor the baby could have been saved. I don't know if I can still do something....'

For the next hour, there was death-stillness in the kothi.

Mansoor stood at the closed door, occasionally walking to the window to light a cigarette. Suddenly, the silence was broken by the wailing of a newborn! The door was flung open and Miss Gill stormed out of the room. With the entire kothi looking on, she lashed out at Qamar Zamani:

'Enough, Begum Sahiba, I have seen enough! It was my fault that I helped you to get an innocent child into your home. Today, she and the child could have died and all because of your obstinacy!'

Qamar Zamani listened in total silence, her agitation evident only in her fingers counting beads. She was looking for the symbolic 'yes'. Two by two, the beads separated and only one was left in the centre. 'Yes!' she said loudly. 'My Maula has given me, His lowly servant, the divine signal.'

She went inside her chamber and shut the door. In a few minutes, she came out with a white folded sheet. Before anyone realized what was happening, she kicked open the door of Shehzadi's room. Miss Gill's nurse had just bathed the baby and was toweling him dry. Like an eagle, Qamar Zamani snatched the bundle, wrapped him in her cloth, and rushed back to her room and locked the door.

History had been replayed. Firozi, her head bowed, came to the anteroom where Miss Gill had been served tea after her ordeal.

'Miss Sahiba, again the same has happened. May Allah save and forgive us. Another wet nurse has been called from Mohammadpur. Our child will again pine for her newborn. Her breast milk will have to be dried with your pills. Miss Sahiba, we are small people. There is nothing for us to say or do. These rich people have their own code...'

Miss Gill's face got redder and redder, listening to Firozi's tearful words. After a long time, she felt an outsider in this household which she had thought of as her own. Tears stung her eyes. She dragged herself out of the chair, suddenly feeling old, and left without looking back once at the zenana where she knew two green eyes would be watching her depart. 'Never again,' she muttered to herself... 'Never.'

Abid informed Mansoor.

'*Mubarak, huzoor*! You have a beautiful boy. But Bari Begum has carried him to her room and closed her doors. Dr Sahiba is very upset and has left without seeing her. Dulhan Begum is getting fit after fit. How long, sir, how long will she survive this injustice?'

Mansoor was furious. He felt like lashing the two women, his grandmother and mother. His heart cried for his young wife. But he could not make himself confront the two women and face the consequences of the showdown—another way would have to be found. He sat for a long time, his head in his hands. Someone placed a hand on his bowed head. Firozi was standing beside his chair. He could see that she had been crying.

'Miyan, I love you more than my blood children. I have eaten the salt of your father and grandfather. Take her away from here... at least for a while. She will go mad if she is deprived of her own flesh and blood, right before her eyes. There is nothing more for me to say, it is for you Miyan, it is for you to do.'

Firozi's words were to haunt Mansoor for days. A thought was taking form... one day, very soon, he would see to it that his wife could breathe freely. He thought of an independent life for himself. Did he have the courage to break his shackles of submission? But he would try. For her sake... yes, also for his own sake!

As a child, Mansoor had been told that naukri was a lowly occupation. He was not allowed to compete for any service or enlist in any commission. When he looked at Shahab, it was with respect and to some extent, envy for his having a job which made him independent of his family. Mansoor found himself totally dependent on his family *jagirs* which meant the will and largesse of his adoring mothers. There were so many reasons to defer to their whims. His lifestyle was their gift, albeit, his two children had been snatched from their birthing bed.....but he could not express or even frame this thought to himself. This last event had shaken him. Something very wrong had been done to his wife. He was unable to console himself that these were benign expressions of nawabi love which should be accepted with humility and never questioned. His mind churning, he decided on a course of action. He thought about his grandfather… What would he have done? He thought of his father, the poet Ammar Ali Khan, what would *he* have done? A sense, an instinct came over him, which made him feel less directionless. 'Firozi Bua, I will do it,' he said to himself, addressing the only 'mother' he knew who did not intimidate him.

Qamar Zamani named Shehzadi's child Asad.

The life of the kothi now revolved around Asad. Sister and brother Rahat and Asad were growing up behind two closed doors tended by two mothers, suckled by two wet nurses. Their own mother's milk was being dried by medications prescribed by a deeply sympathetic Dr Miss Gill.

Once again, Agha Sahib arrived with gifts and clothes for the new baby. He observed the sadness on his daughter's face. Amina whispered in his ear; Firozi looked at him in silence and with pleading eyes. Qamar Zamani and Jahanara Begum kept him at a cold distance. So he decided to speak to Mansoor. So far he had avoided burdening his son-in-law, but now he had no choice.

'I am an old man, Miyan. Shehzadi's condition makes my heart very heavy. She has 'lost' two children. Her womb nurtured them, her body gave them life. Your respected mothers have caused great harm. Miyan, I gave my daughter to you because we valued your high moral character and noble family. But I regret to say that she is withering away in the oppressive grip of your family. Have pity on my child.'

Mansoor was silent. He was not used to being confronted. No matter what was remiss, he was always exonerated. But at this moment, his sense of fairness pointed at his own cowardice. There was no one else he could blame. He placed both his hands together and asked forgiveness. 'Abbajan, I promise I will take her away; just give me time to prepare my mothers for the separation.'

With a heavy heart, Agha Sahib left Shehzadi to return to Lucknow. There his wife was anxiously waiting for news about her daughter and grandchildren. What lies he would have to tell!

Despite his resolve, Mansoor did not take the decisive step. He continued to spend six months in Aligarh and six in the hills during the summer. Ashiana and Mumtaz Jahan Manzil stood side by side, waiting for the occupants. Mumtaz Jahan was expecting her first child. Shahab was very happy and began to personally look after all her needs. When Qamar Zamani and Jahanara learnt about this, they declared that from now onwards Mumtaz Jahan would come under their care. To begin with, they sent maids to Aligarh to tend to her. Shahab had seen too much in Mansoor Sahib's house to allow this takeover, however loving the motive. He tactfully sent the maids back and convinced Qamar Zamani that for the first three months, Mumtaz Jahan would feel better if he looked after her in his own way.

The miscarriage occurred in her third month. Qamar Zamani summoned Shahab. 'Miyan, you repulsed our help. Allah has displayed His will. Who are we to question? But *inshallah* she will conceive again. Come here Miyan, sit next to me. Let me call an *istikhara* to understand His will.' Her fingers told the beads slowly. 'Yes… you will be blessed again, son.' She blew on his bowed head. Shahab left her presence with a sense of relief. Before he was out of earshot, he heard her say to Firozi—'Order Munshi sahib to distribute *sadqa* (alms) to the poor in thankfulness for sparing her life.'

Both Shehzadi's brothers had enrolled at Aligarh Muslim University. Mansoor, had become fond of them, especially of Aamir. Shehzadi was happy because they would visit Mansoor and despite Qamar Zamani's disapproval, she would join their mehfils. Mansoor would ignore Qamar Zamani's summons for Shehzadi and send back word that Dulhan Begum was resting or attending to him. Though she gradually grew much more free and happy, the sight of her two children, now strangers to her, filled her with revulsion against her two mothers-in-law.

It was summer; the 40th day of Asad's birth. A big feast had been arranged for Shehzadi's *chilla*. Qamar Zamani, unlike the norm, had forgotten to select the clothes Shehzadi was to wear for the occasion. Shehzadi was tired of the heavy clothes that were loaded on her day after day. She chose a light green gharara with a matching white and green kurti and light lace dupatta. She had washed her beautiful long hair and was drying it on the veranda. The sun was filtering through the lattice and she was humming a little to herself. Qamar Zamani stormed out of her room in a foul mood—she had caught Asad's Bua feeding the child within sight of a wall lizard; she had heard that lizards were infamous for casting an evil eye!After shouting at the woman, she had come out on the veranda, where she saw Shehzadi drying her hair—the hair that had launched her entire project now became the launching pad for her tirade.

'Displaying your hair in public view,' her voice was stern.

Shehzadi quickly covered her head with her dupatta.

'Whose death are you mourning in these clothes? Are we all dead? May God keep my Mansoor for a hundred years, why are you wearing these damned widow's weeds? Why am I alive to see this day!'

Shehzadi stood still, unmoved.

'Get out of my sight, all of you! Amina woman, hear my orders clearly: No one, I mean *no one,* will go to her room without my permission, nor will she come out. Her food will be placed at the door. Understand?'

This punishment was to last one full month. Mansoor had had enough—he decided to move to Aligarh, using winter as excuse, but actually to get his wife closer to her brothers and out of this daily torture. When she finally came out of her confinement, Mansoor noticed that her face was pinched and her eyes were swollen. His heart sank at the sight of the woman who had borne him two children and had none to call her own. In silent sympathy, he placed his arm around her shoulder.

Mansoor's kafila moved down the hills, towards the plains. After a small distance, their farm lands began to appear, their *jagir* villages.

His arrival created a stir among the villagers! The cultivators came to him with folded hands. Mansoor forgave *lagaan* for the poorest and accepted offerings from the richer peasants. More petitions were received and a few cases were settled on the spot. Lunch had been arranged for them in a haveli which belonged to the village *pradhan*. In the inner courtyard, village women had gathered to see Mansoor's bride. They sat huddled on the floor, holding their children in their laps. They were a huge, noisy crowd of village women and crying children with runny noses and dirty little faces.

The delicately brought up Shehzadi had never seen poverty in its stark form. She felt nausea rising in her throat. Seeing her discomfort, Qamar Zamani decided that she should be trained on the spot in benevolent feudalism. She thrust a glass decanter of rose attar in her hand and ordered her to apply it to the dupattas of these women. Shehzadi did not move. She felt the vomit in her throat.

'Didn't you hear me, child? Go and apply this attar on every single woman!'

Shehzadi had had enough. Today, her patience snapped. She looked Qamar Zamani straight in the eye and refused to move an inch.

'Even if you kill me, I am not going near those women!' Shehzadi shouted at Qamar Zamani. Then she shot out her arm and gripped the fist which was raised to rain the first blow at her. Qamar Zamani was a tiny woman, the girl was towering over her.

Hearing the commotion and at Firozi's beckoning, Mansoor came to see what was happening. He was appalled.

'Enough, Ammajan! Stop this minute! Shehzadi, go to your room, I will deal with you later.' Shehzadi had never heard that note in his voice before.

Mansoor was loth to vent his anger on his wife, but he was equally reluctant to allow his mothers to become a public spectacle. Once more, he took refuge in escape.

'Let us leave this instant,' he ordered the servants. 'This place has upset us all. Let all the peasants get a gift of money from our purse. Tell them Bahu Begum has taken ill.'

He sat with Qamar Zamani in the front seat of the carriage to take away some of her anger. Once they had left the village behind, he placed his head in her lap. Nothing could make the woman happier. Cradling his head, she forgot all about the unpleasant incident and recited prayers in his ears as he slept. Jahanara fussed in the back seat over Rahat. Only Shehzadi, also sitting in the back seat, was angry and tearful. One day, she would get even with all of them! For the first time, she saw how easily her weak-willed husband could be managed. This lesson she never forgot.

In Aligarh, Shehzadi found her old friend Mumtaz Jahan. Once again, there was one in whom she could confide her darkest secrets. Mumtaz Jahan spent many afternoons with Shehzadi, trying to convince her to assert herself, not only before the mothers but equally before Mansoor. 'My brother is too soft; he will never thwart their will. It is your will which will win the day. Believe me you can do it, Bhabijan.'

Mansoor had planned his new house in Aligarh with a lot of thought. The first rooms he built were dedicated to the Imambara, such as he had faint memory of in Akbar Lodge. He asked Qamar Zamani to recollect the details so he could replicate the architecture. During Moharram, when Mansoor sat at the Mimber and recited

'Meer Anis Marsiya' on Imam Hussain's *shahadat* at Karbala, there was not a single dry eye in the audience. Sometimes Shahab recited the Marsiya in his gentle endearing voice but very often, he would go with his family to his ancestral town of Panipat during this period. The kothi itself was set behind the *chaboothra* on which this Imambara stood. It was a long building with Shehzadi's room at one end and Qamar Zamani and Jahanara's at the other. In between were the living, dining and the children's playrooms. There was a long veranda fronting the rooms and an indoor garden where chameli, motia, bela and haarsinghar vines and trees had been planted at the early stage so they would be fully grown at the time of occupancy. There were three pavilions in the garden where the ladies sat and prayed. A *hauz* of water had a tap with cool water which was used for *wuzu* (abolitions for prayers). There were seasonal fruit trees. In summer the jamun tree would be filled with luscious black jamuns and the lemon and mango trees would become loaded with fruit. On summer evenings, water was sprinkled on the garden patio to cool it before the ladies came outside.

Mansoor had designed his portion so that his room was next to Shehzadi's and his grandmother could not keep a watch over his visits. There were a few formal meeting rooms, formal and informal drawing rooms—all of which were tastefully decorated with expensive Burma teak furniture, Iranian carpets and European art on the walls. The official dining room had a long table, crystal chandelier and monogrammed chairs.

At the other end, Mansoor had a large study where he found refuge from all the problems and bickering of the household. A beautifully laid-out garden, filled with seasonal flowers, fronted the house. Shehzadi also had her own small private garden by the side of her room, filled with bonsais and fragrant plants. Shehzadi was very fond of gardening and would spend long hours of the morning walking on the grass, supervising the *malis*. Since she loved to eat ber, there were many ber bushes in the corners. The far side held her little kitchen garden with neatly planted rows of seasonal vegetables. Many cages of colourful birds hung from the trees and two snow-white rabbits frisked around in a large cage, feeding themselves on cabbage and carrot leaves.

This was the first taste of freedom Shehzadi had in all her years of marriage! She spent hours there, feeding the birds, pruning the trees, cutting flowers, tasting fresh vegetables and cuddling the little rabbits in her lap. This was her own world, where she lived freely, without fear or restriction. Even Mansoor could visit her room, not only in the dark of the night, but also in full daylight, without any hesitation.

Rahat was now three years old and Asad was two. All along, they had been kept under the strict supervision of their respective mothers. Rahat would run all over and Asad would follow her. Qamar Zamani and Jahanara were engrossed in the children, they had no time to keep an eye on Shehzadi. The children were getting naughtier by the day!Once, Asad pulled Rahat's thick tresses and entangled them in his tiny fingers. Rahat screamed in pain and bit his arm with all her little might. Hearing them scream, both mothers rushed out of their rooms, and picked up their respective children. Jahanara massaged Rahat's head lovingly and scolded Asad loudly. Qamar Zamani, unable to stand this tirade against her beloved child, screamed at Jahanara. A torrent of words ensued and all the servants dived for cover in case the anger spilt over.

These fights became a daily affair. Jahanara was no more a quiet observer of her mother's imperious behaviour. The fight would begin with blaming each other's child and then turn into an ugly personal altercation. They would then go sit on their *chowkis* and begin reciting their namaaz, praying, praying, praying.

Chapter 12

AMINA WAS GETTING old and increasingly unable to cope with her duties. She asked the begums for permission to call her niece Shamshad, with her husband. They would serve as Shehzadi and Mansoor's personal servants. A few weeks later, Shamshad arrived with her husband and a cartload of luggage. Very quickly, with her aunt's help, she learnt the likes, dislikes, biases and preferences of the family. After that, it took her very little time to gain Shehzadi's confidence. Shamshad was quick-witted and lively, and would amuse Shehzadi with mischievous and lascivious stories. Sometimes, Amina Bua scolded her and asked her to say 'tauba' for her wayward stories. But Shehzadi liked this light-hearted banter that brought some laughter into the grim household. While Amina was fading, Shamshad was was filling her emptying space.

One morning, Shehazadi vomited. She knew the signs. She had noticed for a while that her *kurtis* were getting tight. She had decided not to tell anyone about this pregnancy. For the first time, she confided only in her husband. Mansoor was overjoyed but also very worried. He whispered his plan in her ear.

'This is what we will do,' he confided to Shehzadi, 'but you will not speak about it to anyone, not even to Shamshad. Only Amina Bua could be told as she would rather die than divulge your secret.'

Shehzadi had indeed put on weight but Qamar Zamani was

too preoccupied to notice it. But one day, when Shezadi was unthinkingly sucking a piece of raw mango which she had picked up in the garden, Jahanara got suspicious. She looked up and down at her daughter-in-law's thickening waist line with great interest. She could not say a word to her mother since there was a cold war going on between them due to the children's fights. But the next day, when their play once again turned into a fight and Qamar Zamani snatched up Asad and lightly slapped Rahat on her small cheek saying—'Being the older sister you should be his protector, not tormentor!', Jahanara Begum shot back to get even: 'You are so blind that you do not even know what is happening in your own home. Dulhan is pregnant, do you hear, pregnant! Yes, you have eyes only for Asad—you are blind to the game being played with your family honour.'

For once, Qamar Zamani could not hit back. She pushed Asad into the room and locked the door. She came out and ordered Shamshad—'Hey, you, girl, go to Dulhan's room and ask her to come out immediately.'

Shamshad was trembling with fear as she ran to Shehzadi's room.

'Bibi, the Begum is in a towering rage!'

Shehzadi was afraid. She arranged her dupatta on her head, looked at herself in the mirror and braced herself to go out.

Qamar Zamani looked at her steadily, unblinking.

'How dare you insult our family honour and hide from us word about our own flesh and blood. We will teach you a lesson you will never forget as long as you live.'

Shehzadi saw the hand lifted in the air just as it crashed on her cheek, knocking her off-balance. Amina came running in and threw herself on the girl in order to fend off more blows. The servants stood aghast. Jahanara joined her mother, turning her wrath on the old woman who was protecting the girl.

'*Rahm sarkar*!' the servants begged, pleading before the two women.

Mansoor was playing bridge in Prof. Sharif's residence, unaware of the drama being enacted in his home.

Sharif was professor of English at the university. His wife and three daughters had been brought up with Western values and education; they mingled freely with male friends without too many restrictions. Mansoor liked the atmosphere of the Sharif household, with its intellectual camaraderie between father and daughters. They discussed everything, without inhibition. Mansoor wished he could impart some of these values into his own home, but that was unthinkable while the two women guarded tradition…He started spending more time with the Sharifs, enjoying the freedom to mingle with women who were equally pleased at his undivided attention. Mansoor had wisely designed Ashiana in such a manner that it could be partitioned off, but despite wanting to, he dared not suggest such a division. So the daily visits to this pleasant household became his getaway.

Rosie was the eldest daughter. She was beautiful and lively and showed great partiality for Mansoor. If he did not come to the house even for one day, she registered her protest, much to his pleasure. He justified his feelings as a desire to escape for a few moments of freedom. He did not feel guilty that he was spending time with Rosie at the expense of his wife.

That day, he was engrossed in playing bridge with Rosie as partner. Rani and Ruby, her two younger sisters were playing opposite, trying their best to beat them at the game. Finally, they threw down their cards.

'We are not going to play any more! You seem to get all the cards!'

Mansoor laughed, 'Some people have all the luck, in cards and in love. Isn't that so?'

Rosie got up from the card table, saying 'Let us have some tea.'

Over tea, the talk turned to romance, love, arranged marriages. They lost all track of time till the evening shadows started to creep and the servants came to turn on the lights.

Suddenly, with a shock, Mansoor realized that he had spent the whole day with them! He rose from his chair, glanced at Rosie's face and asked her softly—'Do I have your permission to leave?' Rosie looked at him. 'Not really, but go if you must.' She accompanied him to the car to say good bye, but suddenly stopped. 'Wait a moment please, Mansoor. I had to send a very important letter to Delhi which I forgot to mail. All because of you!' She smiled at him. 'Now you will have to mail it for me as a punishment.'

'With pleasure, but what will be my reward?'

'We shall see,' she said, giving him a quick kiss on the cheek.

Holding the letter in his hand, he got into his new sports car, looked at his watch and smiled. On an impulse he turned the car in the direction of Delhi. In four hours, he was in Delhi looking for the address on the letter. He found the house and handing the letter to the chowkidar himself, he turned the car around. The road was clear at this time of the night and with his fondness for speed, he literally flew back to Aligarh, touching 100 miles an hour!

Ashiana was very quiet and dark, when he arrived and handed the keys to the driver. He knew that everyone must have finished dinner and retired into their own little worlds. Abid was waiting for him. 'Miyan, should I serve your dinner?' he asked.

'Yes,' he replied curtly, sifting through his mail. There were letters from his *munshi* and other workers and the weekly letter from Agha Sahib to inquire about Shehzadi, to which he always replied promptly. There was a knock on the door and as he looked up, Aamir came in.

'Where have you been, Bhai? We did not see you the whole day.'

Mansoor smiled. He did not want to part with the sweet secret of having been to Delhi and back, 160 miles, just because the time of the last postal clearing was over! He moved to the dining room, chatting with Aamir while dinner was served.

'Bhai, I think Shehzadi is not feeling well today. I went to see her but was told that she was sleeping.'

Suddenly, with a pang of guilt, Mansoor got up and without glancing at Aamir or the food, he went straight to Shehzadi's room. The chambers were dark, with Amina Bua sitting at the entrance.

'How is your Begum?' Mansoor asked softly.

Amina spoke very softly. 'Miyan… Miyan, go see for yourself.'

Mansoor went to his wife's bed and switched on the lamp. Her forehead was burning to touch!

'Shehzadi, what is the matter? Do you have fever? I will call the doctor just now.' His guilt-laden voice reached her ears and she opened her eyes and then she turned away without a word.

Mansoor saw Rosie's face hovering at the periphery of his mind. He shook his head to clear it and saw Shehzadi's face in the lamplight, marked by red welts which were turning blue. Mansoor lifted her face and looked at the bruises and at Shehzadi's face.

Amina spoke—'Miyan, she is terrified that this time, again, her child will be snatched—for the third time!'

Shehzadi then spoke quietly 'Please, please, get me away from here, anywhere, any place, but I can not survive here a moment longer. I can't live here, I will die.'

Mansoor tried to calm his wife. He brushed her dark tresses from her face and kissed her cheek.

'Shaddo dearest, stop crying. I promise you that you shall never see any abuse again. I will take you away from here. Do not worry anymore, my darling, It is not good for you, for the child. You don't have to worry. See….. I am with you.'

Running his fingers through her thick hair and wiping the tears from her face, his own eyes became moist. Seeing tears in her husband's eyes, Shehzadi tried to calm herself. Mansoor gathered her in his arms and whispered many endearing words in her ears. She looked at him with hope, much more in control of herself. For the next few days, there was silence on both sides; Mansoor did not pay his customary morning visit to his two mothers.

It was a cold morning. The icy breeze of December was harsh. The first rays of the sun were penetrating through the naked tree branches. Qamar Zamani and Jahanara were asleep in their warm beds, covered with thick quilts. All the servants were also in deep slumber. Only the sweeper, Rati Ram, was awake and sweeping the driveway.

Mansoor emerged from inside, wrapped in his huge overcoat with the collar raised up to shield him from the cold. He was wearing warm gloves and thick shoes. Rati Ram was surprised to see *Sahib* out at this hour. Responding to his salaams Mansoor asked him to go and see if Abid was up.

'Go, tell him that I want to see him.'

Rati Ram stood his broom in a corner and went to do his master's bidding. Mansoor walked towards his car in the garage and waited till the man was out of sight. Then, he turned and beckoned Shehzadi who was standing behind a pillar, covered in her black burqa. Amina Bua was also waiting behind her, wrapped in a warm shawl, holding a suitcase. He settled Shehzadi in the front seat of his car, and Amina Bua and the suitcase were packed in the back seat. Then he got in the car, too. It took a few minutes to start since the engine was very cold, but after a couple of tries, the vehicle started and the quiet of the morning was broken by the sound of the car moving out of the main gate of the kothi.

When Rati Ram returned with Abid, the dust from the car had not yet settled.

Qamar Zamani had just got up to say her morning prayers. She had woken late, so her namaaz was already *Qaza* (the prescribed time having elapsed). Hearing the sound of a car, she covered herself with a big white shawl and came outside. Rati Ram and Abid were standing there, conversing softly.

'Who has driven the car out so early in the morning?' asked Qamar Zamani in annoyance. 'Miyan will be very angry. He does not like anyone to touch his car. Why are you just standing there like idiots, staring at me? Why don't you answer? How dare you allow anyone to touch Mansoor's car?' she shouted at them.

'Master has taken it out himself, *Huzoor*,' Rati Ram stammered.

Qamar Zamani could not believe her ears. In her agitation, she even forgot her namaaz. She turned and rushed inside.

'Where are all the *namak haram* servants who do not even know what happens in the house?' she shouted. This tirade brought the servants rushing out of their quarters in various stages of dishevelment.

'Where is Abid?' she screamed. Abid came forward and saluted her with respect.

'Where has Miyan gone so early in the morning?' she shouted at him.

Abid shook his head in ignorance, which made her angrier.

'Does no one here know where my child has gone so early in the morning, in this biting cold? May Allah protect him!' she screamed again.

No one knew. In the meantime, Jahnara had also woken up and emerged, wondering what this was all about. Everyone was wondering where and why would Miyan go out so early, without informing anyone. Qamar Zamani turned to Shamshad, who was shivering in a thin shawl.

'Don't just stand there. Go to Dulhan's room and ask her! Maybe she knows where he has gone…' Jahanara ordered. Shamshad rushed to Shehzadi's room but was back in a moment.

'Begum Sahiba!' she gushed, 'Dulhan Begum is not there! I have looked everywhere. She is neither in the bathroom nor her garden!'

All hell broke loose. Qamar Zamani hurled full-blown curses at the missing daughter-in-law. 'I knew it! I knew she was up to some evil plan. Who knows where she has disappeared with my *nazuk* child, in this biting cold? May Allah protect and keep my son safe from all evil!' She kept screaming and shouting and finally, exhausted, collapsed on her prayer mat, where she prostrated herself and prayed for Mansoor's safety.

'*Ya Allah,* may I see my son as soon as possible. May my own life be taken to spare him any harm.'

Jahanara also felt sympathy at her mother's condition and tried to console her. Suddenly, she remembered Amina Bua. 'Where is Amina, Ammajan? Maybe she would know something...'

'Yes, call that wretch. Where is she? So much *hangama* and the witch has not even emerged from her quarters!'

This got Shamshad even more excited and she ran to Amina Bua's quarter. Pushing open Amina Bua's door, she saw a neatly folded bed and empty room.

'Amina is gone, Begum, her bed has not been slept in!' Kitchen, store room, dressing room and garden, all were searched, but no sign of Amina Bua. Now Qamar Zamani's full fury turned on the woman. 'May Allah smite her, not even ashamed of her white hair! Always pretending to be *vaari, qurban* on Dulhan, calling her my *bachchi* (daughter), my life. Is she her well-wisher or enemy? Tell me, Jahanara, did she not know that the bumps in the car and the stress of road travel can harm the child in her womb? Her parents should take a cane to the old hag. Let me set my eyes on her and I will make her rue the day she was born!'

Cursing and abusing, Qamar Zamani was not to be silenced. Finally, Jahanara suggested she perform a long namaaz as *mannat* for the safe return of Mansoor.

Chapter 13

IT WAS A long journey from Aligarh to Jaipur. With her usual far-sightedness, Amina Bua had planned well. She had quietly gone to the kitchen late at night and made some *roghni tikias* (soft rotis), fried some kebabs, and made scrambled egg '*khagina*' with plenty of onions, green chillies and mint. Then, she had filled two thermos flasks with steaming hot tea, since she knew Mansoor's addiction to his first cup of tea in the morning. There was also cold water in another large thermos. She had then packed a suitcase with some warm clothes for Shehzadi and had quietly carried them outside when no one was in sight.

After leaving Aligarh far behind, Mansoor had a great urge for his morning tea and started looking around for a tea stall—but it was still too early and no tea stall was open. Mansoor was getting restless. Shehzadi had uncovered her face and for the first time, was breathing the air of freedom. It was a good feeling.

'What is the matter?' she asked her husband gently.

'Nothing much,' smiled Mansoor, 'Just missing my usual morning cup.'

'Here, Dulha Miyan,' came a voice from the backseat, as Amina Bua handed Shehzadi steaming hot tea in a china cup. 'Just stop somewhere for a while—the tea is very hot.'

Mansoor was thrilled and pulled up the car along the roadside.

Amina Bua handed him a cup and also another to Shehzadi. She served rogni roti with kebab and egg khagina with fresh mint chutney. Mansoor was amazed at her thoughtfulness.

He really enjoyed his breakfast—not only was the food tasty, it was a meal with no tension. This simple treat was better than any elaborate breakfast he may have been offered, and he was at peace. They all had their fill and resumed the journey. Mansoor lit a cigarette and drove in a relaxed mood. Shehzadi was content to sit next to her husband and think of the baby, lost in the pleasant dreams of the future, while Amina Bua made *paans* for them to finish off a perfect meal.

The long journey flew by. No one felt tired or bored. They laughed, talked, teased each other and gorged on all the food. Shehzadi's face was glowing in expectation of seeing her parents. The cruel marks on her cheek were fading.

In Jaipur, Shehzadi flew into her mother's arms. They were meeting after such a long time! When Agha Sahib returned from work, he was surprised to see the visitors but he hugged them both, showering his *duas*. After a while, he took Mansoor aside.

'I hope all is well, Miyan? We are so happy to see you, but how did you suddenly decide to visit us?'

Mansoor told him the truth of all that had happened and how Shehzadi was very afraid now about the future of her third child. He had been forced to take this step to allay her anxieties.

'Please keep Shehzadi with you till the child is born,' he said humbly to Agha Sahib. 'Don't you worry, son. This is her home, she can stay here as long as you and she want,' Agha Sahib assured him.

Mansoor wanted to stay on longer, but he realized that he needed to return immediately. The next day after lunch, he asked Agha Sahib's permission to leave, because he wanted to reach Aligarh before nightfall. Agha Sahib tried to persuade him to stay a little longer.

'You know my grandmother,' said Mansoor with a wry smile,

'She must be in a bad state already, so it is better that I leave now.'

Reluctantly, Agha Sahib let him go. Mansoor went to Shehzadi's room to say good bye. Mother and daughter were together—Begum Agha left the room. Mansoor was relieved to see the glow back on Shehzadi's face; he knew he had taken the right decision. He bent down to kiss her right there, in front of the open door. When she protested, he laughed and said—'In this house, I feel so free, dear Shaddo!' He kissed both her hands, saying—'Khuda *hafiz, meri jaan*. Dont be sad, and don't worry at all. I will be back as soon as possible. You just look after yourself and our child and be cheerful.'

Agha Sahib and Begum Sahiba saw him off to the car, and Amina Bua handed him a thermos of tea and a packet of sandwiches. Mansoor started the long journey back to Aligarh, which was very different from the one two days ago. But he faced the long, solitary return journey in an elated mood.

It was late at night when Mansoor's car entered the portico of Ashiana. He went straight to his room. Hearing the car, Abid peeped into his room and found Mansoor reclining on his chair, eyes closed—the fatigue had finally caught up with him.

'Should I draw a bath for you Miyan?' Abid asked solicitously.

As soon as Qamar Zamani heard that Mansoor was back, she rushed to his room. *'Meri jaan,* my darling, my child, where did you disappear without informing us? I nearly died of worry!'

Mansoor was silent, too exhausted to face his grandmother. Qamar Zamani turned to Abid—'Go and tell Saidani Bua to offer *sadqa* for Miyan immediately!' Saidani Bua soon came in with a tray on which there was some rice, Mash Daal and red chillies. She uttered words of prayer and circled the tray around his head three times, warding off the evil eye. The fuss irritated Mansoor.

'Enough, Ammajan! Please do all this in the morning; I just want to sleep now.'

'Yes, my *jaan,* you rest now,' said Qamar Zamani, biting back her curiosity to know where Shehzadi was. Finally, she could not restrain herself from asking—'I hope Dulhan is okay?'

'Yes, she is with her parents,' Mansoor replied shortly and closed his eyes. He wished Firozi Bua was there to press his aching forehead and put him to sleep.

Firozi Bua, unfortunately, had gone to Mohammadpur for her grand daughter's wedding. It was to be her last trip—she passed away peacefully there. Qamar Zamani received the news by telegram. Mansoor was the one most deeply affected by the loss—Firozi had been not only his nurse, but a loving mother, companion and confidante. In a burst of generosity, he decided to call her whole family to Aligarh. Forty days later, both her daughters arrived with their children—no one could replace her, but at least in Laala and Bibban, there was some memory of his beloved Firozi Bua.

Mumtaz Jahan was expecting a second time. This time, Shahab was not able to stop Qamar Zamani from sending her staff to see her through the confinement. Firozi Bua's younger daughter Laala and her husband and son were sent. Laala was the same age as Mumtaz Jahan and there was a natural affection between them because of Firozi. The woman took charge of the expectant mother, and stayed by her side throughout the pregnancy. Even Shahab grew fond of this devoted and hardworking family.

Mumtaz Jahan delivered a girl, who was named Zoya. Qamar Zamani wrote that she was sending a wet nurse for the baby but this Shahab firmly stopped, saying: 'Ammajan, nothing is better for a child than mother's milk. Both mother and child will be better off and stay healthy as well.' No man had ever spoken to Qamar Zamani on such intimate matters as mother's milk! Qamar Zamani had always been in awe of Shahab and Mansoor also advised her not to interfere. 'Shahab knows what is good for his family. It is better if we keep out. Please do not advise or try to influence Mumtaz Jahan.' Qamar Zamani realized she had to give in this time and be content with *duas* and *sadqas*.

The news of Nawab Asad Ali Khan's death hit Mansoor in a different way.

Memories welled up of a childhood spent in his grandfather's loving embrace. He thought of the sudden loss of the only father he had known. Bitter recollections of court intrigues, which had been pushed back over the years, came crowding back. But along with all this, were sweet memories of a young boy who had been his loving playmate, the nawab's second son, Zia.

Akbar Ali Khan had been fond of Zia and had loved seeing the two boys together. He had engaged a tennis coach to tutor them under his supervision. Sometimes, he would take them riding on the best Arabian steeds from the royal stables. There were sports, friendly competitions and camaraderie of the young scions of feudal lineage! Then came the fateful morning when he woke up to find himself not in his bed in Akbar Lodge, but asleep in his grandfather's arms inside a moving carriage. They had left their home far behind, for an unknown destination. 'Naana, where are we going?' he wanted to ask, but did not have the courage to speak. In the dark of the carriage, his small hand reached for his grandfather's face and felt the wetness of his beard.

The replay of persistent memories compelled Mansoor to break the self-imposed exile of his clan from Mohammadpur. The idea of visiting the state took hold of his mind. Abid was summoned to prepare for the journey, in utmost confidence. Mansoor was determined not to reveal his destination to anyone.

'Amma, I will return in a few days,' he said gently to the old woman as he took his leave. She looked calmly at him, spoke the last word of prayer and blew some words gently in his direction. Then, silence.

'Amma, I must go now.'

'Go where, *meri jaan*?'

'Amma, Nawab Sahib is dead. I will go to Zia at this great bereavement. Amma, I will represent all of us in this moment of grief.'

Qamar Zamani looked at her almost beautiful grandson; her heart softened at the sight of his downcast eyes. But when the words came out, they were rasping and harsh. 'Look Miyan, I hope you understand that I can never let you go there so long as I have breath in my body! When I am six feet under this earth, do what you want. Mohammadpur is dead for me, and so is Zia.'

She rose from the prayer *chowki* to stand before him, small and erect. Then she did something he had never seen her do before. She removed the white dupatta with which she always covered her head. Mansoor saw her face framed with silver-grey hair, which instantly softened her patrician features. Next he saw her dupatta lying at his feet.

'I beg you my son and heir to Akbar Ali Khan's fortunes, don't go. It is all a ruse. Nothing good will come of this. Now, go for your tennis game. And let me finish my *Isha* prayer.'

Mansoor bent his head, turned around and left the room. That night, he dreamt of his grandfather.

The very next day, a letter with a royal stamp arrived in the mail. The monogram read—Nawab Zia Ali Khan.

'Dearest friend of my happy childhood, Mansoor Ali Khan,

I cherish our friendship. Too many years have passed. You have lost too much, and so have I. In two weeks, my coronation will be held before the British Resident. Can I expect to see you at my side that day, my blood brother? Believe me, I have no one to call my own.

Your friend and brother,
Zia'

Qamar Zamani saw that she had lost the contest. She was too wise to push her luck further. She instructed Abid not to let Mansoor out of his sight even for a moment. Two armed guards were engaged to protect him. *Sadqa* was given and *Imam Zamin* tied on his right arm for a safe journey and successful mission.

On reaching Mohammadpur, Mansoor turned his car towards Akbar Lodge. There, he stood outside its Buland Darwaza entrance for a long time. It looked like the skeleton of the kothi in which he was born. In Nainital, he had received reports from the servants that all the furniture and draperies of the kothi had been vandalised. He had also heard that all the fineries and precious objects had been removed to the palace. Here was living proof of the rumours he had been hearing all along. Asad Ali Khan had taken revenge for being rejected. There was nothing to do but enter the ancestral mansion which had cradled him for the first impressionable years of life...

He spotted the precise staircase which he had fallen from, grazing his knee. He looked up at the skylights with stained glass, which had been imported from Italy. The *diwan* on which his grandfather once placed him for the studio photograph, had been stripped of its upholstery. Abid had cleaned one of the rooms which had wall mirrors, for his master's use. He had aired and laid out his master's clothes. He wanted him to look his best for the coronation. Abid did not see his master entering the room until Mansoor placed a hand on Abid's shoulder. He saw that the old servant's eyes were red from crying.

'I know, my good man. Too much to bear, isn't it, this sight of Akbar Ali Khan's ruined house...'

Zia's coronation as Nawab Mohammadpur reopened all the doors for Akbar Ali Khan's family. Zia pleaded with Mansoor to come and take possession of his family estate.

'Let the ghosts of the past lie in their grave, brother. Come to the riyasat and take what is lawfully yours.'

When Qamar Zamani heard about this royal edict from her seat in the mountains, she felt she had listened to her death sentence. She had vowed never to set foot in the place from which she had once had to flee for fear of death! She would rather turn blind than let her eyes be witness to her ruined kothi and shrunken estate. The very name of Asad Ali Khan was poison to her ears. She called to her Maula Ali for help: *'Ya Ali, mushikilkusha madad'* was the sound that emanated from her chamber, all hours of the night. So Akbar Lodge with its crumbling foundations, waited and waited for its heirs to return.

After the grand celebrations of the coronation, Mohammadpur settled down to its routine pace.

Zia's temperament was totally different from his father's. While he, too, loved indulging in sensual pleasures, he was also interested in the well-being of his riyasat. From his English tutors, he had been taught the merits of good governance. From his Indian tutors, he had imbibed the importance of education as the best way for the benevolent rulers of princely estates to immortalize themselves in their subjects' memories. So he began thinking about establishing schools and colleges in the name of his forefathers. But there was no one in the riyasat to whom he could entrust this important work. He wrote to Mansoor.

Shahab was in Aligarh as Principal of the Teachers Training College. He had gained a reputation as an excellent teacher. Zia had known him as Mumtaz Jahan's husband, but now he learnt about him as a good scholar, teacher and administrator. He had been witness to the huge opposition to Mumtaz Jahan marrying a 'mere commoner.' He had noticed that while everyone was opposed to Mansoor's selection of a 'poor lecturer' for his only sister, no one had denied the excellent qualifications of the man. Now, the fact that he was Mansoor's family meant that he could be trusted with state affairs. So Zia wrote to Mansoor, asking him to persuade Shahab to take over as Education Minister of the State of Mohammadpur on generous terms and conditions.

Shahab was surprised and flattered to receive the offer. He sometimes felt that he had deprived Mumtaz Jahan of the comforts of her *maika* and brought her into the frugal frame of his life. It was this consideration which tipped the scales in favor of Mohammadpur and he accepted the offer. He was keen to serve in his own field and had decided very early in life never to serve under the British. Here, he saw a good opportunity to educate and influence young minds under the patronage of a benevolent ruler.

Qamar Zamani was dead against his going to Mohammadpur, and tried her best to dissuade him. But Shahab was a principled man, and having once accepted the offer, did not want to go back on his word. So, along with Mumtaz Jahan and Zoya, he left for his new job, after arranging to rent Mumtaz Jahan Manzil to the university.

In Mohammadpur, Zia Ali Khan had a new avenue called *Rah-e-Zia*, built in his name; it started from the palace and went past Akbar Lodge and beyond. He built his own private palace, Dilkusha Bagh, right next to Akbar Lodge. Just opposite both houses, another spacious kothi was rented for Shahab.

During his father's lifetime, Zia had been married with great pomp. One year later, he had been blessed with a son and the whole city had celebrated the birth of the heir apparent. All went well until a few years later when Asad Ali Khan's wrath had descended on his daughter-in-law for a reason that was unmentionable in polite society. For her, it was a free fall into hell.

It happened like this. One day, when he came for one of his customary visits to the zenana, Dulhan Begum found herself the subject of the nawab's deep scrutiny. She feared that she had done something wrong and was dreading the consequences. What escaped her, was that her voluptuous post-pregnancy body was drawing him like a magnet. Her full breasts, covered by the dupatta, pushed roundly from under her tight *kurti*...

The very next day, she received a summons to Asad Ali Khan's chamber. Entering the chamber, she respectfully salaamed him three times. Asad Ali Khan was reclining on his bed. He gestured to her to come closer. Hesitantly, she moved towards the bed, but he beckoned her even closer and suddenly reached out for her, trying to pull her into his bed! She found him naked beneath the quilt and before she knew it, he was thrusting himself onto her, pulling her *kurti* up and jerking open the drawstring of her gharara. She struggled to free herself from the hands which were now all over her body. But the nawab was mad with desire. Suddenly she let out a piercing scream! Her personal maid, who was waiting outside, threw open the door and rushed in.

The nawab was furious. He pushed his daughter-in-law aside with such great force that it sent her reeling. While she straightened her clothes, she breathed the choicest abuses at her father-in-law.

'What an insolent daughter is this!' he shouted, as more servants came in to see what the commotion was all about. 'We are unwell since morning and she cannot even massage our forehead! We will teach her how to respect and serve her elders! Let it be known,' he ordered his Secretary who had hurriedly been summoned to the bedroom, 'she shall be punished for her insolence! Let her be banished to a remote corner of the palace and let Zia immediately marry a woman of our choice.'

No one raised a murmur at this astounding royal edict. Zia was too timid to protest. The nawab's choice predictably fell on the daughter of a Domini (a singing woman) who was attached to the palace. The greatest punishment he could inflict on his daughter-in-law was to have woman of lowly birth bed her husband. After the marriage was consummated, the nawab continued to take a strange pleasure in inflicting pain on the girl, so three more women were brought into Zia's nikah. Had Asad Ali lived longer, Zia's harem, like the nawab's own, would have been filled with women. But the old man had reached a stage that, despite the best efforts of the hakims, vaids and doctors, he had to go. On the very day of his death, even before his *Soyem* (third day), Dulhan Begum was reinstated and the other three wives were relegated to their subordinate positions. Now, it was she, the first wife, who ruled the palace. In the next seven years, she produced seven children, four girls and three boys. People marvelled at the nawab's virility—he seemed to grow younger with every child! All seven children were brought up by governesses who were imported with much aplomb all the way from England, and Dilkusha Bagh rang with their laughter! Hers was the final word in the zenana—as well as in many of her husband's official matters.

In her natal home, Jaipur, Shehzadi gave birth to a girl. The child was the spitting image of her mother, with curly black hair and delicate features. Only her eyes were her father's—green flecked with gold. Shehzadi was overjoyed! For the first time, she experienced the pleasure of holding her newborn in her arms; she loved nursing the baby at her milk-filled breasts. Agha Sahib sent a telegram to Mansoor, giving him the good news. Mansoor shared the news with Qamar Zamani, and said he was leaving for Jaipur. She blessed Mansoor, his wife and child, saying—'Yes Miyan, you must go, but bring them back safely, as our home and heart are bereft without them.'

When Mansoor saw the child in Shehzadi's lap, for the first time, he experienced the joy of fatherhood. He had never seen his first two children in her lap or felt them in his arms. He did not know what it was, that warm smell of a newborn, until he held his own flesh and blood in the form of little Ruhi. He spent a week in Jaipur, but at last it was time to return. He asked Shehzadi to accompany him, but she turned away and hid her daughter in her lap.

'I don't want to be away from you, Sahib. But I am afraid for my child. Please do not ask me to go back where two of my children have been snatched away. At last I have seen this day. God has rewarded my patience. Please, please for God's sake, don't!'

Mansoor held her very close. 'Do not cry,' he said very tenderly. 'I will never force you to leave your parents' home. You are free to come, whenever you wish. But I will miss you terribly!'

Both Agha Sahib and Begum were very quiet as they watched him get into his car. They said farewell with baskets of sweets, fruits and *meva*.

Qamar Zamani was furious when Mansoor returned alone. But since she did not want to greet him with complaints, she only enquired—'Miyan, why did you not bring the child and Dulhan with you?'

Mansoor replied—'She wanted to stay with her parents a little longer.'

Qamar Zamani probed further—'She has been away long enough now. You should have insisted.'

'No, I did not insist,' he replied.

'Why not?' she persisted. 'You have the right. It is not done that she should be away from you so long in her *maika*. You should not agree so meekly to everything she demands.' Too tired to argue, Mansoor quietly left the room.

Time passed and seasons changed. Mansoor divided his time between Mohammadpur, Aligarh, Nainital and Jaipur. He was busy with his tennis, and reading sessions in Rosie's company. He often spent his evenings in Professor Sharif's home where he would play tennis with Rosie and her sisters or take them for long walks. He was also frequently summoned to Mohammadpur by Nawab Zia who found no one better with whom to share his special hobbies. Zia was extremely fond of music and there were always a few renowned musicians resident in the court. He had taken formal training and was well versed in Indian and western classical. His music mehfils started late in the evening and continued throughout the night, ending at dawn. Mansoor found himself becoming attracted to these indulgences of Zia.

Besides music, Zia also inducted Mansoor into the activities of his Masonic Lodge. In accordance with its constitution, the Lodge had very strict rules. Members had to take an oath of secrecy, even from family members. They had one monthly meeting which was held at a secret place and time. All members had to dress in special attire—a formal dinner suit with a broad band round the neck, on which the moon and sun were embroidered in gold and silver thread. All the proceedings took place behind closed doors and two men stood guard outside the door, with naked swords.

An elaborate dinner was served after the meeting. It was strictly a British table, laid with bone china, silver cutlery, crystal glasses… Liveried waiters served each dish with its required decorum.

Mansoor got totally engrossed in this new activity; so much so that he ordered a big hall to be constructed in his own compound, exclusively for the Lodge meetings. All its furniture was ordered from Calcutta and its decor was copied from the Lodges of Britain. Members would arrive from all over India and after the secret proceedings, they would assemble for dinner. Zia and Mansoor became closer to each other through music and Lodge activities. Zia kept Mansoor close by his side for many reasons, including for promoting his personal profile. After all, Mansoor was a graduate, while Zia had studied at home, albeit with private tutors brought from England. Even though he was Master of the Lodge, he needed Mansoor to write his speeches—Mansoor wrote elegant prose and Zia read it with great flair!

Mansoor had never been interested in the matters of land and zamindari. After Akbar Ali Khan, Qamar Zamani had taken over the management and affairs of the Estate. He had no head for numbers and all financial matters were left to the old Estate Managers who steadily siphoned off substantial sums, while professing undying loyalty to Akbar Ali Khan and his progeny. Mansoor's income from his vast properties began to wane. Apart from the daily expenses of the household, the Lodge expenses had also become sizable. He tried not to think about his dwindling income and growing liabilities. His feudal temperament, however, was undeterred by his shrinking income—he spent and doled out as much money as ever!

Shehzadi's brother had gone to Bombay to look for a job but found the big city struggle too hard for his delicate temperament. Soon, he was back at the kothi, looking upto his brother-in-law for help. Mansoor gifted him one whole village, Sultanpur, which was sufficient for all his expenses. Aalam quietly pocketed the largesse, and, no matter what befell Mansoor in later years, never ever returned a single paisa.

Shehzadi's daughter, Ruhi, was now eighteen months old. Qamar Zamani sent Saidani Bua to Jaipur with a request letter for Agha Sahib, to send his daughter back, but the woman returned empty-handed. Mansoor, who visited his wife every month, tried to persuade her too, but Shehzadi refused. For some time, Agha Sahib had been sensing danger in his daughter's long separation from her husband. He had also heard whispers of Mansoor's friendship with the beautiful, educated daughter of a professor. While he had full confidence in Mansoor, he knew that a young, wealthy and good-looking man was unlikely to be left alone by the ambitious parents of single daughters. One day, he talked firmly to Shehzadi, assuring her that there was no danger of her daughter being taken away. He warned her of the consequences of leaving her husband alone for such a long time.

Shehzadi herself was no longer the same hesitant young girl who, for years had meekly endured the tyranny of her mothers-in-law. She had borne three children and had grown stronger and more confident under her husband's love, given freely to her, especially in her natal home. So she agreed to go back. Mansoor decided to drive his family home, just as he had driven them to Jaipur a year ago. Ruhi was thrilled with her first long ride in the car, and kept up a continuous chatter in Amina Bua's lap in the back seat.

The arrival of the mother and daughter filled the kothi with joy; Qamar Zamani and Jahanara seemed over-eager to please Dulhan. Everyone was amazed by Ruhi's perfect beauty, by her docile nature—so much more pliant than Rahat!—having been nurtured in the gentle household of her maternal grandparents. Rahat had equally striking features, but her strict upbringing had made her sharp and quick-tempered while Ruhi was all sweetness and charm.

Qamar Zamani consciously kept Ruhi at an affectionate distance. She would sometimes call for her, but send her back to her mother after a short while. After a long time, there was a truce in the kothi. Mansoor started spending more time at home, playing with his daughter. Both Rahat and Asad were growing under their respective mothers. They had been instructed to call their birth mother 'Bhabi' in keeping with their confused generational relationship.

People began noticing the changed persona of Qamar Zamani. She had been slowly slipping into the persona of Akbar Ali Khan, the former head of the household. She instructed that she be called *Dada* (grandfather) instead of *Dadi* (grandmother). Her voice grew raspy and hair began sprouting on her chin. It seemed that she had willed herself to become the man, thereby negating her own existence as a woman! Her story, which had begun with Akbar Ali Khan, reached its climax in a merged identity. Mansoor, she loved with an obsession which was compounded of many emotions. He had replaced her dead husband; she had lost one and would cling hard to the other. He was hers alone. It was not easy for her to see him love anyone—neither wife nor children. This unspoken fear fueled resentment and anger against Shehzadi.

The second focus of her love was Asad. The intensity of her emotion was identical for both grandson and great-grandson. The childish fights between Rahat and Asad caused huge showdowns between mother and daughter. The children would often leave them to fight with one another while they returned to their games. Shehzadi sat apart and watched the drama. She had lived a very peaceful life in her parents' home, for almost two years and had almost forgotten about these squabbles. It was not long before it all began again.

It was a burning afternoon in the peak of summer. The *Loo,* the hot summer wind, was blowing through the *khus chiks* in the verandah, the vetiver blinds that the servants regularly wetted with cool water from earthen pots. Since Rahat and Asad had started going to school, the family had not yet left for the hills. Shehzadi was resting in her room after lunch, and Ruhi was listening to Amina Bua telling her a story.

Soon, Amina Bua dozed off but little Ruhi was wide awake, and feeling bored, she crawled outside where Rahat and Asad were playing. They were very happy to see Ruhi and asked her to join in. In a little while, there was a fight over some toy. Rahat, being the stronger of the two, hit Asad on his chin. Little Asad promptly pulled a handful of her hair and kicked her hard. Not to be left behind in this skirmish, Ruhi sunk her little teeth into Asad's leg, trying to save her sister. Suddenly, three doors opened and three women emerged. First there was silence. Then, each one snatched her child away. Qamar Zamani pulled at Asad's arm to take him away but Asad screamed in pain, pointing to where Ruhi's little teeth had dug in. 'Dada, she bit me!'

Shehzadi stood quietly, holding Ruhi. Qamar Zamani lunged towards her and spat:

'So this is how you have trained your daughter, to bite the flesh off her older brother?' She gave Ruhi a stinging slap on her cheek.

To the old woman's utter shock, Shehzadi grasped her hand in her stronger, younger grip, and shrieked:

'Stop this instant, old woman! You have trained your son to fight and bully his sisters!'

Both Qamar Zamani and Jahanara were speechless. They could not believe what they had just witnessed! The docile Shehzadi had turned into an unrecognizable version of herself!

That was the moment when the power equation of the kothi was passed on; the next generation had gained control.

It was not only motherhood which gave Shehzadi the courage to hold her own, there was something else. She was encouraged by a visitor who had started to frequent the kothi. Rehana Sharif, mother of Rosie, Ruby and Rani was one of the first women to have graduated from Aligarh University. She came from a family of civil servants who had loyally served the English and thereby risen in official circles. Begum Rehana was in her late 40's—witty, elegant and perfectly-mannered. In her beautiful French chiffon saris, pearls and high heels she became the focus of all eyes when she entered the zenana of the kothi. Her visits were frowned upon by Qamar Zamani and Jahanara, but Shehzadi had the support of Mansoor, who had quietly told her to welcome this extraordinary woman who was, according to him, 'the perfect balance of tradition and modernity.'

'Shehzadi, child, I watch you every day. I see how you are slowly beginning to assert yourself. Remember my dear, you have the power; you have given birth not to one or two, but three children! You have a loving husband and a grand household. You must continue to assert yourself—the minute you relent, the repression will return with double force. Both your mothers carry the fuedal burdens of an era fast disappearing. Understand them, forgive them, but stand firm for what is yours and yours alone.'

Qamar Zamani sat on her *takht* and watched these frequent

visits with disdain. She felt helpless in the face of Mansoor's directive to the servants that Begum Rehana should be escorted straight to Shehzadi's chamber whenever she visited.

'Maula, forgive me,' she said folding her *Ja*namaaz, to no one in particular, 'Protect my household from this *khubsoorat bala*.' The maid who was sitting next to her namaaz chowki bowed her head at these words and said, '*Ameen, summa Ameen*.' Regardless, Begum Rehana not only continued visiting the kothi, she also began drawing Shehzadi out of its confines.

Shehzadi started to occasionally go outside the kothi with her new friend. She shed her burqa and occasionally wore sarees instead of the heavy ghararas. One by one, she broke the rules imposed by Qamar Zamani. Violating the orders of her two mothers gave her pleasure—she discovered that she loved everything they disliked! Mansoor quietly watched this power-play. He loved all the three women in different ways but could not force them to live in peace. Ashiana was wired with tension which would often spark and plunge the household in gloom.

Silently, Mansoor listened to the complaints which were poured before him.

'Her tongue is like the scissors of Meerut, she shreds everything that comes her way, without looking back at the destruction she has caused!' Qamar Zamani said.

'Stop your mothers, Sahib! They breathe fire and spit venom at me and my child!' Shehzadi complained in turn.

Mansoor withdrew into himself, retreating further and further each passing day. He offered no solution, brokered no truce. He took to locking himself in his study with his cigarettes and thermos of tea, responding neither to the summons of Qamar Zamani nor to the pleading of Shehzadi.

In the next two years, Shehzadi gave birth to two more children. A girl and a boy. Now she had three children and total control over them and the household. All the servants followed her orders, and Amina Bua became the chief of the domestic staff. She had the keys of the store tied to her dupatta and gave orders about what and how much had to be cooked. She also looked after the two younger children as Shehzadi was totally wrapped up in Ruhi, her first child and her first love. Amina Bua never stopped saying '*shukr*'... to her *Maula*. She had never dreamt that circumstances would change so dramatically in favor of her Shehzadi.

The schools closed for the summer and Mansoor decided to go to the hills. Aligarh had been burning with hot '*loo*' and brown sandstorms. The children were made to nap in their rooms in the afternoons and warned against going out. Everyone was longing to get away to a cooler climate.

As it happened, two days before departure, Mansoor received a letter from Zia asking him to come to Mussourie instead of their usual retreat to Nainital. Zia had suddenly changed his summer plans and wanted his dear friend to change his plans as well. Hotels had been booked for his entire group of friends, his musicians, his horses and his dogs. Mansoor had no choice but to comply with Zia's programme.

Mussourie has always been called the Queen of the Hills. In summer, most of the royalty arrived there and the city became alive with the nawabs and maharajas of various states. One could see the entourage of the Maharaja of Patiala or the Maharaja of Kapurthala walking on the Mall with their many dogs led by liveried orderlies. Every dog had a monogrammed, gem-studded collar. The royal ladies in their chiffons and pearls would also be seen in the bazaar, going to all the big shops where Sindhi shopkeepers competed with each other to show them their best ware. They would quote high prices and feel very blessed as their business boomed.

Zia had hired a few bungalows along Mussourie's most picturesque Camel's Back Road. Mansoor's place, located next to

Zia's, was an ivy-covered bungalow fronted by a lawn with borders of lilies, pansies, petunias and snowdrops. The nawab had issued strict instructions that when Mansoor woke up, he should head straight for his kothi. The days were spent in leisure, the most important task being to plan for the evening's entertainment. Sounds of music were heard emanating from Zia's kothi in the evening with the lighting of lamps. The mehfils lasted till the first light of dawn. People enjoying late night walks would hear Begum Akhtar mesmerizing the audience, or Jaddan Bai creating magic with her melodious voice. Meanwhile, Zia had discovered a new talent in himself. He had found a new love for composing the *bols* (verses) of the *Thumri* and *Dadra* which he wrote on small slips of paper. In the evening, he would hand the slips to the courtesans, painstakingly instructing them on how to set it to a *raaga*. '*Mora saiyyan mo se bole na,*' had to be set in *Raag Darbari* in *teen taal*. The sarangi and tabla players, eager to please the nawab, listened to him with bowed heads and produced the exact notes on their instruments. The galaxy of the elite, which included the rajas of Patiala, Nabha, Kapurthala, Malerkotla, were regular attendees. They showered money on the musicians and never tired of praising the musical genius of the nawab.

Mansoor would return home in the early hours of the morning and go straight to his room to sleep off the revelry for several hours. He had found this routine useful to avoid the incessant domestic squabbles; he did not have to hear Qamar Zamani's complaints or Shehzadi's tirades... After all, Nawab's orders were Nawab's orders.

The company of Zia, and occasionally Begum Zeenat Zamani, became his refuge. He knew he could not take a firm stand on domestic matters, a quality he admired in his friend and brother-in-law Shahab. In any case, it was too late in life to assert his authority over the three adoring women, his beloved liabilities. So he closed his eyes, leaned back on Zia's *masnad* and immersed himself in music while Begum Zeenat took deep puffs of her hookah and Zia recited his newly-composed verses.

One day, out of the blue, Begum Zeenat turned to Mansoor and asked playfully, 'Bhai, since our families are so close in friendship, why don't we turn it into a permanent relationship?'

Mansoor looked with questioning eyes at Zia who was chewing on his cigar. Zia laughed heartily.

'Dear brother Mansoor, she means that we should join our two beloved children into matrimony so this friendship is secured forever. We know that they are too young at present, but we should get them engaged today, so they can get married tomorrow.' Zia was thinking of his son Munawar and Mansoor's Ruhi, beautiful children, whom he and Begum Zeenat had been discussing as 'a perfect match for each other.'

Mansoor was flattered by this proposal. But he knew the inner rot of riyasat affairs and was not willing to subject his child to these. But royal commands could not be dismissed so easily. He sat quietly for a while, and then, looking at his friend and benefactor with intense eyes, he spoke gently.

'I will have to consult Ruhi's mother.'

'Why not? Do ask our dear sister,' said Begum Sahiba, drawing from her hookah. 'I am sure she will have no objection.'

That morning, Mansoor deviated from his routine and instead of going to his room, he went to the zenana. Everyone was up and busy in their activities. Qamar Zamani had finished her morning prayers and was reading Quran Sharif. Jahanara was struggling with Rahat's long hair to get her ready for school. Shehzadi was still in bed, enjoying a hot cup of tea. Mansoor turned towards her room. On seeing him, Shehzadi sat up. A slight frown was the only indication of her displeasure at his nightly absences.

'Won't you offer me a hot cup of tea, Shaddobi?' She poured a cup and handed it to him. Mansoor sat down on her bed and started talking. She had always found him an excellent raconteur. So she listened attentively while he related the happenings of the night. After a while, he slipped in the proposal of Begum Sahiba.

Shehzadi sat up, throwing off the covers. 'How could you? However could you even think of considering her proposal?' She was on the brink of hysteria.

'No, I told her that I would not consider it, not without asking you. You know I will never do anything against your will.' He spoke very gently.

'Then listen to me once and for all! I will never, I repeat, *never* accept this proposal. I would rather give up my life than agree to give my daughter in a nawabi family. I have suffered enough. I will never push my Ruhi into the same hell. Never!'

Except for a brief stint at Aligarh, Mansoor had lived a nawabi life all along. There was nothing he did not know about the dangers of such a match. As for the royal family, he had seen and experienced enough since the renewal of his friendship with Zia. He had nothing to say in contradiction of Shehzadi's vehement rejection.

But Mansoor knew that he had never shared with her the many-faceted friendship that Zia had offered him on so many occasions. He wondered whether Zia was his brother, his friend, his aspiring lover or all three? He knew about Zia's taste for boys—he had, too often, been witness to Zia's stolen intimacies with youthful serving boys. He had seen the nawab's favourites showered with gifts and favours, their families given truckloads of royal cast-offs. However, if some strapping youth even slightly asserted himself, Zia would turn vicious. Mansoor had seen one beautiful Mewati boy tied to a column and lashed until he spat blood. Somewhere, Mansoor was flattered by Zia's imploring eyes which turned on him at the end of the evening mehfils. But he would embrace him affectionately and before leaving, hand him over to the attendants to be escorted to his bedroom.

The next evening, Mansoor skipped the nawab's mehfil. Zia sent several messages. Abid stolidly turned back the messengers with—'Sahib is not well.' That evening, the music program was cancelled. Two days later, after repeated summons, Mansoor appeared at Zia's place. Zia placed his hand affectionately on Mansoor's shoulder and walked with him in the veranda for a long time. When it became chilly, they moved into the living room which had been warmed with a cheerful log fire. After a while, Begum Sahiba also joined them and listened quietly, sitting on her special chair, smoking her Turkish cigarettes.

'Mansoor, did you talk to your wife about what I had suggested?'

'Yes Begum Sahiba, I did. But she says that Ruhi is too young. You are aware how attached Shehzadi is to her; she cannot bear the thought of her going away. I did not want to upset her, so I left it at that.'

Begum Sahiba was not too pleased at this polite rejection but it also came to her as a relief. She had never liked Shehzadi, who was different from the other ladies of her *zenana* mehfils. She stayed aloof and preferred to sit alone; nor was she obsequious like the others. She did not double over and salaam her seven times, like they did. Begum Sahiba had been observing her and took her dignified behavior as a sign of arrogance.

Zia's personal equation with Mansoor was different. From the servants' gossip, which he always encouraged, he knew the details of his domestic life, so he showed more understanding.

'He is right, Begum, we should not subject Shehzadi to any more trauma. She has got the child to herself after a lot of hardship so we should not talk of her marriage and going away just yet. There is plenty of time, and since you have asked for her, just consider her as yours. Isn't that so Mansoor?' Mansoor only said '*Ji Sarkar*.'

Getting the young and not so young married, was Zia's hobby. He was not interested in multiple marriages for himself but he was very fond of getting others married. No matter who was getting married, he loved making all the preparations. This gave him an excuse for grand parties, musical concerts, dance mehfils and all kinds of celebrations. Whenever there was a long gap between weddings, he would look for an excuse to start something. He arranged a strategic match for his youngest daughter Zarina and Nawab Jhilani's son, Dara. Zarina was 12 years old, which was considered the right age for a girl's marriage. Nawab sahib was in his element—sitting with Mansoor and Zeenat Begum night after night, discussing food arrangements, the choice of musicians, dancers, fireworks display, and the guest list.

The engagement was celebrated with huge pomp, but predictably, it did not last. Nawab Zia and Nawab Jhilani fell out on some small matter and the liaison was broken off. Within months, poor Zarina was subjected to another engagement, this time to her uncle's son, Naayaab. This was again broken due to a burst of royal anger against his younger brother, Naayaab's father.

The cycle of engagements continued. The musical mehfils flourished, as did the patronage of the musicians. Time passed swiftly and the children became young adults. The heir apparent, Munawar, had also stepped into adolescence, and Zia was keen to get him married. Mansoor had not yet given a favourable answer to the proposal and even Zeenat Begum was not too keen on Ruhi now. So she actively looked around for another suitable girl.

Munawar was not at all happy about the idea of marrying someone else. From the time he had set his eyes on her, he had been smitten by Ruhi. He imagined her sitting at his side at his coronation ceremony... Their temperaments, too, were a perfect match. It was not only her beauty but her innocence bordering on naivety which endeared her to him. She made him feel valiant, chivalrous and brave.

'Ruhi, when you visit the palace, why do you only play with

my sisters? Don't you want to play with me?' he teased.

Ruhi would blush and stammer. 'But… but Munawar Bhai, I *can't* play with you.'

'Why not? I can play! I can even play with dolls, if that is your wish. But we don't have to play all the time. We can sit in my room and talk, or you could read some of my books.'

'Books!' Ruhi would be shocked. 'Books are for school! This is *play* time.' She would say seriously—'If you talk of books during play time, I won't ever talk to you.'

Munawar loved her innocent rejoinders. He would see her and her sisters off at the palace gates and think of the day when she would never have to go away from him. 'This is how I will address the matter,' he told himself as he walked back to the palace 'Ammi Huzoor, I love this girl and want to marry her…. simple, isn't it?'

Chapter 14

MUSSOURIE HAD NOW become their permanent hill station. The family spent all summers there, enjoying the nawab's hospitality. Mansoor's life now entirely revolved around Zia. He not only spent time with him in Mussourie, he also accompanied him to his estates and looked after all matters of the Masonic Lodge. He also went along with him on his visits to other princely states. To promote Zia's hobbies, Mansoor was spending a lot of money out of his own pocket. But his resources had dramatically shrunk—to an extent that he was forced to quietly sell off some of the smaller villages of his estate. He could not bring himself to reveal to Zia this growing burden and ask him to pick up the expenses for the Lodge or the travel. He had no choice but to look at disposing off the real estate of Akbar Ali Khan. The munshis brought in secret deals for the properties, and pocketed sizeable commissions. Mansoor knew what was going on but he preferred to keep his eyes wide shut. The golden edifice which his grandfather had lovingly raised was slowly disintegrating to gold dust; and the dust was itself being metamorphosed into dirt.

Shehzadi was now ruling over the household, but she still balked at the intereference of her two mothers-in-law. By now she was mother of five children; three of them were under her care. She had gained control over her family but lost control of herself. Her temper became the dread of the entire household. Even Qamar Zamani and Jahanara were afraid of her flare ups! Qamar Zamani would see in her flashes of her own imperial rages; she would try to calm her down but it was too late—fifteen years of emotional battering had changed the 15-year-old child into a raving, ranting Fury who struck terror in every heart. They were three women with one objective—and this objective, hounded and hunted, was running in the opposite direction, seeking refuge from the chaos that swirled around him.

Shehzadi was in the final stage of pregnancy with her sixth child. Mansoor had gone to Calcutta with Zia. She had made him promise that he would be back before the delivery. In Calcutta, Zia had suddenly sprung a surprise.

'Bhai, have you ever heard about the most beautiful lake in the world, the Inle lake?' Mansoor looked at him blankly.

'Is it more beautiful than Naini lake?' he asked.

'You will see, you will see. That is where we will be tomorrow at this time brother. We will be walking along Lake Inle, in Rangoon!'

Mansoor remembered with dismay his promise to Shehzadi. Never one to spoil the fun, however, he smilingly accepted the nawab's charming impulsiveness.

'But how long will we be there?'

'Oh, not more than 10 days,' said Zia. Mansoor was too timid to protest, he desperately looked for a way out.

Before leaving for Rangoon, Mansoor sat down and wrote ten letters. Each letter described a different sight and sound of Calcutta that he had 'experienced' that day.

'Dear Shehzadi,

Next time, we will come here together. I will bring you to the Victoria Museum. It has some of the best pieces of Indian art.'...'Dearest Shehzadi, in the bye-lanes of Sonagachi, the nautch-girls are dark-skinned and beautiful. There is lilting quality in Bangla music—I will bring Kanan Devi's new record for you.'... 'Dear Shehzadi, the fish here is called Illish; full of bones. You would be afraid of eating it.'...

The packet of ten letters was left with the Manager of the Great Eastern Hotel to be posted every day from the General Post Office at Lal Duggi.

Shehzadi's daughter was born two weeks premature. An express telegram was sent to Sahibzada Mansoor Ali Khan, Great Eastern Hotel, Calcutta. But the telegram lay unopened at the Manager's desk and the letters kept arriving at the kothi every day. For Shehzadi, this was a very difficult delivery. Her blood pressure had shot up and she had bled profusely during childbirth. The doctors had struggled to save her life.

When he returned from Calcutta, the guilt-ridden husband could not look his wife in the eye. This childbirth had shaken her badly. She was worried and bewildered by her own condition. Her fits of anger became uncontrollable and more frequent. She would run out of the house barefoot and had to be physically restrained. When she regained her senses, she would be ashamed, but given the slightest provocation, it would happen again.

Shehzadi's fits terrorized the entire household, including Qamar Zamani and Jahanara. The conflict always started with children and quickly escalated. When she raged, everyone froze in place and listened in pin-drop silence. Cures for her condition were whispered among the servants and found their way to Qamar Zamani. Stories of ghosts, jinns, black magic were exchanged and *aamils* who could exorcise them were summoned from all parts of the state. When the fit abated, Qamar Zamani would make her sit with her on her namaaz chowki and fan her flushed face by flipping the pages of the Quran. Shehzadi had developed permanent red spots on both cheeks where the blood vessels had hemorrhaged. Jahanara quietly stitched *Imam Zamins* and after imbuing them with different prayers, instructed Amina to place them under Dulhan's pillow.

Mansoor had more worries now. He could not leave Shehzadi alone in this condition for long spells, so his escape route was restricted. He tried to look for professional help, knowing that neither Qamar Zamani nor Jahanara would agree to let their Bahu be treated by male doctors. He also knew that Shehzadi's illness could not be cured by domestic remedies and the spell-breaking recitations of *aamils*. She needed to be treated by a professional medical practitioner. So his choice fell on his neighbor, a Hakim, who had become a family friend after he had rented Mumtaz Jahan Manzil. Hakim Sahib and his Begum were an older couple whose affection extended to Mansoor's entire family. Children of both households had become one big family and were always in and out of each other's houses.

One morning, Mansoor announced that Hakim Sahib was coming to examine Shehzadi. His tone was final and brooked no argument. When Hakim Sahib entered the zenana, Qamar Zamani and Jahanara Begum sat on guard on either side. Hakim Sahib conducted the examination with his head bowed, not looking in the direction of his patient. It was in deference to his family friendship and high reputation, that the curtain was not drawn between the physician and the patient.

After he had examined her, he sat quietly with his eyes closed.

'Mansoor Miyan, Shehzadi bibi's condition is serious but not incurable. For years she has endured repression, including the anomaly of losing two children, not to natural but to unnatural causes. The danger of having high B.P. could mean a burst vessel inside the brain and permanent damage or stroke. I advise complete rest and peace and no incident to provoke fits of temper or hysteria. The medicines, I will prescribe for one month.'

These words were spoken loud and clear in the presence of the two mothers. Mansoor looked at the three women while he spoke to Hakim Sahib. 'From this day on, all of us will make every effort to carry out your instructions. We are grateful to you for your advice and words of wisdom.'

Some days later, all the children were playing cricket on the lawn. Asad was bowling, and five-year-old Kamil stood facing him with a small bat. Ruhi, Rahat and Rumina were fielding. Asad suffered from acute myopia for which he wore thick-lensed glasses. He picked up a piece of red brick, mistaking it for the ball, and threw it at little Kamil, catching him straight on the forehead. As the blood gushed, out the boy crumbled. The sight of blood scared Asad who rushed inside to hide, while the little fielders screamed at the top of their lungs. Shehzadi rushed out barefoot; Qamar Zamani frantically looked for Asad and when she found him hiding, assumed that Shehzadi must have hit him.

Shehzadi had picked up Kamil and was wiping the blood from his forehead. Seeing Qamar Zamani with a tremulous Asad hiding behind her, she screamed—'So this is how you have planned to murder my son! I always knew that you would not bear to see my happiness. You have been my enemy from day one, and one day, you will kill me also!' She was in the throes of a full hysteric fit.

'Stop you, mad woman, stop it at once!' shouted Qamar Zamani. By now, Mansoor had come out of his office and was holding Shehzadi in his grip.

'Ammajan, did you hear what Hakim Sahib had said? She is not well. Please control yourself.'

Nothing could rile Qamar Zamani as much as her own flesh and blood siding with a '*ghair*' (stranger). 'So now you are blaming me for your wife's illness? Well done, Miyan! Have you ever heard the sweet words that come out of her mouth? Just listen to me, *beta,* you cannot live your life with a mad woman. Allah and Rasool enjoin a second marriage. I will find you a bride who will give you the happiness you deserve, and as for her, she will learn her lesson and forget her fits.'

Mansoor had had enough. He motioned to Amina Bua to take Shehzadi away. Jahanara had picked up Kamil and was dressing his wound. Mansoor took one hard look at his two mothers. He did not speak a word to them but right there and then, he summoned his Munshi.

'Munshi, call contractor Meher Chand just now, ask him to bring his masons and building materials. I want a wall dividing the inner courtyard to be constructed by the end of the day. Remember, the two sections should be completely separate.' He turned around walked back to his study.

The cup of black tea he was habituated to drinking all day had become cold at his table. The cigarette on the ashtray had turned to ashes. Mansoor took off his glasses which had clouded over during this altercation. He lit a cigarette and smoke rings rose in the air. 'Dada,' he spoke softly to his dead grandfather. 'Today Ashiana has broken in two. This house which was built for one happy family has been developing fault lines for a long time. Today, the earth has moved from its axis and its unity is destroyed. Your family, your grandson's heart and your legacy, have all broken into two…'

That day, Ashiana acquired two separate portions. The wall started in the veranda and tore through the rest of the house, dividing the inner courtyard right until the back wall. Qamar Zamani, Jahanara and their two children were restricted to one section and Shehzadi was confined with her four kids in the other.

Outwardly at least there was peace.

The divided home had three women, each struggling for territory. Each wanted control of the household, control of its members and control of the man caught in the web of the devouring love of three generations of women. The two older children were not allowed to go over the wall, nor were the younger four permitted to come across. The brick wall, for the time being, had soaked all resentments inside its mortar. Mansoor went to his mother and grandmother every morning to pay his respects and be blessed, and then returned to his side. The day was spent in his office, or in the garden, drinking tea, smoking and attending to visitors.

Qamar Zamani never complained about the wall. She felt easily tired these days and was relieved not to have daily conflicts. Asad was growing-up and had to be watched carefully. She could no longer imprison him in her set of rooms. From her prayer mat, she kept an eye on him, counting the beads of her tasbih, invoking Allah and recalling the past. Jahanara would absorb every detail of Qamar Zamani's behavior, but give no inkling of her observation. All her life, she had observed her mother and in trying to be as unlike her as possible, she began to display her very characteristics. Her chance of moving away from Qamar Zamani was lost when Ammar had disappeared two years after their marriage. She would hear about his activities from time to time. There was talk that he lived in Delhi, in a rented house, with a few boys as companions. She learnt that he loved vintage cars, and possessed a fleet of fourteen vehicles. His indulgence in luxuries had become an addiction. She had even heard that once a month, with the help of his boys, he bathed in champagne! Bottles of sparkling Chardonnay were imported from France, only to be flushed down the drain. There were rumours that he had written a *Divan* (book of poems). It had been beautifully calligraphed, lovingly bound in real leather, the pages edged with real goldleaf border. She had learnt that it had been sold at Chawri Bazaar by his boys in exchange for a set of tabla*s*. She had sent her trusted Chhuttan to Urdu Bazaar in Chandni Chowk, Delhi with instructions to retrieve the *Divan,* at whatever cost. She had tried to piece together the bits of paper, on which he wrote the verses which he used to recite to her in those early days. As a shy girl with no exposure to these things, she had not understood the intensity of his emotion and expression. When Chhuttan returned with the *Divan*, after giving the bookseller a large sum of money, she was delirious with joy. She hid it away from the curious eyes of her attendants. It took her a long time before she had the courage to open its first page. The very first poem reminded her of the poetic compositions of Amir Khusro which she used to listen to sitting behind the *chiks* at the mehfil-*e-sama* held in the palace. It was a dialogue between lovers; a poem of *sawaal-jawaab,* question-answer:

Kaha jo usne dawa do kaha dawa kaisi?
Kaha jo mujhko dua do kaha dua kaisi?
Kaha ke waada wafa ho kaha wafa kaisi?
Kaha qaza ko bulado kaha qaza kaisi?
Kaha ye khoon hai mera kaha ke hone do
Kaha hina ye nahin hai kaha hina kaisi?
Kaha ke qatl bhi kardo kaha khushi se abhi
Kaha khata bhi to dhoondo kaha khata kaisi?
Kaha jawan huey tum, kaha ke phir tumhe kiya?
Kaha ke sharm karo ab, kaha haya kaisi?
Kaha ke chhoda hai Ammar ko, kaha chhoda!
Kaha ye kaisi dagha di, kaha dagha kaisi?

That one said, give me a cure; the reply came—what is cure?
I said, bless me with prayer; the reply came—what prayer?
I said, promise to be faithful; the reply came—what is faithful?
I said, call death; the reply came—death, what's that?
I said, that this is my blood; the reply came—let it be.
I said—this isn't hina; the reply came , what is hina?
I said—murder me; the reply came—with pleasure!
I said—search out my fault; the reply came—what fault?
I said—your youth has bloomed; the reply came—so what is it to you?

I said—have some shame; the reply came—what is shame?
I said—have you abandoned Ammar; the reply came—abandoned, yes!
I asked—you betrayed me; ; the reply came what is betrayal?

The news of his death came to her in the form of a letter from his lawyer. Jahanara sent the letter to her mother and locked her door to avoid any displays of sympathy. When the door opened again, her face was calm. She draped her body in shapeless white clothes and wrapped a white dupatta on her dark, shiny hair. Then she sat still for many hours; it was only when little Rahat squeezed herself through a window and threw her arms around her neck, that she moved to hug the child close to her heart.

The dividing wall had insulated Mansoor to some extent. He began spending the evenings with a group of genial men friends. There was his neighbor Hakim Saheb, Shehzadi's brother and his own brother-in-law Shahab, whenever he visited, and a few others.

Sometimes, a young lecturer from the University, Prof. Qutub would also join their mehfil. Qutub was a cheerful young man with one passion—good food. His rounded body was always craving gourmet dishes. This inspired Mansoor to devise new delicacies for him every day. In the process, he began to enjoy cooking; but his fondness for cooking was as intense as his lack of interest in eating it. Every night, he tried out a new dish for Qutub and friends. The servants would bring an *angeethi* with burning charcoal into the outer verandah. All the masalas were freshly ground and placed in small heaps on a large tray. The friends would sit around the fire in reclining chairs, while Mansoor sat on a low stool by the stove, with a spoon to stir the *kadhai* from time to time.

One evening, Qutub brought along a book of recipes called *Shahi Dastarkhwan*. Everyone was most interested in this old-looking volume, which had been through many hands. But Qutub was most possessive. In his anxiety, he sat on the book to safeguard it, knowing that no one could dislodge him. 'Mansoor Bhai, every day you feed us your expert recipes. Today I will make *Pulao Marwarid, Doodhiya Biryani* and *Adrak ka Halwa.*' '*Pulao Marwarid*?' Hakim Sahib asked. '*Marwarid* means pearls, miyan, will you feed us the real or the fake?'

'See these garlic cloves?' Qutub pointed at the small white buds in a basket, 'These garlic cloves will be rendered like pearls through cooking.'

Then he turned to Abid, who stood by for orders. 'I want two kilograms of the best milk for *Doodhiya Biryani*. And ask the *masalchi* to grind 2 kilos of fresh ginger for the halwa.'

By then, the servants from the kitchen had crept into the verandah to listen to this discourse. Behind the *chik*, Shehzadi stood listening attentively. Qutub loved this audience.

'The way an onion is cut, you understand what I mean, the way it is cut, leads to dramatic changes in the pungency it imparts to a dish. Take *Do Pyaaza,* for instance. Most people understand it as 'double quantity of onions'. It is not that at all! What it means is, two *kinds* of onions—caramelized and regular—you understand?'

The admiring crowd of friends, domestic servants and ladies behind *chiks* spoke an approving '*Jee haan.*' Qutub Sahib looked around, pleased at the impact he was having. Then, brandishing the ladle with which he was to turn the rice for the pulao, he further elaborated on the fine art of cooking.

'Folks, Mohammadpuri food has a unique aroma; it is a blend, an unparalled unrivalled, unsurpassed quality! It has hot spices from Dilli Gharana, sour spices from Hyderabad, sweetness from Avadh. From the Nawabs of Murshidabad's spice racks it has *javitri* (mace) and *jaiphal* (nutmeg)... And right from our own *pados* (neighbourhood) Jaunpur, it uses the fragrant sandalwood and khus roots. As the poet said: If there be a cuisine on earth...'

Mansoor smilingly stopped his friend from parodying the Mughal Princess Jahanara's immortal lines written in praise of Kashmir. Everyone joined in Qutub Sahib's hearty laughter!

Hakim Sahib loved Mansoor's mehfils. Everyone loved him, not so much for his *hikmat,* but for his endearing ways.

He had a passion for fitness. He would wake up very early and call his valet Dilawar to massage his body for an hour. Then he would do sit-ups and leg-ups for half an hour. After that, the ritual of dyeing his scanty beard began and then a leisurely bath. He would then emerge in his beautifully starched white Achkan and Aligarh pajamas. White attire had become his trade mark. This was his daily routine. He then visited the zenana before setting out for the Medical College.

'Begum, is my *paan dibbia* ready?' he would ask, even though he knew very well it was always ready and waiting for him. He always had a *paan* in his mouth, and had the habit of keeping his chin up, so the *paan* did not drip, which was just as well, considering his pristine clothes! This gave him a haughty look.

'Yes, of course, Chhote Miyan!' she would retort, 'Why do you ask every day?'

Hakim Sahib's wife was a few years older than him, and so she called him 'Chhote Miyan'. She sat the entire day on a divan, in a flowing gharara and a matching crinkled *mulmul* dupatta, with her huge silver *pandaan* placed in front, making *paans* and issuing orders. She had two daughters, Asifa and Shahida, and one son, Saeed, who were of the same age as the children in Ashiana; all of them were very good friends. She loved all the children of both houses, but would pretend to be angry and scold them all day. Being the wife of a renowned Hakim, all her curses were filled with the names of illnesses.

'*Arre kambhakto,* if you do not listen to me you will get *haiza* (cholera)... or *peelia* (jaundice)...or *shakar* (diabetes). You all are *shakar kay cheentee* (ants of sugar)!'

They all enjoyed her tirade and would deliberately provoke her. When she got started, they would run off, knowing that her bulky frame would prevent her from going after them.

For all his wisdom and distinguished looks, at heart, Hakim Sahib was easily intimidated. Everyone knew it and exploited it whenever possible. Mansoor would often call him to Ashiana at night. Aamir or one of the children would cover themselves with a white sheet and hide in the bushes. When he passed by twirling his cane, they would pounce on the unsuspecting man with yowls and yells.

'*Bachao, bachao*!' Hakim Sahib would scream and run for his dear life.

'What is the matter, Bhai?' Mansoor would ask innocently.

'*B… bh… bhoot*….deo….devils…*djinns*… …'

Suddenly the white clad *bhoot* would appear, salaam him and shed his sheet. Then everyone would enter, rolling with laughter.

Hakim Sahib's daughter, Shahida, and Rumina were childhood friends. During the holidays, they spent their entire day talking and playing in each other's homes. Ruhi considered the girls too childish and preferred to remain aloof. Her good looks and the admiration she got from all quarters, kept her strictly to herself. Shehzadi was not very happy with her daughter going to other peoples' houses and would promptly send Amina Bua whenever Rumina was late. Rumina hated these summons from her mother which invariably came when she was happily playing with her friend. But she had to rush back for fear of her mother's uncontrolled temper.

Aligarh had only two movie theatres. Whenever a new film was released, the ladies would make elaborate plans to see it together. Preparations for the excursion would start in the morning. Khala Jaan (Hakim Sahib's wife) would instruct her special maid Fazeelat Bua, 'Don't forget to make *roghni* roti with *shami kebabs*. Also scramble a few eggs with onions, tomatoes and green chilies. Send someone to Amina Bua to remind her to make tea in the thermos and pack some *halwa*. Begum Rashid from Tarwali Kothi will bring snacks for the children. Where are you rushing off to, Fazeelat? Remember to fill my box with *paan* or ...forget it, woman! You better clean it and give it to me. I will make my own *paans*. And don't forget Miyan's *paans*. If he does not get his quota, he will make everyone's life miserable.'

At last, it would be time to go. Everyone arrived at Ashiana armed with their tiffins. For transporting them, there was one *bhaghghi* and two *tongas*. The older ladies divided themselves in the three vehicles and the girls squeezed themselves here and there, staying as far away as possible from their own mothers. Once, the theatre was playing Ashok Kumar's '*Jhoola*'. The hall was crowded with people. Two large boxes had been reserved for the three families. The servants walked ahead carrying the tiffins and baskets, placed them in the box and went down to take their seats with the public. All the female staff was specially treated to these outings. During the interval, they were expected to come to the boxes and serve their respective mistresses. First, they took out the plates and cutlery. Then they spread the napkins and served the food with proper decorum. Glasses of sherbat were handed around. The women and children loved this outing and the food did not taste half as delicious at home as it did in that ramshackle theatre. The last item was Khalajan's *paan* which was offered around while everyone talked animatedly about the film. Throughout the film, Khalajan would keep up a running commentary; she firmly believed that the reel characters were real! If the villain ever chased the heroine, she would start cursing him loudly, 'Look at him, how he is chasing the poor child. Leave her alone, you rascal! Or... !'

Then her voice would become audible above the dialogue. 'Where has that foolish hero disappeared? Why doesn't he come to save her?' Then she asked all the girls to look for him on the screen. The others would try to hush her and say, 'Baji, it is just a film, don't take it to heart.' But she would get more agitated. 'Poor girl, she is in trouble. And you want me to sit quietly! You can do it, I can't!' Thus Khalajan took everybody's trouble to heart even if it was on the screen.

Hakim Sahib was amused at his wife's antics. Sometimes he teased her by telling her stories of his 'beautiful' female patients. He saw her agitation in the vigorous chewing of her *paan*. When she could not bear it any longer, she would confront him. 'Did she take off her *burqa* in front of you?'

'Yes, of course. How can I examine her when she was all covered?'

'You wretched man, you have lost all shame,' she would spit out the words with the residue of her paan. 'Did you also ask her to show you her tongue?'

'I had to, how else could I diagnose her problem? What a lovely tongue it was!'

'As God is my witness, one day, you will find a black tongue and then you will pay with your entire practice. May Allah never show me that dreadful day.'

The occupants of these four kothis of Aligarh—Ashiana, Mumtaz Jahan Manzil, Tarwali Kothi and Neeli Chhatri—slowly became very close. Men, women and children would seamlessly move through each other's houses and exult in one another's happiness. Eating was a favourite pastime. Sometimes, there would be freshly picked peas from the garden or corn from the fields. These would be fried and roasted on the fire and served along with hot pakoras with mint chutney. The news about the food being served, travelled fast. Everybody trooped in almost on cue. Their activities were planned around the seasons. During the monsoons, *jhoolas* would be installed in the gardens for the girls to swing. The ladies would sit on the wrought iron benches while the servants would serve hot tea and samosas. Small kids played in the rain and enjoyed slinging mud at one another. In the garden, they would compete with each other on who would collect the greatest number of *beerbahoti's* (ladybirds). These little insects with their red velvety coats were placed in a rice-filled bottle and the children would watch how the rice would slowly change from white to red.

At night, when the sky was clear and there was a full moon, they would have a moonlight picnic. Usually it was held on Mansoor's terrace, since it was the largest. Everyone would be assigned a role. Ruhi and Rumina would spread a few mats on the terrace. Asifa and Shahida would ask their mother to make her special chicken patties for the moonlight picnic. The girls would say, 'We have to leave immediately, if we delay another moment, the clouds will gather and the moon will disappear.' Their mother would beat her forehead in despair. 'What is so special about this blessed moon? It comes out every night, so why are you getting crazy about it? The patties are lying in the pantry, take them and go before I change my mind.' The girls loved her reprimand and laughed as they got into the carriage.

The preparation of the picnic would be in full steam in Ashiana. Amina Bua and Fazeelat laid out the food and the jugs of sherbat on the mats. Besides, Asifa and Shahida, there were their brothers, Saeed and Salman. Azra and Munni came with their three brothers Iqbal, Ehsan and Munir from Tarwali Kothi. Khurshid and Jamshed came from Neeli Chhatri. Most of them were now adolescents. While the younger children played on one side of the terrace, the older ones sang and flirted on the other side. All the boys, without exception, were in love with Ruhi. Jamshed played 'tabla' using the table top and Khurshid burst into a Qawwali in which everyone took part. They made up the verses and sang full-throated to the sound of clapping. Across the road, the boy's hostel windows opened towards

Ashiana. Hearing the sounds of music, many of the students would abandon their studies and come to their own terrace to join the singing. To avoid being caught, they would turn off the hostel lights so that even the studious ones could not stay back in their rooms!

One morning, the hostel warden complained to Mansoor. Mansoor apologized and promised that he would not allow them to disturb the students again. So the moonlight picnics on the terrace were eventually banned. But youth found other ways and the fun continued, unabated. Inevitably in these mehfils, serious romances were also blossoming. Jamshed fell madly in love with Ruhi and could not conceal his feelings. Everyone knew of his lovelorn condition. He urged his mother to go to Ashiana with his proposal for Ruhi. His mother went at least three times, but all Shehzadi said was that Ruhi was too young and Jamshed needed to finish his studies. Jamshed could not take this refusal: he started behaving like a jilted lover, sighing, crying, and singing sad songs, until he was banned from Ashiana.

Chapter 15

IT HAD ALMOST been a year since the wall had been erected, dividing Ashiana into two. On either side existed two different worlds. Laughter on one side and silence on the other. While the children on Shehzadi's side were free to move around, the children on the Qamar Zamani side were caged in. They dared not play with their siblings for fear of their mothers. The highlight of their day was when Mansoor visited in the morning to pay his respects to his mothers. Sometimes, Qamar Zamani asked about Shehzadi. She expressed her concern that it had been six years since she had borne a child.

'Has she become barren? Miyan, it has been a long time. Even your youngest is in school. I am worried about Shehzadi...'

Mansoor smiled, 'Ammajan, she has had five children, is that not enough?'

'This big house and only five children? They all go to school and the house is empty all day. I am sure she must also feel lonely. If only there was a small child to look after, she would be much happier.'

Mansoor was quite amused. He knew his grandmother and it was not her concern for Shehzadi, it was her own loneliness that she was talking about and thereby looking for an excuse to break the wall. Her ego stood in the way of a frank expression of her feelings.

Every time she saw Mansoor, she would bring up the subject.

He had decided that she would have to speak three words, 'break the wall' before he took action. But she could not bring herself to utter the words.

One morning, when Mansoor appeared to greet her, she had just finished her prayers. As he bent down to embrace her, she held him away from her and looked him straight in the eye. 'By the grace of Allah, ours is a small family. Your grandfather was an only child of his parents. And I the only child of mine. You are our one and only heir, but I want to reverse this condition. I want this house to be full of children. If Bahu is unable to bear a child, we can get you married again to whomsoever you want, from anywhere in the world, from Iran or Turan. There is nothing that prevents you from marrying a second time.'

Mansoor found her suggestion amusing and thought, 'Iran and Turan is the limit of my grandmother's world.' Smilingly, he put his arms around her and said, 'How about a wife each from Iran, Turan, Afghanistan and Azerbaijan!'

Planned or unplanned, the very next day, Amina gave tidings that Dulhan Begum was '*mashallah,* in the family way.' Nine months later, Shehzadi gave birth to another son. On that very day, in compliance with Qamar Zamani's orders, the wall came down.

Qamar Zamani met her daughter-in-law after a long time. There were affectionate greetings on both sides and for the time being, all acrimony was set aside. Asserting her right as a head of the family, Qamar Zamani named the child Yusuf Ali Khan. To recite the *kalima* in his little ear, she reached out to pick up the baby. But Shehzadi placed both her hands on the child. Qamar Zamani did not say a word; after placing her hand on Shehzadi's head and mumbling the *kalima,* she left the room.

The house fell into a set routine; all five children were going to school. In the evening, Rahat, Asad, Ruhi, Rumina and Kamil had their tutors to help them with their studies and homework. They took turns playing with Yusuf who longed to join the siblings but was too little for this robust crowd. At night, the beds would be placed in the courtyard, each under its own mosquito net which also served to hold back the dew. In the centre, was placed the bed of Baji Begum, decidedly the best storyteller. She had an unending repertoire of adventures and fairy tales. She would tell them the stories of Nargis Pari, Mehtab Jadoo, Umar Aiyar, Malika Gulnaz and the five children imagined themselves as incarnations of these denizens of a fantasy world. They loved the disguises of Umar Aiyar who would appear as a beautiful sorceress, an old woman, a nymph, a hunchback—in whatever form he wanted to appear he just had to wish for it and thrust his hand deep into his magic '*zambiel*'. In a flash, he was transformed! They were fascinated by Malika Bemisaal, seated on her flying throne. Each of its corners was placed on the shoulders of her flying women attendants. One by one, the children fell asleep, transported into a land spinning with dreams...Only Rahat, the oldest, would stay awake until the end.

At the dining table, they would all sit together and learn table manners.

'Don't hold the glass with the soiled hand, or it will slip and run away.'

'Finish all the food on your plate or it will get up and chase you forever.'

'Don't drop a single grain of food, or on the Day of Judgment, you will have to sweep it up with your eyelashes.'

'Only if you clean your plate, can you ask for *meetha*.'

In that household, which now had six children, three mothers and one Mansoor, there was one who had become a human machine. Jahanara Begum had filled her empty life by devoting every single moment of her waking time in doing something with her hands. Cutting and tailoring for the entire family became her obsession. Not finding it enough, she began knitting sweaters, mufflers, socks, mittens for all the children. She was never seen without her hands busy in creating something 'useful'—useful, to her mind, was strictly utilitarian. Mansoor was too wrapped in his cares to notice that his mother had sentenced herself to manual labor. But Shahab, when he came to visit, often remarked that his mother-in-law had become a *neher ki panchakki.*

'Baji Begum, please give these hands a rest. Every child has a new sweater for the winter; all their winter clothes are ready even though winter has not even started. Come with me to Mohammadpur, you can spend time with your daughter and grandchildren.'

Jahanara Begum was grateful to Shahab but obsessive work was the only way she had found to navigate her intense loneliness.

The day when Rahat returned early from school and dashed into her room, banging the door behind her, life in Ashiana took a new turn. Jahanara found the girl, doubled over, her clothes blood-stained. Amina was summoned to explain the menstrual cycle to Rahat since this subject was never discussed between mothers and daughters. For three days, Rahat was prohibited from playing with her brothers and sisters. She was also exempted from offering namaaz. The younger children were told 'Apa is not well.' Rahat was angry at being thus afflicted and isolated. The only consolation she was offered was that similar affliction would be experienced by Ruhi and Rumina in due course.

On the fifth day, when Rahat completed her first period, she was given a ritual bath by Amina. That day, Qamar Zamani summoned Jahanara and Shehzadi to her room.

'Rahat is no longer a child; we must begin to look for a suitable match. It is not advisable to keep a girl at home one single day after she has started menstruating. I was married at the age of 9 and it was in my marital home that I had my first *maheena.*'

Shehzadi announced, 'I will take this up immediately with her father.'

For the past few months, Shehzadi had become kindly disposed towards the two mothers. Whenever she had to make a difficult decision, she would ask Qamar Zamani to find the solution through *istikhara*. Whatever the *istikhara* indicated, Shehzadi would follow it to the letter. If a child was sick, a new servant had to be hired, or a trip had to be taken, the answer was sought in the counting of the beads. The beads had thus become a bond between Qamar Zamani and Shehzadi. She had also begun to indulge herself in the hobbies of her childhood. She loved animals—in her backyard, she had separate enclosures made for cows, buffaloes, goats, dogs, cats, rabbits and birds. She personally tended to all the animals and early in the morning she would supervise the milking of the cows and buffaloes and preparation of fresh butter and *chhaachh*. She would then ensure that it was filled in earthen pots and distributed among the neighbours' houses. Whatever time she could spare from the animals, she would tend to the vegetable garden and fruit trees. She had a passion for fragrant flowers, so there were bushes and creepers of champa, chameli, mogra, motiya, raat ki rani and harsinghar. The frequency of her hysterical fits had abated but still, from time to time, they erupted, directed at the servants, children, and other family members. But by now, they too had learnt how to cope. They listened to her tirades quietly, waiting for the storm to blow over because they knew that at heart she was generous and kind-hearted and unable to refuse anyone who came to her in need.

Of all the servants, it was Shamshad who found her way into her favour. Spying and carrying tales was the best way of pleasing her gullible mistress. Shehzadi was quite interested in the servants' tales. And Shamshad's first target was Amina Bua.

'You know Dulhan Bibi, Amina Bua has lost her mind. She gives the best food to Rumina and Kamil but if Ruhi Bibi asks for anything, she turns her down. This morning when Ruhi asked her for some cream to spread on her paratha, she pretended that there was none left but I had seen her locking it up in the *nemat khana*. When I reminded her, she almost slapped me and said, 'Mind your own business.' I saw Ruhi crying in the corner; it really broke my heart.'

This was enough for to bring on a tantrum. Shehzadi summoned Amina Bua and burst out 'Who are you, old woman, to deny my child anything? Do not cross the limit of your authority or… or just get out!'

Amina was too shocked for words, she tried to say something but bit back her words; she knew Shehzadi was not in a state to listen to reason.

'Leave, I said!' Shehzadi screamed.

Amina wrapped her belongings in her prayer mat, placed the bundle under her arm, put on her slippers and walked out of the door. When Rumina and Kamil saw their beloved Amina Bua leaving, they ran to her and pinning her down, refused to let her move. By this time, Shehzadi's fit was ebbing. She looked sheepish and began to apologize.

'Please don't leave us. You should not take my anger to heart. You know, I don't mean it. You know, Amina.'

Amina was dragged inside by the children, but she had had enough. That day, she handed over her precious household keys to Shehzadi, marking the end of her rule over the servants. She stopped participating in household affairs and took a kind of *sanyaas*. All morning, she would stay on her prayer mat; sitting, eating, and sleeping, all on the same *chowki*. Only when Rumina and Kamil returned from school, did she get up.

Shehzadi transferred Amina's duties to Shamshad. All the staff were now under her control. She was the one who gave orders and she was the one who held the keys to the stores. With her new-found power, she ingratiated herself into Shehzadi's favour by carrying more gossip than ever. Every morning, there would be a scene between Shehzadi and the servants, instigated by Shamshad's words. The children would plug their ears and duck under their quilts to block out the noise and only emerge when things had quietened down. Since her husband was employed in a nearby city and came to visit her only on holidays, Shamshad was totally free from any personal responsibilities and on the lookout for new stories with which to regale her mistress.

Into this scene, one fine morning, a new person walked in. Mansoor's agent in the estates of Akbar Ali Khan was an old family retainer, Munshi Nisar Husain. He had come to explain the condition of the estates to his master. Shehzadi asked Shamshad to open a room in the servant quarters for the duration of his stay. Nisar Husain had charge of collecting the *lagaan* in Mansoor's estates and villages. He would distribute the money between estates and household expenses, which he did with utmost probity. Mansoor did not even take a second look; he had implicit trust in this old servant of his grandfather.

In the sober Munshi, trusted by the whole family, Shamshad saw a future which would relieve her of an absentee husband and anchor her firmly within this household. Over the next few weeks, she built up a story about a cruel husband, a womanizer, a wife-beater, to whom she was forcefully married even before she had matured. She hinted that even her three daughters were not safe with this man who would often return home drunk. Shehzadi was fed this packet of lies; and slowly began to feel sorry for the woman. She fancied herself in the role of a savior and became convinced that the only way out was to arrange for a *khula* since she could not make the husband give Shamshad *talaaq*. Shamshad was only too eager to sign the papers absolving her husband of *meher* and taking custody of her daughters who would henceforth be looked after by her kind benefactress. Having won her freedom, the next step was to make Shehzadi propose a match between her and Munshi

Nisar Husain. Playing on sympathies and vulnerabilities, Shamshad succeeded in making Shehzadi believe it was her own idea that a marriage be arranged between these two lonely people.

In a simple ceremony, Shamshad and Nisar Husain became man and wife. With the signing of the nikahnama, it seemed that the future of Ashiana was also signed and sealed. Inside the house, Shamshad became the undisputed head of the domestic establishment, and outside the house, Munshi controlled all matters related to income and disbursements. Between the two of them, they began to chip away at the inheritance of Akbar Ali Khan. They did so until it was completely hollowed out and only the outward shell remained.

Chapter 16

AGHA SAHIB HAD retired and moved back to Lucknow. Husband and wife were keen to get their sons married. The elder one, Aalam, was not yet ready so they planned to get the younger, Aamir, married first. There was a proposal for him from Agha Saheb's brother for his only child, Arifa and soon, the wedding date was fixed. Mansoor and Shehzadi arrived in Lucknow with all the children. It was a grand family reunion.

The day after the wedding, Mansoor prepared to leave with his family. He saw Shehzadi's puffed eyes and the strained look on Agha Sahib's face. Begum Agha was stitching the *Imam Zamins* and wiping her tears.

'Abbajan, why don't you and Ammijan move to Aligarh? Aalam is unlikely to move back to Lucknow and Aamir is applying for a teaching position at Aligarh University. You can be close to him as well as to Shehzadi, and all the children will be there to keep you busy!'

Agha Sahib became thoughtful. 'But there is so much a move like this will involve... At my age ...'

'You don't have to worry, Abbajan. You just say 'yes' and leave the rest to your daughter and me.'

It was decided that initially, they would move into the annexe of Ashiana till their own bungalow was ready. Mansoor had built a little guest cottage, so he proposed that this is where Agha Sahib and family should stay. Agha Sahib looked at his wife, there was a silent exchange between them; suddenly all the children burst into the room and threw themselves on the grandparents. 'You have to listen to our papa, we cannot bear to be away from you and Nani, please.... please, for our sake, say yes!'

The responsibility for building the house which was already named 'Shabistan' was given to Mansoor. This had always been Agha Sahib's dream—to spend the evenings with Mansoor, Shehzadi and the grandchildren. Soon, the construction began and Agha Sahib became involved with its daily supervision. For the children, the annexe became a holiday home. They would spend every free moment there and return home with great reluctance. Amina also loved to spend time with her old mistress. She finally had someone with whom to share her worry about Mansoor's growing indebtedness, due to the trust he had placed in Munshi Nisar and his new wife, Shamshad. Begum Agha shared some of this with her husband and both of them tried to warn Shehzadi. They could foresee the impending doom.

It was fear of Shehzadi's intemperate outbursts which prevented them from speaking to her more openly. Every morning from their verandah, they heard her shouting. Sometimes, the tea was not hot enough, or the eggs too hard, or the toasts burnt. Most of the temper tantrums were inflicted on the servants but sometimes even the children bore the brunt. If ever Shehzadi decided to help them with their school work, all hell broke loose. A poorly learnt lesson or incomplete homework, meant a painful cane on their open palms. If ever she found their rooms untidy, she picked up whatever lay around and set it on fire. When they saw her approach, the children ran to their refuge in their Nana-Nani's house. In a few months, Shabistan was completed, but the children were sad. Their Nana-Nani would be now living a whole mile away, and they could not just run across there anytime they wanted as they had been doing in the annexe. Now, their visits were restricted to once a week.

That weekly visit was like *Eid*. Their Nani spent all morning preparing their favourite food so when they came, the table would be laden with the most tempting *nashta*. Shehzadi was amazed at the sheer joy with which they pounced on the food.

'How is it—' she asked her mother, '—that they relish the food here, but at home I cannot even make them finish what is on their plate! Look at Rumina, at home she never touches her roti and only eats dessert, but here she quickly finishes two rotis and does not even bother about the dessert.'

'Dear child,' her mother answered with a smile, 'children are plants which need to be nurtured with gentleness and with love. Don't scold them and keep laying down rules. They will eat as much as their system requires, but if you force them, you will find them digging in their heels and resisting.'

Shehzadi wanted to follow her mother's advice but was unable to keep herself in control. Most days, she felt ill. She spoke to Hakim Sahib who prescribed some pills and pastes. She even wrote to Miss Gill:

'I have a burning sensation in my chest, it becomes intense when anything annoys or upsets me...'

Miss Gill wrote back suggesting that she show herself to a specialist in Delhi. Shehzadi took one look at Miss Gill's letter and shook her head, 'Nobody can cure me, and nobody can diagnose my ailment.'

Both sisters-in-law were by now expecting—Arifa her first and Shehzadi her seventh. There was a sense of weariness in the household; the very matriarch who had suggested a second marriage to Mansoor when Shehzadi had not borne a child for six years, was now thoughtful at the prospect of yet another grandchild, another set of expenses.

Mumtaz Jahan, meanwhile, had borne three beautiful girls within five years. She was becoming desperate for a boy. When she became pregnant for the fourth time, there was not a single *mannat* that she spared to ensure it would be a boy. Shahab often teased her saying, 'I am praying for a fourth daughter.'

Mumtaz Jahan could not bear to think of a fourth girl child. She had overheard Miss Gill saying to her husband that it seemed difficult for Mumtaz Jahan to carry a male fetus full term. When she learnt about Shehzadi's pregnancy, she wrote an imploring letter to her sister-in-law, 'Dear Bhabijaan, there is such wonderful news about a new life which is stirring in your womb. I am praying, dear Bhabi that you have a little boy, and if that happens, can you think of giving it to your unfortunate sister who is destined never to bear a male child? Please talk to Bhaijaan, although I know that my happiness is paramount in his heart.'

Both Shehzadi and Mansoor spoke about this letter and agreed that their seventh child, if it was a boy, would be placed in the lap of his sister and her husband.

The atmosphere in Shabistan was peaceful. Begum Agha was very efficient in the household affairs, especially when it came to Agha Sahib's needs and comforts. She had brought her old servants with her, but there was no one like Amina Bua. Since the move to the new house, Amina could not visit her as often as she did earlier. Begum Agha had learnt all her cooking from Amina and was, therefore, a very accomplished cook. Agha Sahib loved her cooking and would often ask her to make his favourite dishes. She would act coy and pretend that she was annoyed at his demands, although she was in fact, very happy at his '*farmaish*'. He would instruct the children to go and ask her to cook his favourite dishes; but not to mention his name!

'Ruhi Bitiya, don't you feel like eating *kali gajar ka halwa* today? It has been a long time since your Nani made it.'

'Not really, Nana, I like *kheer* better,' she would say innocently.

But Rumina would catch on. 'I want to eat *halwa*,' she would say.

'So? Why don't you ask your Nani to make some?'

Rumina would run to her Nani. 'Nani, Nani, can we have *kali gajar ka halwa* today? Please Nani Amma.'

'You! You don't even like *halwas*. I know who wants to eat the *halwa*, and I am never going to make it. Go and tell him!'

She would pretend to get angry, but sure enough, there would be a dish of *halwa* garnished with almonds and covered with silver waraq at the next meal.

Time passed pleasantly. The children blossomed in this loving atmosphere. Arifa gave birth to a little baby girl who became the favourite of the entire household.

It was a cloudy monsoon evening when Shehzadi returned from her parents' house. She was thoughtful after her mother had spoken to her about her uncontrollable temper. She had promised both her mother and herself that she would try to control her emotions and not allow them to rule her. From a short distance, she heard the muezzin call the *Maghrib* Azaan. As she entered, three women were spreading their prayer mats. Shehzadi, who was not a regular namaazi left them praying and wandered into her private garden. Rumina and Kamil were playing outside. They returned indoors, since they were not allowed to play after the azaan had sounded. The children looked at the three women bent with their foreheads on the floor in their respective *sajdas*. Rumina playfully climbed on Amina Bua's *chowki* and sat on her back. This was her favourite game. She loved the sound of Amina saying '*Hun*... *hun*...' Knowing that Amina Bua would not talk during the namaaz, Rumina knew that she was free to do what she liked. So she sat astride her favorite 'Amma', pretending she was riding a horse. Surprisingly, Amina did not utter a single word, not even '*hunh*.' So Rumina became even more playful. Shehzadi came out of the room and scolded her daughter for bothering Amina during her namaaz. Rumina climbed off and ran away, but still, Amina did not stir. Shehzadi came closer and shook her a little... But there was no response. Shehzadi screamed and collapsed next to the dead woman. In moments, everyone crowded around Amina's lifeless body.

The children had never seen death before. They had assumed that Amina would live forever. Now they all held on to her worn-out white dupatta and refused to let go. Mansoor rushed in with Hakim Sahib, who declared that there was no pulse.

'*Inna lillahe wa inna alaiha ra ja'oon.*' From Allah we came and to Allah we return.

Amina was buried with great outpouring of grief and hundreds attended her *namaz-e-janaza.* She was hailed as a true 'momina' for the fact of dying during namaaz. Both households went into mourning; both had different reasons. Agha Sahib's family had lost the woman who had faithfully served them for fifty years, having come into the household as a child of five. Qamar Zamani's household had lost a woman who had never made any claim on them other than a corner of their home from where she could shower her love on all the children. But little Rumina's entire world had been shattered—Amina was not just 'Amma' she was her real mother. For months, she did not allow anyone to take away that worn-out white duppatta which smelt and felt like Amina's affectionate embrace.

After the mandatory mourning of 40 days, life in Ashiana slowly returned to normal. Baji Begum took over the responsibility of Rumina and Kamil, trying to fill the void created by Amina's death. The children were growing, and so were their demands. The three mothers placed many restrictions on them, especially on the girls, but Rahat, the leader of the gang, was always thinking of new ways of breaking the rules of the house.

There was a *churan* seller who used to come every day and call out '*Damadam churan wala*'. The children loved his *churan* and would run out when he arrived. But there were more flies on his cart than *churan,* so they were very strictly forbidden from buying anything from him. It was Rahat found a way out—she told him to come in the afternoon when everyone was asleep and without his customary call, so they could sneak out and buy whatever they wanted. There was also the *Malai Kulfi-wallah* who was much in demand. He would also come at the same time and call, '*Sawan ki phuhaar aiyee kulfi ki bahaar aiyee.*' The children loved it when he sliced cold, creamy kulfi and placed the pieces on green leaves. The best part was licking the leaves before throwing them away.

One afternoon, suspicious Shamshad followed the children when they sneaked out and saw them eat their fill of *chooran* and *kulfi*. She ran to Baji Begum and told her horror story of how dirty the ice was, and how many flies were hovering over the *churan*. Baji Begum picked up her iron *guz* (yardstick) and stood behind the door, waiting. Rahat was the first one to get in and the first one to get a hard stroke of the *guz* on her shoulder. The younger children tried to run away, but ultimately they were all rounded up. They were told to vomit out everything they had eaten: 'Put your fingers in your throat and vomit all the rubbish in your stomach.' Shamshad was ordered to get the bottle of castor oil, which they hated, and pour a tablespoon of it down each child's throat.

The children were fed up of these restrictions and orders. Rahat, the oldest and the naughtiest, always got the major share of scolding. Yet, she was continuously thinking of ways of breaking free. One afternoon, when everyone was asleep, she quietly rounded up Ruhi and Rumina. 'We cannot tolerate this prison anymore. Here, we can neither drink nor eat what we like and they torture us by pouring castor oil down our throat. Today, we will run away and work to earn our own living. To begin with we will beg, but we will not stay in this prison hole for a single moment longer.'

Ruhi and Rumina did not understand the implication of *begging* and *earning*, but they were happy at the thought of living a free life. They each filled a bottle with water, picked up bedcovers as chador*s* and walked out in the hot sun. Before leaving the house, Rahat made them remove their shoes. 'Beggars don't wear shoes. So hide them in the bedcovers,' she ordered. The three girls walked out barefoot onto the hot pavement, pretending not to care for their burning soles. An hour later, they were hungry and thirsty. So, without thinking, they knocked at the first door they saw. Rahat called out like she had heard the beggars calling: 'Please give us some alms in the name of Allah!'

She suddenly realised that the house looked very familiar. Quickly, she hid her sisters behind the wall. They peeped out cautiously and saw Qutub Sahib's wife coming out with some roti*s* in a *thali*. She looked around and not finding anyone, shrugged and closed the door. The girls ran as fast as they could from that area, realizing that most people who lived in these big houses would know their parents and would recognize them. So they walked on till the familiar big houses were left far behind and they had reached the Railway Lines. They had to cross these lines in order to reach the inner city. This was even worse, as the metal lines blistered their feet, and the stones pierced the blisters. Little Rumina's nose and Ruhi's delicate feet started bleeding and even the water bottles got emptied. But they continued to walk in search of freedom. Somewhere they had read a slogan, 'Do or die! Now or never!'

By this time, everyone in Ashiana had woken up from their siestas and the servants were bringing cool glasses of raw mango and falsa sherbet. The children were called but no one answered. Shamshad was sent to their room but she came out saying the girls were missing. Suddenly, the news that the Ashiana girls had disappeared was all over the city. Mansoor drove around the city searching, the servants combed the estate, Qamar Zamani sat on the prayer mat, Shehzadi and Baji Begum rushed to the front gate.

Even the university students from the nearby hostel rode out on their cycles looking for them. It was almost dark, when a slight commotion was heard at the gate. They saw three girls sitting on a bicycle which was being wheeled in by a young student. Munir was one of several needy students supported by Mansoor. He had been offered a scholarship and a place in the servant quarters so that he could pursue his studies. Returning home that evening, he had spotted three little girls walking along the railway tracks. They were dirty, bleeding and dazed. Shehzadi, almost fainting with anxiety, rounded up the girls for a sound thrashing. But Qamar Zamani and Baji Begum, looking at their wretched condition, held on to both her hands and stopped her, imploring her to forgive. Rahat was the only one who was still coherent. Even at this critical moment, she thought up a story of how a beggar had come to the door and when they went to give him some coins, he thrust some sweets in their mouths which must have been laced with a sleeping potion. They all immediately fainted and the next they knew, they were on the railway tracks. While spinning this tale, Rahat even managed to spill few tears. Everyone's anxiety transformed to sympathy; the girls were cleaned up, fed, and tucked into their beds. But after this incident, orders were given to lock them up in their rooms during the afternoon naps.

Chapter 17

WHENEVER SHE SAW Rahat, Qamar Zamani always remarked, 'At her age, I had already given birth to Jahanara. And look at her, unaware of her maturing body, behaving like a *sar phiri bachchi*...' Every day brought new complaints about her pranks and escapades. Even Jahanara had lost control over her and realized that some drastic measures had to be taken to restrain the willful girl. A suitable boy would be the only way to curb her.

There were many proposals from good families, but Mansoor was not keen on any of them. He was against interrupting her studies and getting her married so young. But Jahanara, and now Shehzadi, were both insistent.

Shabistan had a new visitor who caused some excitement in both houses. Naved was Begum Agha's brother's son, recently selected for the Indian Police Service. He had been very young when his mother had died and his father remarried. Naved had been sent to a hostel where he was left to fend for himself. Begum Agha had taken the boy under her care and ensured that he would spend his holidays in her home. Shehzadi was very fond of Naved, treating him like a little brother. Unlike Aamir and Aalam, he was quiet and gentle.

That evening when he opened the gate, Mansoor saw a tall, slim youth bent over a small puppy who seemed to be hurt in the leg.

'*Adab,* Bhaijan,' said Naved, standing up with the puppy in his arms.

'Naved? I would not have recognized you—how tall you have become!'

Watching him tending the hurt animal, Mansoor thought of Rahat. He had often seen her in the inner private garden, tending the rabbits, feeding the squirrels, scattering birdseed. Once, he had watched as she fed a baby deer with the milk bottle stolen from her baby brother's crib. When he had summoned her, she had said simply, 'Papa, he is so small and has no mother. Baba will get another bottle, but if I don't feed him, this baby will not live.' Suddenly, like a flash the thought came—Naved and Rahat… Rahat and Naved. The image slowly settled in Mansoor's mind.

Everyone rejoiced at this proposed match. When he was summoned by Agha Sahib, Naved just said, 'Bhaijan, as you wish.' But he smiled to himself; he had caught a few glimpses of Rahat and thought—'she is quite an eyeful'.

All those who mattered were taken into confidence. Qamar Zamani's prayer beads gave the 'go ahead' signal; Agha Sahib and Begum Agha were thrilled that a new bond would be created between the families; Baji Begum was satisfied for a totally different reason—she knew Rahat's volatile nature would only be accepted and managed by a gentle partner. Much as she hated losing the only anchor she had, she told herself strictly, 'Naved is the perfect match for her.'

Soon, the wedding preparations were in full swing. This was the first wedding in the family since Mumtaz's. Mansoor wanted it to be a grand affair, so, he personally invited his dear friend Nawab Zia Ali Khan to attend. The man arrived with his entourage of musicians, mirasins, cooks and khidmatgars.

The whole day the beat of the dholak, the ribald wedding songs of the Mirasins and the sound of the shehnai were heard. There was a musical soiree each evening and the musicians and courtesans sang late into the night. The royal cooks outdid each other with dishes of varied cuisines. The fragrance of *ittar, zafran, kewra* and *gulab jal* hung in the air. On the back lawn, Mansoor had tents pitched and neighboring kothis were borrowed to accommodate the guests, many of them members of the Masonic Lodges from all over India.

The list of ceremonies to be performed was long—engagement, *Manjha, Sehnak, Bari,* Nikah, *Rukhsati* and *Chauthhi.* Shehzadi happily conducted the arrangements on both sides.

The festivities began with *Mangni.* From Shabistan arrived trays of Mithai, a set of clothes, and the ring for the bride. Baji Begum brought a small carved tray on which the ring was placed and a brocade *Imam Zamin* plus 5 gold guineas. Rahat was asked to sit still with her eyes closed. Qamar Zamani pronounced 'Bismillah', tied the *Imam Zamin* on Naved's arm and placed the gold ring on his finger. Begum Agha tied her *Imam Zamin* on Rahat after also pronouncing 'Bismillah'. When she presented the diamond ring, the girls chorused: 'Naved Bhai must place it on Rahat's finger!' Qamar Zamani was aghast at the idea of 'an outsider' touching Rahat's hand; he was still unrelated, a *namehram*—but Mansoor laughingly told her it was 'allowed' because he was also a relative. So Naved began to place the ring on Rahat's finger, but she stiffened it so he could not slide it down. He whispered in her ear that if she did not ease the little bone, he would have no choice but to break it. The ring slid into place.

The next day was the mehndi and *oupton* ceremony in Ashiana. The girls flitted around everywhere in rainbow-colored ghararas. Ruhi and Rumina had been allowed to get mehndi applied on their palms for the first time after which they went to the *Chooriwali* for matching glass bangles.

Rahat was brought to the mehfil in a yellow gharara, *kurti* and a long yellow dupatta. Saidani Bua carried in the silver tray with a blob of '*oupton*'—a paste of *besan* ground with jasmine oil and perfumed herbs. Shamshad's contribution was a large basket laid with seven pieces of jewellery—*jhoomar, teeka,* earrings, necklace, bracelets, anklets, ring—made from fragrant flowers. Rahat sat on a *takht* and seven married women were asked to place *oupton* on her palm with a silver coin.

Next, they placed, in turn, one piece of floral jewellery each on the bride and one morsel of sweet in her mouth. Then—there was bedlam! The girls began to uninhibitedly smear *oupton* on each other. Even the boys got their share!

As for the bride, instead of retiring like a traditional dulha*n* for her *oupton* massage, Rahat was right there with her friends, throwing yellow flowers and *oupton* on everyone, especially on Naved who had quietly slipped into the zenana.

The nikah and the *rukhsat* the next day were more dignified ceremonies. Begum Qutub, Begum Rashid and Khalajan arrived early. Khalajan put herself in charge of the dowry room. Seated on a *takht,* she gave orders. 'Don't keep that yellow gharara set with the red one, you silly girl. What is your name? Don't you see the colours are clashing? Move the red gharara set next to the green *Benarsi joda ...*' Clothes, jewellery, linen and all the household goods had been displayed.

The *Sehnak* ritual was performed in the afternoon. A special meal was laid on a white *dastarkhwan.* Seven married Saidanis had to sit around it in a circle and recite some verses from the Holy Quran. Fateha was recited for the Prophet's daughter, Hazrat Fatima, who was asked to bless the bride. After they had eaten, the bride's mother, dressed in her own bridal gharara, had to wash their soiled hands and dry them with the corner of her ornate dupatta. This water could not be poured into the drain, it had to be poured into a flower pot.

After lunch began the decorations. Begum Rashid with Rumina, was in charge of the flowers. Strings of gulab, mogra and chameli were hung from the roof and doors and wound around the columns. The floors were covered with carpets and lined with brocade cushions for the guests to lean on. Then the guests started to arrive in their finery. There were elaborate brocade Farshi Ghararas, the long trains carried by the maids. Diamonds, rubies and emeralds glittered on men and women alike, and khus, henna and amber ittars perfumed the air. The climax of the arrivals was when two tall *Khwaja Saras* came with their maces and announced '*Ba adab ba mulahiza hoshiar*: Zia Ali Khan of Mohammadpur is arriving.'

As expected, Zia arrived with spectacular fanfare! Mansoor was busy overseeing all the arrangements, but once Zia had made his formal entrance, he felt at ease. The nawab was all over the place—one moment instructing the cooks, the next asking the domnis to sing all the cheeky wedding songs, most of them written by himself, teasing the bridegroom's party.

Friends of Asad and Kamil were helping Naved to dress. He wore a cream brocade sherwani, a silk pajama and a golden turban. Begum Agha and Arifa tied a long floral *sehra* on his turban, after which he mounted the white Arabian steed. University boys joined the baraat and added their singing and dancing to the celebrations. As the baraat arrived in Ashiana, they were welcomed by a police band. Shehzadi came forward and, now, as Naved's sister, placed the corner of her dupatta on his head to escort him inside.

Rahat dressed in the traditional nikah *jora* of plain red silk gharara, *kurti* and red chiffon dupatta embellished with nine small gold guineas sewn on the edge where it covered her head. The guineas would be given later to her sisters and cousins. After the baraat arrived, the Qazi was called inside and he asked Rahat if she accepted Naved as her husband for one lakh rupees as Meher. A traditional bride manages a barely audible 'yes' and that too, when asked the third time. But Rahat being Rahat, said a quite clear

'*Ji*' the first time. The Qazi then asked for Naved's consent. When Naved said '*Qubool*!' a chorus of '*Mubarak*' rose from the gathering. *Chhuwaras* (dry dates) wrapped in red muslin were distributed to all the guests.

The bridegroom was then brought inside. He was now allowed to see his bride, but only through a mirror, sitting across from the red bundle of a bride! Shehzadi placed a mirror and Quran between them and covered the couple with a big red dupatta. The Mirasins asked Naved, 'Mian, now you have to say, 'Biwi open your eyes. I will be your slave forever.' Naved had no choice but say the words—but Rahat's eyes were already open and twinkling under the dupatta! Next he had to place a bit of *kheer* in his palm and ask the bride to lick it off. When he placed his palm near her mouth, Rahat bit his finger—Naved yelped, saying 'something bit me!' and, struggling to keep a straight face, everyone commiserated—'Too many mosquitoes.' When he got up to leave, he found his shoes missing. After much haggling and parting with a large sum of money, the little thieves brought them out of the hiding place.

And so, to the strains of Shehnai and Babul, Rahat was escorted outside, walking under a star-studded dupatta to mount the bridal palanquin. With Naved on his horse, the wedding procession left for Chhatari Manzil, where a bridal chamber had been decorated for them.

The next morning, Asad and Kamil were sent to escort the bride back for the Chawthi ceremony. Seven kinds of fruit and vegetables were placed in a tray between the bride and the groom who sat opposite each other. First, they had to gently hit each other with seven delicate branches from flowering bushes. Then the bridegroom was to throw the seven fruits and seven vegetables, one by one, at the bride and she was to do the same. Naved threw his lot very gently. But Rahat's friends held her hand and pelted him hard, to which she also added her might. Being assaulted by brinjals, potatoes, apples and pomegranates was tough but Naved bore it cheerfully, waiting for his chance to get his own back at his mischievous new bride. After the couple were done with their ceremonial fight, it was a free-for-all. Many old grudges were squared and secret lovers had a chance of venting their pent-up emotions! Even Naved took revenge on his tormentors. The room was filled with squashed tomatoes, crushed oranges and gooey bananas! Everyone had worked up a ravenous appetite for the lunch that followed after all this vigorous exercise.

Agha Sahib had organized a grand Walima dinner on the lawns of Shabistan. All the gentry of Aligarh were invited. Rahat wore the heavy brocade *Farshi gharara* Qamar Zamani had given to her mother at her wedding. She also wore Qamar Zamani's ancestral diamond-studded *jhoomar, teeka* and *nuth*. Naved wore a *kimkhwab achkan, pagri* and a diamond *Kalghi*—head ornament with a jewel and feather—which belonged to Mansoor. Aligarh had never seen a more resplendent wedding!

As the evening drew to a close, the guests started leaving. First Shahab and Mumtaz Jahan left with their three daughters. After her last miscarriage, Mumtaz Jahan was expecting again, and Jahanara Begum was keeping a hawk's eye on her. Then Zia left with his entourage. And finally, Naved left for Agra with Rahat to report for his new posting. Ashiana was again quiet, too quiet. The three women recited the words of Shukrana to Allah, and returned to their routines. At that time, no one could have dreamt that Rahat's was the only formal wedding they would ever see in Ashiana.

1947 saw the partition of India which shattered and splintered families all over the country. Free India was born, mired in human blood; Hindus, Muslims and Sikhs went on killing sprees—or were themselves killed—in fields, in standing crops, on roads, in chaupals, on trains, and in houses. One million human beings, women, children and men, were killed and three million were rendered homeless. It was an unprecedented human tragedy which created two blood-soaked nations, Pakistan and India. Cities and villages were deserted, roads were blocked with dead bodies, and madness prevailed... Every morning brought a new day of destruction, and the shadows of death blackened the daylight. Cries of revenge rose from every corner and in that frenzy, people lost their reason, rationality and sanity. Newspapers and radio flashed horror stories, whipping up emotions to breaking-point. Friends slaughtered friends, brothers destroyed brothers, neighbours burnt each other. Muslim families trying to cross the border to go to Pakistan, and Hindus moving to India, were slaughtered enroute. Children were separated from parents, wives from husbands and women, young or old, were raped and burnt. All semblance of sanity was destroyed in the fire of hatred and revenge.

Ashiana could not remain immune to this dance of death. Aamir, who was in Delhi for some work, went missing. Asad who had gone for a trip with his friends, did not return home as scheduled. Qamar Zamani tore her hair and clothes in anguish. The whole day she sat like a stone and and for once, could not even pray. Her *sijdagah* (prayer stone), made of the dust of Karbala, began melting with her tears.

In that one week, Mansoor's face changed. At forty-five, he began looking old. Shehzadi bit back her rising hysteria. Death was everywhere. The University students set aside pen and paper and picked up knives and sticks. People, too, gathered sticks and stones and hid them on their roofs. Mansoor took out his rifle and cartridges, which he had not used for a long time. People took turns holding vigils at night. In case the marauders come from the city, they were prepared.

The Aligarh Collector had assured Mansoor that he would not allow any riot, and he and the Police Commissioner would constantly patrol the city. But Mansoor was distraught about Aamir and Asad and sent messages to all the high officials in Delhi to try to locate them. He had been assured and reassured that they would be safe.

Hindu friends made it a point to visit Mansoor everyday. Dr Lall, the renowned ophthalmologist who Shehzadi called 'brother', promised them that they were safe and would be harmed only over his dead body. Major Singh, recently retired from the army, moved inside the house to guard them around the clock. All this gave comfort to the family, especially to the children who were badly traumatised by the anxiety of the adults. In their innocence, they made the horror into a game and would often pretend to attack each other with butter knives or a toy gun. Major Singh would join the game to amuse the kids, but Mansoor put a stop to it, saying that such games were not in good taste, not even in fun!

Gradually the tide of hate and revenge began to subside, but the damage was done forever. Life began to be restored to 'normal' but people were still trying to find their lost relatives and loved ones. A few weeks later, a letter arrived from Aamir saying he was in Karachi and had joined the Pakistani army. He asked that his family be sent to join him there. Agha Sahib and Begum Sahiba laughed and cried at the loss and gain...Gaining and losing—that was the meaning of partition! They arranged for Arifa and her daughter to sail for Karachi.

Mansoor got word that some boys from India had been found in Lahore, but no one had claimed them as kin. Mansoor immediately dispatched Aalam, who went to Lahore and identified Asad. Apparently the boys had been trekking near the border, when they were picked up by the Border Security Force and on finding that they had Muslim names, they were sent to Lahore. Mansoor solicited Zia's help and together, the two of them managed to get the boys back. Qamar Zamani's skeletal frame rested on her own bed after 60 days spent on the wooden chowki.

Many of Mansoor's close friends went to Pakistan. There was no one left in Neeli Chhatri. Many inhabitants of Aftab Manzil had also migrated. Aligarh slowly seemed to be emptying out. The university students also scattered like autumn leaves—many disappearing, the few remaining behind, forlorn and without friends. Overnight, people started looking old. All the festivities and mehfils were folded away in albums and autograph books. Aligarh, a university town which was bound together like one large family, was left desolate.

Fear of riots spreading to the Civil Lines had made people secure their precious assets. Mansoor handed a safe box filled with all of Shehzadi's precious jewellery to his dear and trusted friend Lala Karam Chand, for safe-keeping. Lalaji was a friend and brother who he could trust with his life. He could never have imagined the scenario that later unfolded... Lalaji died suddenly of a heart attack and Mansoor was heartbroken at the loss. After the mandatory waiting period of 40 days, he asked Lalji's eldest son to return the jewelry.

'What safe box, Chachaji? Babuji never mentioned any such thing to me. When I opened his safe three days after he had passed away, there was no such box in it.'

Mansoor felt his heart sink and lurch up to his throat. There was no witness to his transaction with Lalaji, only trust and a 40-year-old friendship!

'Are you sure, beta?' Mansoor tried to smile through the churning turmoil inside. All the family jewels of the royal house of Qamar Zamani, were lost forever! For a long time, Mansoor could not reveal this loss to Shehzadi.

Thus, the cycle of misfortune began for Mansoor Ali Khan, beloved grandson of Akbar Ali Khan and only son of Ammar Ali Khan, the man who was the rightful heir to the Nawabat of Mohammadpur. The next blow came from Munshi Nisar Husain, the trusted family retainer and keeper of the purse. One day,

Mansoor learnt that the Munshi had disappeared. He had migrated to Pakistan, taking with him all the funds that were deposited in his trust by the farmers as *lagaan* for the lands they cultivated. Shamshad increased the booty by tying in a *potli* whatever jewels of Jahanara Begum that he could lay his hands on. When Mansoor got a blow-by-blow account of the heist, the feeling that those closest had betrayed him, began to gnaw at his heart. He closed the door of his library and sitting at his Burma Teak writing desk, so lovingly carved by the best artisans of the walled city, he placed his head in his hands and wept alone.

From the village of Akbarabad, Munshi Banke Bihari was summoned. Banke had opted to stay in the village and personally supervise the cultivators. He had seen through Nisar Husain's treachery, but was unable to transmit this to either Mansoor or Shehzadi. He had come all the way to the city to try to warn Mansoor, but both Shamshad and Nisar made sure he did not meet Mansoor. Nisar had asked him in Mansoor's name to transfer a large sum of money for Rahat's wedding but Banke had refused and before more lies and intrigues were spun by the couple, he had returned to the village. Now he returned to salvage the remnants of Akbar Ali Khan's estate.

Mansoor sequestered himself in his study and racked his brain for a solution. The edges of his two fingers were nicotine-stained yellow and his gums black from chain-smoking. He could not share these worries with anyone, neither friends nor family. He was ashamed to expose his impending poverty to a city where he had lived a good life. Not that there was anyone left in the city whmo he could turn to for advice!

One evening, after they had retired to their room, Mansoor fell into an uneasy sleep. He dreamt of his grandfather who seemed to be holding him on horseback, instructing him to stay firm on the stirrup and not let go of the reins. He could feel the horse under him bucking as if he would throw him off.

'Nana, Nana!' He woke up in a cold sweat. He found his wife anxiously bending over him, 'Sahib, are you alright?'

Mansoor sat up in bed and looked at the anxious face which was now finely marked and lined. 'I am alright,' he lied. 'But why are you still awake?'

'I want to tell you something,' Shehzadi's tone was anxious. 'I am four months pregnant.'

The news which at one time would have given him a surge of joy, was a blow. An eighth child coming into a household which had been robbed clean of all its ancestral wealth! But he did not allow a shred of his dismay to show. Smilingly, he said, 'Good news! Qamar Zamani will be happy and will not pester me to get married again!' A slight blush rose on Shehzadi's tired face; he noticed it, and marveled that she could still blush so beautifully.

The news of Shehzadi's pregnancy was spoken about in whispers. No one seemed very happy and there was no sign of celebration or thanksgiving. The only person who was overjoyed, was Mumtaz Jahan. The time had come for her to redeem a promise made by Shehzadi and Mansoor two years ago at the birth of their seventh son, Raza, also called Babloo.

Mumtaz Jahan had come for the birth with her daughters and baskets of fruits and sweets and many parcels of gifts for the child. She had lifted Saleem from the cradle, kissed his forehead, and despite her generally reserved nature, had spoken words which she had been framing in her mind for a long time, 'Bhabijaan, Babloo is God's gift to you and Bhaijaan and who can be happier than me, for whom you both mean so much. But today as I hold this child in my arms, please fulfill the one desire of my heart which only you can. If you have another child and if it is a male, you will place him in my lap. I have four daughters who I love but you know that by now, I have had seven miscarriages and each one has been of a baby boy. Bhabi, I am not destined to bear a male child.'

Mansoor and Shahab had by now entered and had heard Mumtaz Jahan. Shahab spoke, 'Bhai, I have always tried to convince Mumtaz Jahan that my daughters are as good as, if not better than, sons. But she has this burning desire for a male child. I often find her in a state of depression, sometimes she gets fits and needs to be restrained. I am saying all this in front of her and Bhabijaan because after a lot of thought, I have come to the conclusion that the cause of her trouble is her desire to have a male child.'

The four of them had sat for a long time together, talking over Mumtaz Jahan's proposal while the newborn baby slept peacefully next to his mother. It was a pact between them. If another child was born and was a male, he would be given to Mumtaz Jahan and Shahab.

Mumtaz Jahan arrived two days before Shehzadi gave birth to her eighth child. The boy weighed eight pounds, had golden hair and was the spitting image of Mansoor. Mumtaz Jahan lowered her head in sijda when she heard about Saleem's birth. When she rose, her face was radiant and her eyes misty with tears. She looked at her husband and removed the cover under which she had hidden the baby clothes, the quilts, the knitting that she had prepared in case today was the day of *Qubooliyat*. Together with Shahab, she walked to the room where Shehzadi had given birth. The nurse had cleaned the child and placed him at Shehzadi's side. Mumtaz Jahan entered with a towel and smilingly bent over to gather the little child. Suddenly, Shehzadi's face became contorted with pain and she shouted, 'Never! You will never touch my baby, I will never part from him!'

The next moment, she was holding the child tightly to her heart. Mumtaz Jahan stepped back in fear of the madness she saw on Shehzadi's face. The baby was gasping for breath; the nurse tried to gently prise the child from her grasp. The lady doctor also rushed in. Shahab firmly turned Mumtaz Jahan away from the bed and led her out of the room. Mansoor looked at his wife, who seemed momentarily transformed into a dreadful creature, and asked the doctor to examine her.

'Mansoor, miyan, you had better advise your sister to give up her claim on this child. If Shehzadi is separated from the child at this time, I am afraid she may burst a vessel in her brain. Just let her be.'

Even in this state, Shehzadi was conscious of her irrational behavior. In a flash, she saw the worried looked on Mansoor's face, she heard the words of the doctor and felt a surge of shame.

'I don't understand what comes over me,' she said to Mansoor. 'I have let everyone down—you, Shahab, Mumtaz Jahan and in a way this child too. I do not have the face to confront Mumtaz Jahan again. Please don't let her see me in this wretched state...'

In another room Mumtaz Jahan was crying, unable to come to terms with what she regarded as an 'empty lap'. It took Shahab a long time before he was was able to convince her that she had to rise above her personal grief and think of others. He prepared her to go to Shehzadi and tell her that a child had to remain with its mother and that she would love him regardless of the fact that he would not be 'hers'.

And so it was that in her quiet, dignified manner, Mumtaz Jahan spoke these words to Shehzadi. Neither Mansoor nor Shahab could hold back their tears. Shehzadi begged forgiveness from her husband's younger sister, with hands folded in supplication. 'You, dearest sister, have given me this gift of dignity, for which I will be ever grateful.'

Mansoor's disappointment at Shehzadi's change of heart was, most of all, for his own child. He had been hoping to see this child thrive under the care of Shahab and Mumtaz Jahan; he had hoped that the child would thus imbibe the values that were practiced in Shahab's home—values so different from his own. When he honestly assessed his eight children, he wished he had given them a different upbringing. In the stifling atmosphere of Qamar Zamani's home, with its lack of academic rigor and work ethic, they had all slid into varying stages of indolence. He recognised his own inability to guide their upbringing. Their school and home tutors, most of them products of a feudal mindset themselves, , could not inculcate the scientific temperament which had become the national slogan for modern education. Shehzadi never realized how badly she had hurt the two persons she held dearest in her life, by changing her mind. Her inability to control her emotional outburst had damaged the future of her youngest child.

Despite her own steadily worsening condition, Shehazadi continued to anticipate Mansoor's every need and every mood. Yet she did not see what was there, stark before her eyes every day. Her husband was counting the last days of his life.

Shehzadi's change of heart about Saleem had hurt him deeply. Few could see through the mask that Mansoor had drawn over his sunken face. His pleasant smile was deceptive and went some way towards hiding the trouble in his heart. He tried to hide his emaciated body by wearing loose clothes and a hat, even inside the house, to conceal the haggard face that stared at him in the mirror. His body had lost its sporty spring and turned into a hunched frame. The fact that he could not eat, and could not digest the little that he did eat, was beginning to worry him. He longed to place his worries before Qamar Zamani, his strong link to the grandfather whose memory he still invoked in moments of despair. But Qamar Zamani had become a shadow of her old self.

He thought of a day many years ago when his maths tutor, exasperated at his carelessness, had slapped him. Akbar Ali Khan who happened to be passing by, had walked into the school room and seen his grandson's flushed face and angry eyes, full of unshed tears. His heavy hand had crashed on the hapless tutor. For hours,

Akbar Ali Khan had held the child and gently rubbed the cheek marked by the slap. Curiously, this memory triggered the thought of similar recent incident in his own house. During their visit one summer, Shahab's daughters were studying with the tutor who taught Rahat and Ruhi. During the lessons, there was another slap. This time it was not the teacher who slapped the student, it was the other way around! Butool, Mumtaz Jahan's second daughter, had slapped the tutor out of a sense indignation at the teacher's making a snide remark about her father. Shahab, instead of praising his child's loyalty, had sent her to her room and forbidden any food or water unless she humbly apologized to the teacher. 'No matter what,' he told the nine children of both families who had gathered together for a lecture, 'disrespect to a teacher is unforgivable in the eyes of man and God.'

Mansoor was unraveling his upbringing and juxtaposing it with the childhood of another cohort of children. Where had this road led him and where was it leading the new generation?

Despite the tightening purse, the household still ran smoothly. To keep up the semblance of genteel living, Mansoor slowly disposed of parcels of his precious land. Shehzadi avoided asking him where the income was coming from—she preferred not to know so long as her needs and those of her children were met. She was still able to help the needy supplicants who came to her door. Closed up in their limited world, Qamar Zamani and Jahanara Begum were unable to see the larger picture. So long as Mansoor smiled during his daily visits to their chambers and gathered their prayers in his cupped hands, they felt satisfied. They did not notice the tremor in his fingers or the weakness of his embrace. He knew, even if they did not, that neither his body nor his mind was now capable of being restored by their recitation from the Quran or the extra prayers dedicated to his well-being.

It was Shehzadi who discovered the gravity of his illness. At night when they retired, Mansoor always turned off the lamp and pretended to be asleep long before Shehzadi came to bed. One night, she found him shivering in a crumpled heap. Taking out a new *razai* from the cupboard, she gently removed the chador in which he was wrapped. Mansoor held on to the chador, but she playfully yanked it off. What she saw was the form of a man who resembled her husband, but was an emaciated skeleton, covered with loose skin. Mansoor covered himself with the *razai* and tried to pass the incident off as a joke, 'What is the matter my dear, have you seen a ghost?' But by now, he knew that he could not hide any more. 'Okay, I promise I will eat well from tomorrow. And if you insist, I will show myself to Hakim Sahib. I will do exactly what you want, but just stop crying. Nothing will happen to me. I have you, I have my beautiful children. What more could I possibly desire?'

He stopped for a moment, to catch his breath. Then he continued, 'But there is something else I have been thinking of. I want to return to our estate. Akbar Lodge has been vacant for many years. The place has been neglected; how much can the old chowkidar do? I know Ammajaan will agree if I implore her and so will Baji Begum. Its only you I am afraid of asking.'

Then he sat up, fully covered by the *razai* and made his wife sit by his side. 'Look at me. A change of place will make a world of difference. You will see how quickly I will recover… We will have horses for the children to ride…There will be walks in the fields and picnics by the river.. And the fruit will be fresh off the trees and vegetables from your very own garden. Please, my love, say yes!'

The momentary vigor in his voice created by the urgency, deceived Shehzadi. She closed her eyes and said, 'yes.' As if her 'yes' would work magic and life would go back to its start.

Mansoor had spent hours thinking about this move. In Aligarh, he was well known and his changed circumstances would become the subject of local gossip. Moving to Mohammadpur would distance him from Aligarh and it would take a while before people began to notice things. He was acutely conscious of his rapidly failing health and that each day brought him closer to what he described to himself as the 'precipice.' He wanted to explore new means of income for sustaining Shehzadi and the children and that would not be possible in a known place. Time was running out and he could not stop its downward slide. He did not even want to stop it.

'I am tired,' he said to himself when alone in his study. 'All I want is to rest; to find peace, where there will be no more of this nagging pain.' His cancer had been confirmed by the surgeon at the university hospital.

Sometimes the pain was unbearable. He would press his knees to his stomach and double over on the couch in his office. The servants would say, 'Sahib is busy in important work.' Shehzadi often walked past his door but finding it locked, would not dare to knock. Once in a while, she questioned him, 'What is it that keeps you busy for such long hours? At least leave the door open, I start having all kinds of suspicions.' He would smile. 'There is so much accounting and estate work to be done. I can only do it when there is peace and quiet; the children make too much noise. Stop worrying, there is nothing wrong.'

Shehzadi was not entirely satisfied with these explanations. Something told her that he was hiding his illness. A strange dread had enveloped her heart; it was now obvious to her that her husband was a very sick man.

One evening, Mansoor appeared before Qamar Zamani and sat on her *namaz chowki*. Placing an arm around her shoulders, he began to reminisce about the past. Qamar Zamani was surprised by this visit, because he very rarely came to her at this time. Sensing his hot breath on her neck, she made him lie on the *chowki* and pulled a chair close to him, cradling his head in her lap. Mansoor felt a strange sense of peace.

'Ammajan, when Nana built Akbar Lodge, how did he see his future?' The tone of his voice brought a lump to her throat and Qamar Zamani found her eyes filling with tears.

'He dreamt of bringing you up in that kothi and engaging resident tutors from London to give you lessons. He dreamt of getting you married from the kothi and watching the children come... He dreamt of enjoying a large family till the end of his days. He used to say, 'I have planted a big garden and many fruit trees. I want Mansoor's children to climb the trees, break all the fruit and eat them fresh from the branches... He had ordered fruit tree saplings from all over India. ...'

'Do you remember the little elephant calf who used to play hide-and-seek with you?' She was lost in her memories... 'Your Nana used to say that by the time he becomes a full elephant, Mansoor's children would be old enough to ride him.'

Mansoor also invoked his own memories. 'Ammajan, do you remember, once you told me there was a djinn who used to live in Akbar Lodge?'

'Yes, my love, it is a very old story. I was newly married and all of us women were in very strict purdah. To give me fresh air, your grandfather had a terrace garden planted for me. He ordered flowering bushes to be placed around the garden so that we could inhale the fragrance when we walked there every evening. The whole terrace used to smell of bela and chameli. Every evening the gardener had orders to make flower garlands and place them on a tray for my wrists and neck. There was an old amaltas tree in the courtyard below, which had been planted by my father-in-law. By the time the terrace garden was built, that tree had reached the top of the terrace. One night when I was in a deep sleep, I heard a voice—'Stop visiting the terrace and disturbing my abode in the Amaltas.' I opened my eyes and saw an old man standing at the foot of my bed. I thought it was a dream because the next thing I remember, it was morning! I told your grandfather about this man, and he laughed it off as my imagination. Every evening, he and I visited the terrace and every night, the man appeared to warn and admonish me. Being young and impetuous, one evening I decided to go to the terrace by myself before our usual time, to verify this 'dweller' in the amaltas tree. When I reached there, I had a vision that the garden had turned to wilderness, the flowering shrubs burnt by frost. The garlands in the tray appeared as coiled snakes. The amaltas itself had become an old man with a flowing beard! Oh, it was a dreadful sight!

'The next thing I remember was lying in bed with an intense pain in my abdomen, and your Nana bending over me. 'You fell from the terrace and landed on the concrete courtyard! It is a miracle, Qamar Zamani, that you are alive. Not only that, you have suffered no injuries or broken bones! I am ashamed not to have heeded the warning delivered by the venerable elder in your dream. Allah has given us a new life, for which I will offer my thankfulness and feed a hundred people and send one deserving family to Makkah for Haj this year. From today, the terrace garden will be padlocked forever. No one will disturb the sanctity of the djinn…' '

Her voice faded and both grandmother and grandson were quiet for a while. Each was trying to unravel the lesson behind this incident and accident. 'Ammajan, I have been thinking that Nana wants us to go back to Akbar Lodge and make his dream come true. The place is desolate. The trees in the garden need to be rejuvenated; age has turned them senile and a little care will revive them again. Nana's spirit will watch over your eight grandchildren, let them enjoy the fruit of the trees and fresh water from the old step well. Ammajan, Akbar Lodge is waiting for us to return to its protective embrace.'

Qamar Zamani felt a winter chill entering her bones. 'No Miyan, I cannot return. I did not tell you that when I fell off the terrace, I was seven months pregnant with my second child. After that accident, I could never conceive again and your grandfather's dream of a big family remained unfulfilled. The night we fled from the kothi is still fresh in my mind, as if it happened only yesterday. Please my son, sell that house! Never, never open a door which has been closed for 30 years. Let us remain here in this town which has given us so many years of shelter.'

'But Ammajan, I don't feel well here. A change of environment will be good for my health. Maybe the open space will give me a new lease of life; please, please Ammajan.'

Qamar Zamani sensed the urgency in Mansoor's voice and saw the tightening of his facial muscles as he spoke. Her large green eyes, framed by hundreds of fine wrinkles, had been travelling over Mansoor's wasted face and form, as he lay stretched on her chowki. All these months, she had been trying to ward off the evil by her prayers and supplications but had not permitted herself to name his illness, lest it become a bad omen. But today, her resistance broke and her tears began to flow. Hugging his head which lay on her lap, she spoke the words which she thought she would never speak and which he was longing to hear, 'Whatever you wish, my child. I am ready.'

A great burden had been lifted from Mansoor Ali Khan's heart.

Preparations for the move started. Ashiana was slowly being divested of life—things were packed or put aside to be given away. What would soon remain would be only a shell. Most of Mansoor's friends had dispersed over the last two years; only Agha Sahib and Hakim Sahib were left to say goodbye. Agha Sahib and Begum Agha were heartbroken at the thought of Shehzadi and her children leaving. All the joy had gone out of their lives, to the extent that the man stopped asking his wife to cook his favourite dishes. Nothing was fun without the children. They often talked about their impending loneliness. 'We left our beloved Lucknow only to be near the children. It is meaningless to live in Aligarh now.'

On the day of departure, everyone felt the agitation in Mansoor, as if he wanted to leave as soon as possible. Hakim Sahib tried to lighten the depression, 'Mansoor Miyan, why are you in such a hurry? Are you really so tired of us? I know this separation is only temporary, I cannot imagine life without you.' His affectionate words brought tears to Mansoor's eyes, which he did not show. He looked at his friend and placed a hand on his shoulder, 'Yes, dear friend. Let us hope that we will be together one day. But as the poet said:

Chund lamhon ki mulaqat ghaneemat jano
Chund lamhon mein ye sheeraaza bikhar jayega
Apni yadon ko sameiteinge bichadney waley
Kis ko maloon ke kal kaun kahan jayega

(These few minutes together, consider them well
In a few minutes this company will scatter
Those who are parting will gather their memories
And who will go where…who knows?)

Hakim Sahib turned his face away to hide his tears.

Rati Ram, the sweeper was standing in a corner, sobbing into his *gamcha.* His wife, Phoolwati, was sobbing loudly. For the last twenty years, when the household was fast asleep, she used to sweep the veranda and the courtyard in her twelve-yard *lehnga.* The children would be woken up in the morning by the tinkle of her anklets—'this is our school bell,' they would joke.

'The kothi is now in your care,' Mansoor told the crying couple. 'Make sure that you keep my garden blooming by planting seasonal flowers all year round.'

Rati Ram fell at his feet. Mansoor lifted him up and embraced him. Everyone was amazed to see the scion of a nawabi family embracing a menial and that too, a *maleechh*—the one whose touch was 'polluting'. Handing the keys of the house to him, Mansoor and the family left for the railway station.

The children had thankfully bounced back to their cheerful selves and were determined to treat the journey as a picnic. As soon as they boarded the train, they declared they were hungry! Jahanara Begum opened the tiffin carrier and gave them kebab, roghni tikia and omlette on picnic plates. Through the windows, they summoned the hawkers and wanted to buy everything, colourful clay toys, fresh fruits, *chai* in earthen *kulhars* and freshly fried *pakoras* with chutney. Rumina bit on a chilli and demanded some milk to cool her burning tongue. Shehzadi filled a silver glass and took it to her lips. Just then she saw a little girl's grubby palm at the window begging for alms. Rumina's heart melted at her plight and as the train pulled out of the station, she thrust her sliver glass into the begging hand.

Jahanara Begum scolded her and ordered that they all move away from the windows. As the train left the station, they stuck their heads out to enjoy the wind on their faces. Ruhi got coal dust in her eyes… 'I told you not to stick your head out,' said her mother, taking out a handkerchief and warming it with her breath before applying it to the child's eye.

Throughout the journey, Mansoor was in pain. But he suppressed it, and with his arm flung over his eyes, pretended to be asleep. The only thing he asked for was black tea and an occasional cigarette.

Zia's cars were waiting at Mohammadpur station, As soon as the car entered the gates of Akbar Lodge, Mansoor experienced a sense of relief: the end of a long journey! The first thing that his eyes fell on was the amaltas tree. It had grown majestically and rose far above the terrace. Mansoor placed a hand on the tree and resting his forehead on its trunk, asked for the blessing of its occupant and also of his grandfather. The rest of the family waited for him to place his foot inside the house before they all trooped in.

'You must look after this garden and make it as lush green as it was in my grandfather's days,' he told the old caretaker who had been waiting to receive him. He noticed that the house had been cleaned well and everything was in order. Shorn of splendour, room after room had bare floors and walls. But there was a sense of neatness and a cared-for look. The bed in the master bedroom was bare. Mansoor asked Abid to prepare the bed for him to lie down and rest.

Behind the closed door of the bedroom, Mansoor felt intense pain in his abdomen. He clutched his stomach and tried to breathe evenly, hoping that regular breathing would reduce the pain. But it continued, unabated. Mansoor shouted for Abid. Shehzadi, who was outside his door, rushed in and found him doubled over. Her string of questions—What is wrong? Why didn't you call out? What are you hiding? Where is the pain?—elicited no answer. Mansoor could not speak. Shehzadi called out to Abid. Qamar Zamani, hearing her cry, came running from her room. The sight of her grandson lying pale and inert, was more than she could bear. For once, her daughter-in-law sank to her knees and, holding the old woman's hand, begged her to recite *Dua-e-Mashlool* which is said to cure the most serious illness. Placing her hand on his head, Qamar Zamani began reciting; Shehzadi sat at her feet, her head bowed. Having finished the prayer, Qamar Zamani consulted the beads on her tasbih and having framed her question, began to count. 'Shehzadi, my *istikhara* says, 'don't delay one moment. Call for a doctor now.'

Abid was dispatched with a message to Zia's palace. Within the hour, the Civil Surgeon appeared. He examined Mansoor for a long time, saying nothing. At the end of the examination, he turned to Shehzadi and asked for a record of all previous tests and medical examinations.

'Sahib never got any test done, I have no records to show.'

Turning to Qamar Zamani, the doctor spoke words which would ring in their ears for years to come: 'I have never in my medical practice seen a case where the disease has spread and caused such unbearable pain and the patient has coped on his own, never complaining or revealing his condition. I will try to do my best, but I regret, Begum Sahiba, it may be too late now.'

For immediate relief the doctor gave him an injection and left after offering to come at anytime, day or night. The injection subdued the pain and made Mansoor drowsy. Shehzadi did not move from the floor by his bed, holding his hand firmly in hers and not moving her wrist lest the tinkle of her bangles woke him up.Qamar Zamani sat at the foot of his bed, reciting verses on her tash bih. Jehanara brought her gilded copy of the Quran and began flipping its pages to fan his face.

Outside, darkness was swallowing the last light, and the man on the bed was barely visible.

Abid came in quietly and whispered, 'Begum Sahiba, should I turn on the lamp?'

Shehzadi placed a finger on her lips, 'Quiet, don't you see, he is asleep?'

'Please Begum Sahiba, come and eat something. The begums have been waiting for you at the table, not touching the food. I promise, I will sit with Sahib and not move an eyelid. For his sake, please go, Begum Sahiba.'

In the darkness, Abid could not see the flush of anger on her face but he heard the harshness of her voice, 'Go away from here, at once. And do not come back unless you are called.'

Abid left quietly. Night deepened. Even the children were awake; no one complained of being tired. Qamar Zamani and Baji Begum spread their prayer mats at Mansoor's door and kept vigil throughout the night. The house was wrapped in darkness and there was death in its air. As the night breeze passed gently through the branches of the amaltas tree, it seemed to be soothing the terror of death.

Shehzadi watched each passing moment; it was too dark to be able to see Mansoor, but his smiling face was right there before her eyes. She was counting the hours until the morning and planning that when he woke up, she would fight with him about hiding his condition from her. Her eyes never left his face, trying to pierce the dark curtain of the night... Finally, the darkness seemed to be slowly lightening, leaving the morning to witness what was becoming inevitable.

Outside, it was still pre-dawn. It seemed that the sun did not want to rise and was hiding itself in the clouds. Then the clouds took the matters in hand and they dispersed as suddenly as they had gathered. The sun had no option but to appear. It first rays touched the highest branches of the amaltas. The leaves twitched and threw back the sun's gold.

The burden of the night gave way to the brightness of day.

Abid, who had sat outside the door the whole night, opened it a bit and peeped in. Shehzadi was still sitting on the floor at the side of the bed, holding Mansoor's hand, her eyes fixed on his face. Mansoor was in deep sleep. Seeing the ash-white of his face, Abid was greatly alarmed. Heart thumping, he moved silently in the dark. Shehzadi did not even notice him. He softly placed his hand on his master's forehead—it was ice cold.

'Miyan, get up please, it is morning.'

There was no life in the inert form.

'Allah!' Abid shouted, '*Ya Ali Madad*!'

The entire household rushed into the room. Only Shehzadi did not move from where she sat, holding his hand. Abid fell at the feet of Qamar Zamani who was feverishly counting the beads of her tasbih. She looked at her grandson's lifeless eyes, placed a hand on his forehead and closed his eyelids. Then she turned around, saying in a flat guttural voice:

'My child has gone.'

With Jahanara at her side, Qamar Zamani stood by Mansoor's bed for a long time looking at the extinguished light of her love, hopes and dreams. Then she turned to Shehzadi, but Shehzadi refused to leave Mansoor's hand. Neither Qamar Zamani nor Jahanara could loosen her grip. When they managed to pry her fingers loose, she dashed her wrists on the floor, smashing most of her glass bangles, piercing her wrist with glass shards, spattering her dupatta with blood. Qamar Zamani placed her hand on her grandson's forehead to brush away a few strands of his golden hair. Her heavy rasping voice was heard above the sobs of grieving men and women. The *nauha* on her lips was Hazrat Shehrbano's lament at the martyrdom of her six-month-old baby, Hazrat Ali Asghar:

Kehtein thein Bano, Ashgar Jani kab tum rann se aaoge
Darya par se peekar paani, Kab tum rann se aaoge
Yaad mein tere pyare pehni kafni kaali hai
Bhooray baalon waley aaja jhoola tera khali hai

'Bano says

Asghar my love, when will you come from the battlefield
After drinking from the river, when will you come from the battlefield?
In my longing for you, I am wearing a black shroud.
My brown-haired one come, your cradle lies empty.'

As soon as Zia learnt about Mansoor, he rushed from the palace to say farewell to his dearest friend. He looked at his face silently for a while, then he raised his hands in Fatiha.

'Phupijan,' he addressed Qamar as his father's sister, 'Have courage, *Inna lillah-e-wa-nna-alaihe-raja'oon ...*' (From God we come and to God we return).

There were crowds gathering outside Akbar Lodge. People

spoke in whispers:

'What an unfortunate homecoming for Akbar Ali Khan's grandson.'

'He was summoned by death. His grandfather wanted him by his side.'

'We hear that the sahib of the amaltas tree claims the best in the family; Mansoor Ali Khan was the Kohinoor of this clan.'

Mansoor was carried to his last resting place, wrapped in a white shroud. Shehzadi did not utter a single word or shed a single tear. With blank eyes and stony face, she bid a silent farewell to her beloved husband with whom she had spent 35 years.

Jahanara Begum tried to brace herself to console the children. For the second time in her life, she felt her breasts harden with milk for the child who was born from her, but who she never had a chance to breastfeed. Her breasts were aching and no amount of hugging the little children gave her any relief.

The doctors informed Qamar Zamani that Shehzadi needed to cry, otherwise the pent-up emotion would burst a vein in her brain. It was the arrival of her parents that made her finally break down. The sight of their daughter in the white clothes of a widow was more than they could bear. They tried to suppress their grief and console the daughter they had watched over so carefully all these years. Cradled in her mother's arms, Shehzadi finally gave in to her grief. Once the tears started flowing, there was no stopping them. Quietly, the room emptied. When Qamar Zamani entered the room an hour later, she found her daughter-in-law with her head on her mother's lap in an exhausted sleep.Again, the room quietly filled with people—Shehzadi's parents, her two mothers-in-law, the children, Rahat and Naved.

Qamar Zamani's voice broke the silence. 'My beloved child is gone, this was the will of Allah. He has gone into the arms of his Nana. That world is a happier place for them. It is we who are condemned to live out our days with his loss weighing down on us every moment. Shehzadi, child, you have the responsibility for eight lives now, the children who are his legacy for you. Immerse yourself in bringing them up and fulfilling your duty as a wife and mother. Thirty-five years ago, when his grandfather died, I was exactly where you are today. By the will of Allah, I managed to fulfill my promise to Akbar Ali Khan.'

She walked up to Shehzadi and to the shock and surprise of all present, instead of the usual gesture of blessing the younger woman, she placed Shehzadi's hand over her own head.

'You are now head of the household of Akbar Ali Khan.'

Chapter 18

AFTER THE MANDATORY 40 days of mourning, the first thing Shehzadi did was to call Munshi Ram Lal. She knew nothing about her estate and finances. But she was anxious to learn. 'Tell me frankly, Ram Lal what do we possess in terms of land, properties and cash? Do we have any assets left after the government passed the Land Ceiling Act?'

Mansoor had told her how the Land Ceiling Act had taken away the bulk of his property. Ram Lal was impressed with her keenness to learn.

'We don't have much left, Begum Sahiba. Sahib sold off property after property to meet the daily living expenses. All we have are these paper bonds from the government in lieu of all our property. They have also demanded a huge amount for death duty. As for the cash, Munshi Nisar Husain absconded to Pakistan with all the cash he could lay his hands on. Our only income now is from the fruit orchards, and some meagre rents from a few shops in Bareilly. But our entire assets will not pay for the household expenses and certainly not for government duties.'

For Shehzadi, it was a losing game—her husband had given her no inkling of their financial crisis. She looked out the window at the amaltas tree, trying to find some inspiration. When she spoke, her voice had a new determination:

'Munshiji, please arrange the sale of Ashiana.'

'Sale of Ashiana? But Sahib had built it with such care, I cannot *think* of placing it on the market!'

'Sahib has gone, Munshiji. It makes no difference to him. We will never return to live in Aligarh. Our happiest memories will lie buried in its soil forever. Please do as you are told.'

Ashiana was sold and most of the money was used in paying off debts and other duties. Mansoor's collection of books was given to the university library. He had often told her, 'I do not see anyone in my family taking care of my precious collection of books. I have acquired them from all over the world and want them to go to an institution that would appreciate their value and ensure their use.'

For the first time in her life, Shehzadi understood the meaning of austerity—but a lifetime's habits could not be changed by a change in circumstances. She was used to spending whatever she got, she had no idea of economizing or cutting corners. She was also not willing to compromise on the lifestyle the children were used to. Her parents tried to help, but she was too proud to accept their offer. Zia neither offered to help nor would she have accepted had he done so...

The seemingly unlimited wealth of the house of Akbar Ali Khan had dwindled from a heap of gold to a pinch of dust. The large family that he had dreamt of, daughters and sons, was there, each demanding a share of the treasury which was completely empty.

Shahab and Mumtaz Jahan were living in Delhi during those trying times. Three of their daughters were married and they had four grandchildren whom they both adored. Their third daughter had given birth to three boys in three years. Mumtaz Jahan's lifelong desire of having a male child was fulfilled not once, not twice, but thrice!

And while Mumtaz Jahan loved all the children, her special favourite was the youngest, Shahid, who had never left her side since the day he was born.

This is how it happened. After two children in two years, Mumtaz Jahan's third daughter Zainab, became pregnant a third time. 'Ammi,' she confided, 'How will I cope with another baby?'

'Dearest child! So long as I am alive, you have nothing to worry about. But I may not always be with you, *meri jaan*. Sooner or later, you will have to be on your own.'

'Never... Ammi. I cannot imagine living without you.'

'Zainab, I know you are very keen to have a daughter, but everything is in the hands of Allah. But if you have a third son, will you ... will you...?'

Zainab looked at her mother, and knew the words before they were uttered—'If you have a third son... will you allow me to bring him up? He will always be yours, no one can alter that. But I will look after him even as his *ayah*, his *anna*!'

Mumtaz Jahan's burning desire for a male child was never as evident as it was in the humility and beseeching manner in which she uttered these words. Zainab was overwhelmed. At that moment, she made up her mind that she would fulfill her mother's dream if the child in her womb was male. So, from the time Shahid was born and Mumtaz Jahan lifted him in her arms, he became the center of her life. She looked after all his needs with her own hands, and would not allow in any ayah or attendant. Her days and nights had only this one focus.

After his retirement, Shahab was getting teaching offers from many foreign universities. He refused them all, because for the first time, he saw a new Mumtaz Jahan. Gone were the fainting fits and hysterical outbursts. He had never seen her so completely happy! When Shahid was eighteen months old, an offer came from a prestigious university in the USA. This time, Shahab broached the subject to Mumtaz Jahan:

'It is two years since I retired, but I have not taken up any job offer because I did not want to take you away from here; you are so happy where you are. But my love, now I want to go to teach in the US for one year!'

'One year...!' was all she could say.

'One year is a long time, my dear. I will understand if you want to stay behind with the children. I promise to come for a visit after six months.'

Mumtaz Jahan became thoughtful. Since Shahab's heart attack she had never left him alone. She could not allow him go alone now.

'You know Sahib, I will never let you go alone, But....only if we can take Shahid...'

'Not yet. I do not know the arrangements there and you have never lived without domestic help. It will not be easy for you to look after a small child. Let me go first and as soon as I settle down, I will call you both.'

'No, no...You cannot go alone,' she said decisively.

The day came when Shahab and Mumtaz Jahan were to leave for the USA. Till the last minute, Mumtaz Jahan did not let go of Shahid's little hand.

Away from all her loved ones, Mumtaz Jahan felt lost. After Shahab left for work, she filled her time conjuring up images from the past. The most prominent of them was of the little boy who she had held in her arms until she had boarded the aircraft. She began to neglect the house work. Sometimes she stood by the door and called out 'Bua Firozi!' Sometimes she had imaginary conversations with her daughters and grandchildren. At other times, she heard Shahid's little footsteps and imagined him appearing at the door. She continuously thought of her brother, Mansoor—he seemed to smile from all the windows of her apartment, that characteristic lock of hair falling across his forehead. In this self-created world, she even forgot her loneliness.

Shahab realized the gravity of her condition for the first time when he returned home one evening to see everything exactly as he had left it. Dishes were in the sink, the bed was unmade and Mumtaz Jahan was asleep. When he had left for the university, she had been fast asleep, exactly as she was when he had returned. It was clear that she had not gotten up even to eat. Shahab's heart was filled with foreboding.

The next day, Mumtaz Jahan was taken by ambulance to the University Hospital. Shahab held her hand along the way and on arriving at the hospital, he wired his daughters, asking them to come immediately.

All the top specialists examined Mumtaz Jahan but they could find nothing wrong. Physically, she was alright. All the tests were done, but even the brain X-Ray did not reveal any abnormality. It was the consultant's opinion that unless the brain was opened up, they would be groping in the dark. Shahab was asked to sign the consent slip—which he began to do, his hand shaking as he picked up the pen. So he went into Mumtaz Jahan's room to steady his nerves, wanting to look into her brilliant green eyes. But her eyes remained hidden behind her eyelids and he came out with a heavy heart and signed the paper.

The operation was performed without any complications. She was still unconscious when he went to see her in the recovery room. The surgeon told him that they had found a very small tumour at the base of her brain, which was removed. The doctors were hopeful that she would regain consciousness soon. A few hours later, Shahab was overjoyed to see the blue-green eyes open at last. Mumtaz called out to her daughters one by one. There was only one question in her eyes and on her lips—'How is my Shahid?' Then everyone noticed that her restless eyes had became glued to a spot as if she was seeing someone. Her lips quivered and Shahab bent over to listen to her words. She whispered. 'Sorry ... but Bhaijan has come and wants to take me with him.' This was her last sentence and then she closed her eyes. The doctors tried to revive her, but she had gone.

Shahab looked at her for a long time. She seemed to be in a deep sleep. He recalled how, in the second week of her marriage, she had cried secretly because she was leaving him to return to her parental home. And today....after being with him for 33, years she had left him forever. What now?

Shahab did not want to bury his beloved wife in alien soil. Maybe he could not build a Taj Mahal for his Mumtaz Jahan, but he could at least take her to the land where she belonged.

When the family arrived with a wooden casket carrying Mumtaz Jahan, the entire clan had assembled. Shehzadi recalled her confidante and sympathizer, who had befriended her from the first day she had stepped into this house.

Mumtaz Jahan's casket was placed in the central courtyard. She looked beautiful, her face showing no sign of illness. Framed in her golden brown hair and with her flawless complexion... she seemed just asleep.

Watching her daughter's bier being carried out, Jahanara Begum pressed her breast to stop what felt like the twist of a knife in her chest. She had developed this pain since Mansoor died. The sound of women wailing filled the air. Only one person sat with eyes that were completely dry. Qamar Zamani. This was the second time that the light of her life had been extinguished. But she was neither lamenting nor crying.

Mumtaz Jahan's body was draped in a red shawl, a sign that she was a *suhagan* (one whose husband was still alive.)

Suddenly a cry pierced the air; it was Jahanara. A doctor emerged from the crowd to examine her and suggested that she be taken to Emergency. Shehzadi sat with her in the emergency ward, holding her hand.

'Dulhan, have both my children gone?' Jahanara asked, writhing in pain. 'I could not even nurse them. But now I have so much milk in my breast and no one left to nurse.'

Shehzadi had herself experienced this pain and the woman who lay helpless on the emergency bed had been instrumental in inflicting it. She wiped the sweat off Jahanara Begum's forehead and tried to ease her pain by gently massaging her chest.

Jahanara Begum was diagnosed with advanced carcinoma of the breast. She only had one prayer on her lips. 'Allah, call me in your presence. Let me be united with my children like I never was in my life time.' Exactly one month after Mumtaz Jahan's death, Allah did have mercy and her soul left her body. Rahat was inconsolable. She was, for her. the real mother.

The news of Jahanara Begum's's illness had been kept secret from Qamar Zamani but the matriarch never asked about her. She even stopped praying. What was left for her to pray for? After some time, Shahab told her gently, 'Ammajan, Baji Begum has expired.'

She just looked at him with blank eyes, muttering—'Good for her, she always blamed me for taking her children away, now at least she will have them to herself without my presence. At last, she has scored over me.'

Normalcy returned to the household in one sense of the word. In another sense its normal rhythm had been altered forever. Qamar Zamani became increasingly paranoid. She began to ask for Asad as soon as she heard him enter the gate. She held him in her embrace for a long time as if fearing that if she let go, he too would disappear from her sight. She hardly spoke to anyone. She was often found in the garden, standing near the amaltas tree, her lips moving as if she were conversing.

Shehzadi's golden brown hair was turning grey.

After Mansoor's death, she had persuaded her parents to move to Akbar Lodge. They had sold Shabistan in Aligarh and divided the money equally between their three children, sending Aamir's share to Pakistan. Agha Sahib's pension and *wasiqa* were enough for both of them. Begum Agha had secretly kept some money aside from household expenses. One day she called her husband for a secret exchange. 'Sahib, over the last 40 years I have been saving money from our household expenses. It is kept in a *chor* compartment of the big wooden chest lying in the attic. It is so well hidden that in all these years, despite having been opened a thousand times, no one has spotted it. Tomorrow I will tell Shehzadi how to take it out of the chest. Together, we will bestow our life's savings on her; she needs it now, more than ever before.'

Ever since moving to Akbar Lodge, Begum Agha had been confined to her room on account of her failing health.

The next day, Shehzadi brought chicken soup which she had prepared for her mother. Begum Agha looked with wistful eyes at her daughter and said, 'Why did you bother, dearest child? You should have asked the cook. But let me tell you about the secret compartment in my wooden chest.' Mother and daughter spoke for a long time, while Shehzadi fed her spoonfuls of soup.

Agha Sahib and Shehzadi remembered this as the last conversation they had with Begum Agha. That night, Agha Sahib lost his companion, and Shehzadi lost her mother. When she heard the news, Qamar Zamani came to the room and stood looking at her *samdhan* lying on her pillows. Begum Agha looked exactly as she did when Qamar Zamani and Jahanara Begum had visited her for the first time carrying the *Imam Zamin* in the hope that she would agree to their proposal of marriage.

'Khuda *hafiz, samdhan,* sleep peacefully. You are fortunate to have died a *suhagan*. Your daughter is now in my custody and I will look after her as long as I am punished to be alive.'

The amaltas tree had watched over the loss of another beloved life.

Shehzadi looked around at her gradually emptying home. After losing his wife, Agha Sahib had become restless for Lucknow. His departure was now imminent. The last three years had turned Akbar Lodge into a well of depression. So Shehzadi had decided it would be better to send the children to a residential school in the hills. The boys were duly admitted to a boarding school in Nainital. All except Asad. Qamar Zamani refused point blank. No amount of persuasion by Shehzadi and Asad himself, would move her. She arranged for a tutor to help him with preparation for the board examination from a local school. Both intelligent and hard working, Asad assiduously applied himself to his studies, but Qamar Zamani constantly interfered; she would walk in during his lessons, 'Are you tired?' 'Are you hungry?' 'Are you straining your eyes?' The final exam began and Asad had to go to the examination hall every morning. Then night before his last paper, Asad studied late into the night. Qamar Zamani sat up with him, watching the clock all night long. When it struck 3, she decreed that it was time to sleep. Asad looked up from his book, saying—'You are right. I am tired, Dada, so I will sleep now, but you must wake me up at 7—my paper starts at 9.'

'Yes, my darling, I will,' she said, switching off the lights.

When Asad woke up, the sun was high in the sky. It was 10 o' clock!

'Why did you not wake me up, Dada?' he asked, choking with anger. 'I've missed my paper!'

'How could I wake you, *meri jaan*? You had gone to sleep so late. I did not have the heart to disturb you, my child.'

Asad ran all the way to school and pleaded with the principal to be allowed to write the exam. The principal had known Mansoor and well understood the obsessive nature of Begum Sahiba. He gave Asad special permission.

When Qamar Zamani learnt that Asad had rushed off without eating anything, she began shouting at the servants. Her screams brought Shehzadi out from her room. Lately, she had become kinder to her mother-in-law, but this incident had triggered all the old resentments.

'Did you know that Asad went hungry and no one had the sense to feed him? Everyone in this house is my child's sworn enemy!' Shehzadi understood only too well, what this word 'everyone' meant.

'Ammajan, who is his enemy and who is his friend, only time will tell. Today was his last paper, and you have ruined his whole future by your obsessive affection! You did the same to your own grandson—your husband had set aside a large sum of money for his education abroad, but you preferred to buy him luxuries rather than the best education with that money. Yes, he told me this himself; and where did this leave him? He wasted all his natural talents and kept his longings locked in his heart, for fear of hurting you! Ammajan, you killed him and now you are killing Asad—how long will we go on re-enacting this history?'

After writing his exam, Asad returned home with a new determination. He would no longer let Qamar Zamani run his life... never! He would never let himself be suffocated and suffer as he had seen his father do. Qamar Zamani's love was a noose around his neck. He would break out of this silken cocoon. Once before, he had tried to escape when he had quietly left for Pakistan, but he had returned when he was summoned. He would never again repeat the mistake of returning.

One day, very quietly, Asad left for Bombay and never entered the door of Akbar Lodge again.

The pinch of golden sand that was left, was slipping away grain by grain, only two grains were now left. Two grains, Qamar Zamani and Shehzadi. Their struggle had begun on the day when Shehzadi had first entered the house—for Qamar Zamani, she had always been the rival, never a daughter. And they were still pitted against one another.

All Shehzadi's hopes had faded away one by one. The old chest, whose secret she was told, when opened, revealed packets of moth-eaten notes which crumbled as soon as they were exposed to fresh air. Mansoor's lifelong investment of friendship with Zia, about which she had held some hope, yielded only an occasional invitation to a function or a marriage, and nothing more. Agha Sahib had packed his belongings and left for Lucknow, unable to live in the kothi without his dear wife. Her brother Aalam lived off Mansoor's generous gift of village Sultanpur, but never once asked what his widowed sister needed.

The only exception to this growing list of disappointments was Munawar, Zia Ali Khan's oldest son. His love for Ruhi continued unabated despite his being married and the father of two. Shehzadi herself had become very fond of Munawar. His presence in their household was the only stabilizing factor. She gradually began to lean on him and in his gentle manner, he took on the responsibility of sorting out her financial affairs. Ruhi's presence gave Munawar the impetus to come day after day and sit with Shehzadi and Munshi Ram Lal, trying to navigate a way out of this financial mess.

The big kothi in Nainital was badly in need of repair. Munshi Ram Lal had brought a letter from the municipality which directed her to repair the retaining wall of the Bari Kothi, since it was endangering the entire the hill-side settlement. Failure to repair would result in government acquiring the property, the notice said. The magnitude of the work was frightening. Shehzadi neither had the money for it, nor the prospect of raising it.

To sell the shops in Bareilly was the only way out. Both Munawar and Munshi Ram Lal were opposed to the sale, since that was their last means of income. Besides, it would be a distress sale since they had no means of negotiating the sale price with their tenants.

One evening, as was his routine, Munawar arrived in Akbar Lodge, bringing with him his usual cheer and good humour. Behind him came his driver and orderly, carrying elaborate containers of food, desserts and savouries. For Ruhi, there was *halwa sohan* and *kali gajar ka halwa*; for Rubina, *ande ka halwa*; for Shehzadi *rasawal* made from fresh cane juice and rice, cooked on coals in an unbaked clay pot. They all sat together, forgetting the impending doom, and urged him to tell stories—Munawar had a great knack for storytelling and could keep the mehfil entertained for hours. Sadly, he could not use this talent in his own home—his wife had been chosen by his mother, without asking his consent; he had two children, a girl and a boy; and though he was gentle and protective of his family, and had never divorced his wife, he had a sterile relationship, bordering on separation. At Akbar Lodge, his natural warmth and quest for love found a niche. With Ruhi as his tether, he gradually became a favourite with all the children. Shehzadi rued her short-sightedness in rejecting his proposal of marriage to Ruhi. Not all *nawabzadas* are identical, she mused in hindsight. Munawar was different from them all. Perhaps Mansoor saw that quality, that is why he, who had rejected feudal *nawabzadas'* proposals for Mumtaz Jahan, had hesitantly broached Begum Zeenat's proposal of Munawar for Ruhi. It had been her own diffidence and obstinacy which had killed the idea.

'You have no one to blame but yourself…' Shehzadi thought wistfully, watching Munawar and Ruhi playing scrabble while the children cheered them on.

Shehzadi was now on the last lap of her journey, a journey she had started the day her husband had died. She did not feel like struggling anymore. Mansoor had coped with his pain alone, and she wanted to follow his example.

Late at night, she would remember how the lock of golden hair would fall on his forehead and she would remark—'How obstinate is this lock of hair, always clinging to you like my *sauten* (rival)!' Her beautiful thick hair which had once ensnared so many suitors, was now mostly snowy white. Her hazel eyes were dimmed and her slim form had lost its pride.

Sometimes she would hear a footstep. This was the footstep which touched her ears when, as a bride, she was waiting for Mansoor. She wanted the footsteps to halt at her side but they passed on and her loneliness remained embedded deep within.

Munshi Ram Lal brought her the money from the sale of the Bareilly shops. With the money in her hand, Shehzadi decided to go to Nainital herself and get the *pushta* repaired. She went to Qamar Zamani's room to say goodbye, with a sense that they may be seeing each other for the last time. She searched Qamar Zamani's face for a sign of affection, but found it expressionless, as always. She sat for a while in silence, then, getting up, said: 'I am going to the hills, Ammajan, to get the big kothi repaired. I do not know how long I will be away. Look after yourself. Khuda *Hafiz*.'

Qamar Zamani looked at her as if seeing her for the first time. Was it Shehzadi's imagination or was there a glimmer of moisture in her stony eyes?

'Khuda *Hafiz,* Dulhan, may God protect you,' she said.

Then as she was leaving, Qamar Zamani called out—'Dulhan, don't forget to water the champa tree. It must be full of flowers. Do break off all the withered flowers on the tree—they do not let the new buds blossom. And only pluck those flowers that have yellow petals, not the half-open ones.'

Shehzadi stopped and turned around, realising that the old woman was even lonelier than her. She had been so wrapped in her own grief that she had forgotten that Qamar Zamani's sorrow was a mountain. Suddenly, she felt the need to come closer to the woman who had been her lifelong adversary. She walked back and before a contrary thought could intervene, she threw her arms around her mother-in-law.

Qamar Zamani took Shehzadi's face in her trembling hands, brought it closer. Tears were streaming from her eyes, finding their path along the creases on her face. Her lips quivered.

'Khuda *Hafiz* my moon, the light of my household and the treasure of my family.' She stroked Shehzadi's hair and ran the silver locks through her fingers. 'However did your hair turn grey?' she mused. 'Where are the thick, dark clouds which made Mansoor desire you? Did you know that the sight of your thick hair cast a spell on us? Like the magic of *Zulf-e-Bengal*... You were just a little girl when all of us watched you for hours through the telescope... Did you ever know?'

'Yes Ammajan, he told me everything.'

'*Shaitan*! I told him not to mention it to you... Let him come and I will...' she could not continue, and the two of them mourned as a single soul.

Shehzadi left for Nainital.

ଓ

The mountains were beautiful; sloping greens dotted with clumps of wild flowers. The trees were rain-washed and the water in the lake shimmered. Shehzadi had the small kothi opened up—she had bought it from Shahab after Mumtaz Jahan's death. That is where she planned to stay while the big kothi was being repaired. She walked up and saw where the retaining wall was showing signs of collapse. A contractor had been arranged who had promised to start work from the next day.

She had not yet sent word of her arrival to the younger children in the school hostel. She would do it the next day. She had brought along her personal servant Bashir to attend to her. The man knew each habit of his mistress, and anticipated her every need.

In the big kothi, she walked around with Bashir, taking stock of all that had to be done. She did not feel like walking back to the small kothi and decided to sit here for a while. The evening shadows lengthened and a cool mist rose from the lake. She wrapped herself in a shawl and walked up and down the gravel driveway, her gaze fixed on the veranda where all the windows were dark. Suddenly, the lamps of her memory lit up and she heard and saw people milling around in a festive mood, laughing, talking. Then she saw Mansoor playing the perfect host, smilingly, looking after everyone. His smile held her attention and she could not tear her eyes away from it until aloud noise and a streak of lightning distracted her—Shehzadi looked up at the top floor where she saw herself sitting as a bride. That image faded and another rose—the days of her solitary confinement. Thoughts chased each other and memories drifted in and out of her consciousness. The sky lit up again and there was a great clap of thunder. This play of lightning and thunder continued for a long time, at times lighting up the whole kothi. Again, the sky was illuminated with a great streak of lightning and roll of thunder. This time it flashed over an old battered telescope.

It had rained heavily the whole of the previous night. Streams of water had flowed in small torrents towards the lake. Shehzadi saw that all the flowers were broken and the smaller trees uprooted. The champa tree had been devastated, the old flowers blown away and even the new flowers and buds broken at the stem. One part of the retaining wall of the big kothi had been torn away and was lying in rubble at the foot of the hill.

Bashir saw that his mistress had walked to the precipice to look at the wall which had crumbled down. He brought out a table and a chair. She sat down, without taking her eyes off the broken wall.

'I will serve your tea here.'

He went inside and brought out the tea service on a tray. Arranging the tray neatly on the table he asked, 'Should I pour your tea Begum Sahiba?' There was no answer. Shehzadi, leaning back in the chair, was staring intently at the house. He waited and then asked once again.

'The tea is getting cold, should I pour?' Still, she did not answer. Very hesitantly, Bashir bent over to touch her shoulder. Her head fell lifelessly to one side.

❧

In Akbar Lodge, Qamar Zamani all alone, watched the last grain of the golden sand slowly turn to dust. Fixed on the door, her glazed eyes were waiting for her dulha*n*. Unknown to her, the bond between the two women had finally snapped.

And there was nothing left.

Shehzadi had won, and Qamar Zamani was left, to wait.